TALITHA

A Haunting

RACHAEL RAWLINGS

Hydra
Publications

ISBN: 978-1-942212-89-8

Hydra Publications

Goshen, KY 40026

www.hydrapublications.com

To my wonderful Facebook friends, my crazy parrot people, and all the dreamers out there who like to travel with me.

PROLOGUE

Eddie's truck belched a final cloud of exhaust as the engine rattled into silence. He opened the door slowly, his eyes trained on the car just ahead of him. A sleek silver foreign job was parked at an angle and blocked the drive, its nose tucked almost to the basin of the huge fountain. He couldn't see a person behind the wheel, so he figured the owner was already out.

"Shouldn't be walking around here," Eddie muttered. "Break his fool neck." He struggled out of his seat and dropped the few feet onto the weed strewn ground, his boots hitting the earth with a muffled thud. He was huffing from tobacco stained lips by the time he had mounted the stairs to the front porch. His heart jumped as a figure separated itself from the front of the house.

"Didn't see you there, sir," he said keeping his voice even. "I'll have the place open in a jiff." There was no audible response, but he thought he could see a nod. He dug into the deep pocket on his jacket and pulled out the old key. It was oversized, ridiculous really, but with the formal ornamentation, the key matched the overall look of the house. He tried not to think of the shadow beside him. Pale skin, dark hair, shadowed eyes.

With a harsh intake of air, Eddie struggled to open the door, the hinges protesting as the crack widened. Inside the foyer, clouds of dust stirred by the draft of air swirled up the staircase like a figure racing for cover. A sweet stench of mold and mildew drifted out, and Eddie turned his head away in disgust. It was his job to take care of the lawn, to slice through the rapidly growing weeds that led up the pitted driveway to the collapsing front porch. It was not his responsibility to get near this cursed house. Talitha. The name seemed too sweet to belong to a place such as this. But here he was, standing next to a man that looked more like a ghost than flesh and blood, opening the place up.

He coughed and covered his mouth and nose with the stained collar of his work shirt. "Well, here we are, Mr. Edwards. If you need anything else, you let me know." He started to back away, heading down the porch steps.

"Do you have a light?"

The voice was as dry as the wind gusts, scarcely loud enough to be heard over the buzz of the insects nesting in the weeds. But Eddie knew the man had been sick so he paused, handing over his flashlight he had tucked in his work belt.

"It works. The batteries are fresh. But as I said before, I don't think I'd be going in there. No one's been caring for it, and I've seen some serious signs of rot."

"That's all right. I'll be careful." The voice was cool and dispassionate. "I'll give this back as soon as I'm finished."

Eddie took this as a dismissal and was grateful. He paused on the steps as the man opened the door wider and flicked on the flashlight. Briefly, the figure of the man was outlined by the failing glow of sunlight leaking in through the windows, then the door was closed. Eddie shook his head and descended the rest of the stairs.

Never in his days would he have thought anyone would want to go back in that house. And now he was back. The only remaining member of the family that had been cursed by that house had come home.

CHAPTER ONE

An ant moved purposefully across the floor, so tiny it was barely visible against the scuffed linoleum. Climbing determinedly up the cabinets, it stopped at the rim of the mustard yellow countertop and paused. The 13 others following it did not and ran rampant over their companion and the counter, searching for crumbs. Claire felt an uncomfortable sympathy with the trampled ant. She knew what it felt like to be downtrodden.

Claire knew there were 14 ants. She had counted them. She also knew there were three tiny holes in her tee shirt, just around the collar, caused from excessive use of bleach, and four stray threads at the bottom where the hem was coming undone. Even her jeans were starting to wear thin at the knees. Her hair hung in a straight ponytail down her back, almost to the waist of her jeans, and she pushed her hands through the soft strands in silent frustration. With slow deliberation, she stood and began mopping the counters with the cheap paper towels. Sitting here and waiting for the inevitable would do her no good. She was still scrubbing at the table, a pile of towels on the old tabletop, when the door was flung open and her roommate backed her way into the tiny kitchen.

"Hey, give me a hand, will you?" Noel questioned as she held the door open with an elbow.

Claire quickly got up and took a grocery bag dangling from Noel's fingers. She held the door open as Noel nudged a third bag in with her foot. The odor of spicy chicken filled the air as Noel pulled the top container out of the bag at her feet and pried the lid off.

"I'm starving. You know, you're never supposed to go grocery shopping when you're hungry. I can see why now. I think I bought too much." Noel took a large bite of chicken and put the container in the middle of the table.

Claire frowned at the bags. Then she looked up at her impetuous roommate. "Where did you get the money? I thought you were broke for the rest of the week."

Noel looked innocently at Claire. "I found a $20 in the couch cushion. I might have emptied the penny jar. I knew we needed to eat…" Her smile was contagious, and Claire decided to drop the subject. With the bind they were in now, no $20 was going to save them.

"We got our eviction notice," Claire said calmly.

Noel didn't look surprised. They had been expecting it, dreaded it, with no way to catch up on their bill. They had been skating on promises and smiles for long enough, and they both knew it wasn't going to last forever.

"Okay, now don't panic," Noel said, pacing the kitchen." Don't panic" had become their theme and echoed hollowly in Claire's ears. Noel stopped her pacing abruptly, and her hands dived into the grocery bag and emerged with the daily newspaper. "I've got two really good ads for today." She opened the paper and spread it out on the table. "I scanned it while I was checking out."

Claire sighed and sat down in the nearest chair. For weeks, they had been combing every want ad and newspaper, website, and email posting they could find in the Louisville area, including the small towns that radiated from the larger Kentucky city, hoping to find a situation that would allow them work and a place to stay. But it was a tight economy, and jobs were hard to come by, especially if someone could only work part time and hadn't finished her degree.

"Listen to this," Noel continued, pointing to one of the tightly printed ads. "'Wanted, help for light house work, care of senior citizen'," she stopped and scanned the ad quickly, "some cooking involved. It looks like it's located in J-town, so not a far drive from campus."

Claire bent over the paper, elbows on the table, and wisps of hair tickling her cheek. "Does it include a room?"

"Yes, I think so." Noel examined the ad, using a thick red marker to outline it with a bloody loop, her brow marked with a frown. "Now that one would be a live-in situation for one of us, but listen to this..." She flipped to the next page and paused dramatically. "'Wanted, housekeepers for large renovation' see, it says 'housekeepers,' plural, right? I figure we can both apply for this one. And it provides a room, flexible hours... It sounds perfect." She repeated the mark, circling the other ad as well. "I was reading this in the car and nearly peed myself, I was so excited. I think this might be it!"

"I don't know about perfect," Claire responded, glancing at the text. "Large renovation. I wonder how large they're talking about. And I wonder who lives there. And, where is it? It just says Shelby County. The 'Talitha' house. I've never even heard of the place."

Noel made a face and took the paper again to fold it neatly. "Okay, Debbie Downer, I see where you're going with this. But it sounds good to me, and our options aren't exactly wide open. Besides, it can't hurt to phone them and ask our questions. I'm going to call about both jobs tomorrow morning." Her face sobered. "How long do we have here?"

"One week starting tomorrow. Mrs. Chambers gave us an extension, but if it was up to George, we'd be out tonight," Claire responded, taking a piece of chicken for herself.

"How could a nice lady like that end up with an ass like him?" Noel was on her feet, rinsing her hands in the sink before pulling more groceries from the bag.

"I don't know. Maybe he was a real looker in his day."

Noel rolled her eyes dramatically, and Claire chuckled at her expression.

"There must have been some reason," Noel said absently. "Remember her apartment? Sad how it was, like, so empty."

"Just her and her old man," Claire agreed. "It was sad."

Noel nodded and then shook her head briskly as though shaking the thoughts from her head. "Are you going to start packing?" she asked stowing the paper bag under the counter as she neatened up.

"No, don't have time," Claire responded between mouthfuls. "I've got to study tonight for the exam. I won't be able to call on any ads either." She looked apologetic.

"It's okay," Noel responded. "I'm going to call tonight and follow up whenever they'll see me. We'll get it figured out. Worst comes to worst, is there any way you can ask your folks for some help? Just for a few months?"

"No," Claire interjected, frowning. "Definitely not. I can't go back to them and ask for money..." she trailed off, feeling defeated. She only had until May, then she could go home, master's degree in hand, and help her parents. "Just not now."

"You're right," Noel said quickly. "I sometimes forget how rough things have been for them." She turned and pushed a lock of hair out of her eyes. "How's your dad doing? I haven't seen him in a month at least."

Claire's father had had a sudden and severe heart attack at the beginning of the summer, and it had changed the world dramatically for their family. Claire shuddered at the memory. She had been walking the University campus early in May, one final exam left, her mind full of equations from the last test she had taken. All her troubles had seemed so simple then. Just passing the classes, going to the cozy bookstore where she stocked the shelves, getting the first glance at books she would get to read during her free time. The sun had been glaring and hot, and the heat had been a heavy pressure in the air. That hadn't bothered her though. The sun was hot because summer was coming. But for a moment, a sudden splash of panic, she felt a bone deep chill rush along her skin and then beneath it, into her flesh, muscles, organs, the marrow of her. She knew something was happening. A stutter of the sunlight, like a flash of shade darker than night, made her catch her breath and hold it. Her panicked gaze had revealed nothing, but she had stopped and stood so very still, feeling the weight of the air, now cold, the chill that came from within. The sensation was quick and now gone. She had forced her feet to move on, traveling over the smooth green lawns without seeing any of the students passing around her or hearing their chatter of conversation. She had reached her classroom building and was mounting the front steps when her phone had vibrated in her pocket. Her mother's number was lit in sour green, and her fingers trembled as she answered the call. Heart attack, surgery, called in family, calling a priest, all a terrifying reality she never wanted to experience again. The memory alone could bring her to her knees, in prayer and in desperation.

But her father had miraculously and successfully undergone the surgery and was progressing through rehabilitation with only minor setbacks. Her mother had aged frighteningly during the ordeal but the little family unit that was she and her brothers had stitched up tightly into a rigid support for her parents. Because of the surgery, her father had been off work for several months and still able to tolerate only part time. All the spare money had gone into paying the medical bills, leaving little for Claire's tuition.

And Claire would have been fine with her student loans and her own paycheck if her part time job hadn't gone up in smoke, literally. When the small book store in the Highlands where she had been working burned to the ground a month ago, it had taken with it all the money the owners had, and insurance was only going to cover part of the rebuilding. Claire had said goodbye with regret.

Now, unemployed and up to her neck in student loans to cover tuition, books, and living expenses, Claire was losing her apartment. Noel wasn't much better. Her hard-earned money from waitressing covered groceries and the car insurance for the tiny Ford Escort parked out back.

Together they had made enough to eke by and continue to go to classes. With Claire's lost income, the rent money had disappeared. Noel's family was unable to help much but had generously donated the car and some of the furniture.

"Dad's fine, getting better every day." Claire pushed a stray lock of hair from her face, forcing a smile, and picked up another piece of chicken. "Mom says he'll go back to work full time in a few weeks, but only on light duty."

"Well, that's still good news. I know he's driving your mom crazy while he's home. He'll be happier when he can be back in the office." Noel had spent much of her senior year at Claire's house and had seen the family in action.

Claire smiled and stretched her arms above her head, easing her stiff muscles. "Yeah," she said and then looked at her watch. "I'd better hit the books, and you've got calls to make," she said. Seeing that the kitchen was mostly picked up and the few groceries were put away, Claire took her mug into her bedroom to work.

An hour later, Claire was still reading, a half-empty cup of cold coffee at her elbow. Noel came in, a smile of victory illuminating her face.

"Well, calls are done and guess what? The house sitter job is already filled, but the guy about the house cleaning seems interested in us." She paused and looked at her notebook. "His name is Charles Danwood, and he's managing the renovation of the house, or rather, the 'estate'." Noel's gesture indicated the term was the one Charles had chosen. "They're going to turn it into a hotel, like an upscale bed and breakfast with all the amenities. I think they're considering the horse racing crowd." Noel shrugged. "Anyway, the workers are there already and have been muddling around in their own mess. They need someone to clean up after them as they go so they can avoid tracking in construction dust into the finished spaces. It would be easy work, you know, dusting and sweeping and keeping the bathrooms decent. He said he could use as many people to help as he could get, so we're both in if we want it."

"No interviews?" Claire interrupted.

"Well, yes. I'm going in tomorrow to talk to him, but I think it's just a formality. They seriously need the help and apparently there haven't been many responses."

"I wonder why," Claire said, raising an eyebrow. Instantly she could envision a bleak old house perched atop a hill, a single light shining from the window like the house in the movie "Psycho."

"I don't know, but I'll find out tomorrow," Noel responded. "Now, let's break out the ice cream! I feel like celebrating."

The next day, for Claire, was one disaster after another. She arrived late for her first class because her bus was running behind schedule, and Noel had taken the car for her interview. By the time Claire had sat down in the classroom, her hair was falling loose around her face, and she could feel the sweat inching down her back from the run. Her books felt as though they weighed 50 pounds each, and the cute sandals she had gotten on sale had rubbed a painful blister on her heel. After settling into her seat, she realized she had forgotten her breakfast bagel and spent the next two hours in agony with her stomach burning from a cup of coffee and too little sleep.

During lunch, Claire studied while she ate, her mind wandering to Noel and the interview. On one hand, it could be the answer to all their problems. A place to stay, part time work, and they wouldn't need to ask for help from anyone.

But on the other hand, the idea she would be moving into an old house, an old house with a long history, made her a little sick inside.

The voices flitted through her mind, and she physically shook her head as though to dislodge the thought.

There was no reason it should come back. That tiny chemical imbalance that had descended like a black cloud in adolescence, puberty rearing its ugly head. The whole thing had been ridiculous. It had started as an accident, a stupid kid prank that had gone terribly wrong. Her mind flashed to a quick view of scenes, the empty house with the papers taped to the windows, Noel's pixie face alight with mischief, the odd murmurs, lights, and shadows. Haunted. Dead. A dead house. She shook her head again and forced herself to focus. Her hands felt damp and cold and she stood up quickly, a wave of lightheadedness making her sway on her feet. She grabbed the tabletop and just stood for a moment, getting her balance back. Slowly, she grabbed up her purse and slipped into the bathroom as quietly as she could. She stood at the sink and turned on the hot water, waiting for it to warm. Staring at herself in the mirror, she had studied the blue eyes rimmed with red, and the wild hair falling around her shoulders. Her face was angular and her expression tended to be too serious. She had been called plain or striking, but never pretty. But this was fine with her because she was generally unconcerned with her appearance. She wore little makeup, and that was only on special occasions. She was often too busy to check the mirror at all. Now the girl in the mirror looked haunted, frightened, and frightening. She had to remind herself she was far from that long-ago event, that house exploration when she was a teenager.

Realizing her lunchtime was ending, Claire put her chilled hands into the heated water. With quick efficiency, she grabbed a wad of paper towels and soaked them in the warmth. She pressed them to her face, her cheeks and eyes, feeling the tension drain. She dabbed at her face with another dry towel and checked her watch. Not much time. She scooped up her purse and returned to her table. Quickly she stuffed her books and notebooks back in her bag. She heaved a sigh. She was ready for a break, a break from the stress and worry, worry about her family, her job, money, and her future.

Her irrepressible roommate was already there when Claire got to the apartment. It took only a minute to realize Noel was pacing and wringing her hands with excitement. She had changed from her waitressing clothes into her favorite jeans with painted hearts trailing down one leg. Her tee shirt was several sizes too small, showing her figure to an advantage, and a rainbow peace sign emblazoned across her chest. Her dark hair was close cropped around the sides and back with a longer layer on top that fell in attractive waves around her face, but now it was standing up in choppy locks where she had run her hands through it.

Claire dropped her book bag to the floor and, getting a glass of water, sat at the scarred kitchen table. "Okay, what's the story? You've hit pay dirt, right?"

Noel sat down opposite and paused dramatically. The sunlight from the window framed her like a halo. "Our problems are solved. We met over at Applebee's to talk. He even paid for lunch."

"He who?" Claire interrupted.

"Oh, Charles, the man in charge of the renovation." Claire nodded and Noel continued. "He asked me some background questions, our experience and all that. But really, I don't think it mattered that much." Noel's hands fluttered as she spoke, her nervous energy fairly bouncing off the walls.

"That desperate?" Claire asked suspiciously.

"Well, I'm not sure about that but..." She looked cautiously at Claire, "I did get to see the house. Talitha."

Claire had grown accustomed to reading her roommate. It became surprisingly easy after being friends with someone for 10 years to know exactly what someone was feeling. Noel was good at covering her thoughts generally and had managed to build up a protective face for most people, but Claire could see through her with almost no effort, and she was holding something back.

"The house?" Claire prompted.

Noel frowned. "You know, maybe it's better if you see it for yourself."

"I will soon enough," Claire responded. "Just tell me what it's like."

Noel's expression cleared. "I think I'll just wait and let you decide."

Claire looked surprised. "Well, at least tell me something about it!" she demanded.

"It's like nothing you've ever seen before," Noel responded cryptically.

The rest of the evening Noel remained determinedly reticent. She refused to elaborate about the house or Charles and instead, decided to let her serious friend stew for a while. She knew Claire well enough to realize by the time they actually saw the house, it could never be as bad as Claire had imagined it.

CHAPTER TWO

The next morning both girls slept in late and woke to the sound of the phone ringing. It was Charles on the line, and Claire listened to Noel's side of the conversation.

After she hung up, Noel wiped her face slowly and yawned. "So, we're meeting Charles at McDonald's, and he's going to lead us out to the house. It's kind of hard to find, and I got a little lost when we went out there before."

"What time?" Claire asked curling up on the tattered couch.

"10:30. We've got an hour. But we might want to leave a little early to grab some coffee."

Claire agreed and slowly stood. "I'll be ready in a few," she reassured Noel, and headed toward her tiny room.

The weather had warmed up slightly when they left the apartment, and they kept the windows rolled down as they drove. Their building was close to downtown Louisville, one of the many larger residences that had been chopped up to provide apartments for the ever-growing University of Louisville student body. The morning air was comfortable with the fading scent of exhaust and cut grass rushing in as Noel increased speed. The antique Escort rattled in protest, but continued forward, the whine of the engine making conversation impossible. Claire took the extra minutes of silence as a time to lean back against the seat and close her eyes, relishing the breeze brushing her face and stirring the strands of hair drifting against her cheeks. They arrived early and got breakfast and a cup of coffee as they waited in the car. Noel kept the window rolled down and let the warm air flavored with the spicy smell of sausage surround them. Claire carefully reviewed the information about the job with Noel before Charles arrived. She wanted to be forewarned of any possible catches before facing the house. Noel continued to smile as she answered the questions.

"It's not as though we're doing brain surgery. All we have to do is clean where they tell us to," she said wryly. "Trust me, you're worrying for nothing. I think we were the only applicants so far."

But Claire didn't feel so secure. Something still hovered in the back of her mind that warned her nothing in her life was ever as easy as it first seemed. She just hoped this time she was wrong.

Charles arrived exactly on time, which appealed to the perfectionist in Claire. He was a tall man with an average build, leaning toward the middle age spread that came with a happy marriage and good food. He was nicely dressed in a pair of casual slacks and a dress shirt. He wore no tie and the top two buttons were unbuttoned, revealing a tanned V of skin. His face was also tanned with sandy brows and hair, lightly tipped with gold highlights from the sun. Claire thought he looked as though he was working on maintaining a business-like demeanor, but was failing miserably. Claire noted when he smiled, deep dimples appeared, giving him a boyish charm when combined with the lock of hair that was continually falling onto his forehead.

"So, Noel tells me the two of you have been friends for a long time."

Claire smiled and pushed the wisps of hair out of her face.

"We met in middle school. We weren't as close then. We kind of bonded in high school. We've been friends since then," she replied, nerves making her give a little too much information. She found she was watching his expression for a sign of what he was thinking. But he appeared genuine, mildly curious and slightly amused, as his eyes skimmed back to her roommate.

"Has Noel told you much about the house?"

"No, actually she's been holding out on me. She said it was something I needed to see."

Charles grinned boyishly.

"Well, if that's how Noel wants it, I guess we'll have to go along." He turned back towards his car and disengaged the locks. "If you are ready to go, we'll be on our way."

Claire noted as he pulled his car onto the road he had two car seats in the back and a brightly colored duck stuffed into the back window, its felt eyes pressed against the glass.

"I think I'm going to like him," she told Noel, smiling.

Noel drove their car with more excited style than finesse, and they followed Charles out of town. Although she had been there once before, Noel admitted she didn't think she could find it again without help, so Charles drove slowly to avoid losing them in the Louisville traffic. They caught Interstate 64 and headed away from the city, watching as the busy streets and neighborhoods gave way to open fields lined with stubby pines or clumped forest trees bending and beckoning in the wind.

Charles followed the interstate until he had passed the Jefferson/Shelby County line and exited at the Simpsonville sign. This was mostly new territory for both the girls. They had grown up in Northern Kentucky and hadn't ventured this far from the city of Louisville. Now as the road stretched away from the main thoroughfare, the scenery changed again. Paved roads split curved hillsides of farmland and pasture. Fences of wood and wire stitched the landscape into quilted patterns, and stately horses or staid cows meandered in their own personal kingdoms. They turned off again, the tires bumping over the less smoothly paved track. Here the road narrowed until no dividing line for the lanes could be seen. The trees closed in more closely and hung over the road like a tunnel of greenery with the sun shut out in places and showing like a bright squinting eye farther down the lane. Driveways became few and far between, and the road began a progressive ascent. There was a parting of the trees, and Claire was surprised to see a one-lane concrete bridge crossing a tumbling spring. The water widened into a frothy marsh to their left as they passed. The bridge was in poor repair, a white concrete painted structure so chipped and beaten it looked more like a skeleton stretching over the water. The road turned abruptly after the bridge, hiding it from sight, but Claire still felt its presence, like a Déjà vu. Where had she seen it before? The car was still rattling from the rough pavement when the road had given way to a gravel drive that wound its way for another mile of rough terrain.

This ended at a gate, huge and forbidding, which blocked the drive. The walls were bent in a curved arch ending in a line of hedges, growing wild and blending into the forest. Beyond the black iron bars of the gate, a cleared drive could be seen going uphill to the most indescribable house Claire had ever seen. She felt her heart speed up slightly and her palms grow damp. She had another feeling of Déjà vu, as though at some other time, in some other life, she had seen the house at this angle, the light dappling the darkened face of the old structure, the windows like empty wells.

Charles slid out of his car, unlocked the gate, and pulled it open towards the cars. Noel waited impatiently until he had pulled his car through so she could follow. Claire watched with something like dismay when he closed the gate behind them. The ring of metal against metal made her shiver involuntarily.

The house towered in front of them, rising four stories of stone centered in a large plot of cleared weeds. The lawn was sadly overrun with brambles and coarse vegetation, which choked off the grass leaving tangled vines with bare patches of earth beneath. The vines continued to the gravel drive and stretched out their spiny limbs across the steps and crept up the walls. The driveway ended in a large loop in front of the house with a fountain rising in the center. The fountain had once been a group of wildly rearing horses, heads thrown back, eyes rolling, hooves pawing at the air. Two of the horses had lost pieces of their heads or ears and several others had lost legs or hooves over time. Streaks of dark gray and black ran down their faces like tears, and the sleek mains had been worn by wind and rain. The water pooling at the base was a dark oily green.

Behind the fountain, steps rose in two flights to the front door of the house, a black railing that matched the curved metal of the gate on either side. The door was a double panel, heavy dark wood with a strip of stained glass flanking each side. The main part of the house rose in a solid block, a large square window in the center over the door winking crimson and blue. The other windows were narrow; some with colored glass and others with thick clear panes. There were visible cracks or broken panes in some of the upper floors, but the windows on the first and second floor were in good condition, and some showed recent scrubbing. No ornamentation could be seen around the windows or at the roofline, and the stone was a light gray, which caught the color of the sunlight. The impression was austere, almost to the point the house reminded Claire of a prison.

The two wings stretching out from the center hall were very different in style. The walls to the right and left were made of the same stone, but a deep porch supported by carved stone columns broke up their façade. A narrow balcony accessible through French doors on the second floor stretched the entire length of the wings. The windows in the wings of the house were large rectangles with clear glass, which sparkled when the morning light stuck them but would be shadowed as the sun rose overhead.

The walls ended with an angular roofline above broken only by large chimneys. On the far end of the wings were rounded turrets, topped with whimsical pointed roofs like witches' caps. Each of the turrets boasted four long narrow windows with beautiful stained glass that glowed in the flickering sun as the beams cleared the tree-tops. French doors had replaced the windows in the first few rooms on the bottom floor as well, and above, the small balconies with ornate railings added a gingerbread effect. The clash of the two architecture styles should have been unattractive, but for some reason it seemed right to Claire, and she found herself both attracted to and repelled by the house.

They parked both cars in front of the house and Noel turned to Claire. "What do you think?" Her eyes were fairly dancing, and she smiled as though she had a great secret.

"We're supposed to clean that?" Claire asked. She couldn't help but smile back. For all her dread about the house, her first impression was benign after they passed the entry gates. The house was big, no huge, and cleaning it would undoubtedly be challenge, but it held none of the dark feelings Claire had expected. Perhaps she had been overly sensitive, and the stress from exams had impacted her more than she had thought.

Charles had gotten out of his car and was approaching the front door, moving briskly. Claire and Noel scrambled out after him, leaving their purses in the car. They had purposely dressed casually in jeans and loose shirts because Charles had warned them about the condition of the house, and now Claire was grateful for her old tennis shoes. There was mud mixed with the gravel, and the long grass painted stripes of muck on the cuffs of her jeans.

Now, seeing it close up, Claire was glad she hadn't gotten any descriptions from Noel. It would be nearly impossible to put the overall impression of the house into words.

They caught up with Charles on the porch. It was obvious that work had already started as soon as he opened the door. Tools were piled in untidy groups just inside the doorway. Walking into the front room, Claire was struck again by the size. The ceiling rose several floors high with two curving staircases descending from above to join at a landing on the bottom step. The floor was marble, a few tiles cracked or scratched, but still very elegant. The tiles ranged in color from a pearly gray to a soft taupe and formed a pattern that was difficult to discern due to the protective mats that had been thrown on the floor from the front door to the stairway and beyond. The stairs themselves were wooden, the spindles and railing carved into ornate loops with great lions displaying sharp fangs at the newel posts above and below. A threadbare runner covered the center of the stair tread, and it was gray from traffic and age.

To the left and right were doors leading to adjoining rooms, but Charles continued straight back to open the door behind the stairway. This next room appeared to be a huge dining room stretching across most of the middle of the house. In the center was a long table, as heavily carved as the stairway, with mismatched chairs. Only two of the chairs appeared to belong with the table, the rest a variety of seats from card table chairs to cushioned armchairs that must have belonged to the parlor.

The dining room appeared to be relatively untouched with dark paneled walls and scratched wooden floors. Great pieces of furniture flanked two of the walls, but sheets had been thrown over them to protect them during the renovation. A layer of dust covered every surface except the tabletop and spider webs hung in lacy ribbons from the crown molding.

Charles did not hesitate but continued into the adjoining room, the kitchen. This room had been renovated extensively with gleaming stainless-steel appliances and granite counter tops. The floor was a utilitarian terra cotta tile, and the walls a shiny white gloss. He stopped and looked around the room, clearly pleased.

"This is the first room we finished. We knew some of the men would be staying over and would need the facilities. It will eventually be used to make all the meals for the hotel."

Noel looked around with awe. She was a closet cook, someone who loved to try new recipes but seldom had the time or money to indulge herself. At her job in the restaurant, she had been known to whip up a special dish for certain customers, and the results were delicious.

"This is great," she said enthusiastically, running a finger over the slick surface of the counter. "Can we use it to cook?"

"Of course," Charles responded. "You're welcome to use it as long as it's kept in good order. It's already stocked with utensils, pots and pans, food basics," he listed as he opened the cabinets to reveal the contents.

"Great," Noel repeated, clearly enthralled with the set up.

"If there is anything else you need, we can make sure and get it," Charles continued. Then they moved through the kitchen to the next room. This was obviously the office for the hotel. Tasteful wallpaper covered the plaster, and the hardwood floors had been refinished. Three large bookcases lined the back wall with a wooden desk in front. The window was open, letting in a soft breeze that ruffled the papers on the desk. Building plans, catalogs, and printed receipts were scattered carelessly, and a laptop computer was pushed off to the side of the desktop. Charles sat behind the desk, apparently most comfortable in this room.

Claire decided the interview was about to begin. And 15 minutes later, Claire found Charles was more serious about the job than Noel had alluded. His pointed questions reviewed her education and work history as well as her goals for the future. Claire found herself discussing her major, her plans for her life after graduation, and her family. Both girls had brought their resumes, and Charles appeared to be very familiar with those as well.

Charles seemed to be satisfied and went on to discuss the terms of the job. He wanted them to agree to stay at least four months. After that they were welcome to stay on as long as they wanted since he was sure it would take longer to complete the renovation.

Claire was reluctant to agree to an extended contract that specified time, but when Charles mentioned the hourly wage, Claire was pleasantly surprised. It was more than twice as much as she'd been paid at her other job, and this job included a free place to live. Charles also agreed to give them mileage money due to the commute to and from the University.

When Claire left the office she felt as though, once again, fate had taken a hand in her life. *There was no question*, Claire thought grimly. They would take the job and smile, even if they had to clean the toilets with a toothbrush. They hadn't any choice.

Claire quickly realized why Charles had sealed the deal in the renovated office when they continued upstairs. Halls stretched out in either direction, angling at the wings to continue to the end of the corridor where it widened into an ornate doorway. Beyond that were the turrets, which Charles explained contained a wooden spiral staircase that led to one room at the top of each tower overlooking the landscape below with enormous glass windows.

Charles backtracked down the hall and paused to open the four doors to the right, throwing open each rather dramatically. He stepped back with a flourish.

"These are the first bedrooms we've completed. You can have your choice to stay in, these or one in the wings. We've got six completely ready. You can bring any furniture you need or take

some pieces from the other rooms. Just let us know what you need
or what you have found, and we can help move some of the heavier
stuff."

Claire and Noel walked doubtfully into the first room. The ceilings were impossibly high giving the room a feeling of unending
space. The walls were neatly painted with neutral colors, the
wooden floor polished to a mirror shine. A carved wooden fireplace
dominated the room and massive bed, carved from the same wood,
stood built on a pedestal. The windows were small, and the light
was colored in a dozen shades by the stained glass. The carvings
appeared to be related to the ones seen on the staircase out in the
hall with hunting scenes of wild animals, hounds, and formally
dressed hunters.

Claire suddenly felt a strong draft and turned to look behind her.
But the hallway was still, and the house was silent. She turned with
an odd feeling of distaste and walked out of the room to the next. To
her disappointment, all the rooms in the cluster appeared to be alike
with the violent scenes being played out on the headboard of the
bed and the fireplace.

"You don't have to choose your rooms now. We've got several
others that are close to being finished in the wings, but these are the
largest. It was the master suite for the older part of the house and
rooms for the first sons. The people who completed the house a
little later built their own suite in one of the wings and gave these
rooms to visitors. Our architect, John, has chosen one of these
rooms to stay in." Charles turned and led the way down the hallway
and up the stairs at the center to the next floor. It was an almost
exact copy of the hall below with long rows of doors opening to the
right and the left.

They trudged over most of the public spaces, went out one of
the back doors to look at the lawns, and back in to front foyer. By
the time Charles had shown them some of the unfinished bedrooms

and dressing rooms, both girls were tired, overwhelmed, and hungry.

Claire checked her watch and noted it was after 2:00 in the afternoon. She and Noel both needed to get back in town for classes and explained this to Charles. Charles instantly agreed to lead them back into town.

"I don't want to chance ruining your grades this early on," he said cheerfully. "Now that we've got you, we want to make sure to keep you."

"Well, thanks," Noel said, looking decidedly satisfied. They wound their way over the stone and weeds of the driveway and stopped at the parked cars.

"Let me take you to lunch in town before you go back to class," Charles offered.

"Sure," Noel responded before Claire could say anything. Not that she minded too much. She was hungry and the fact was, they were short on funds. A quick lunch would be a nice ending to their adventure.

"We'll follow you," Noel assured Charles and slipped into the driver's seat.

Charles nodded and pulled open the gate before climbing into his own car. They had to pause again once through the gate so Charles could close it after them.

"Okay, so what do you think now?" Noel asked, glancing at Claire as they started crossing the one-lane bridge.

"Umm, well, it's going to be a whole lot of work, but the money is fantastic! We'll be able to pay our bills off and start on our savings." She looked out the window, squelching a stab of unease as the trees closed around them.

"This is going to be a whole new life for us," Noel said confidently. And Claire felt a cold breath trace her spine.

CHAPTER THREE

The morning sun pierced the yellow curtains and cast a soft light over the bedroom. The carpeted floor was littered with papers and boxes, the drawers of the dresser hanging slightly open.

Claire and Noel had begun packing days ago, pulling posters off the walls, boxing up books and papers, and cleaning out closets. They had managed to empty several boxes into the car but had quickly run out of space.

Claire squinted against the light and rolled over to bury her face in her pillow. Today was the big day, moving day.

She heard Noel already moving in the kitchen. The sputter of the coffee maker blended with the sound of the news over the radio. The smell of the coffee drifted across the hall and into the bedroom the two girls shared. Claire couldn't imagine what it would be like to have a room of her own. She had shared a space with someone for the last six years, and the idea of her own domain was a luxury she couldn't wait to indulge in.

Claire swung her feet to the floor, bending over to roll up the braided rug at her bedside. She dropped it into a box as she went out into the kitchen. The carpet under her feet was gray with large stains of brown in the hallway. The kitchen linoleum's yellow surface was also graying with burn marks near the stove. Claire sat at the table slumped with her head in her hands, and waited as Noel poured their coffee.

"Are you ready to start loading things into the truck? Ben said he will be here at 10:00."

Claire looked up at Noel wearily. "How can you be so cheerful? We only got four hours sleep, and we worked all of yesterday. I feel like the truck ran over me."

Noel grinned. "A new day. Come on! Let's get going. We have a lot of packing to finish before we can start loading the boxes into the cars."

Claire looked after Noel as she started into the living room. Then she looked back at her coffee cup and took another sip. She groaned and got up to dump another spoonful of sugar in the cup. She was going to need all the energy she could get.

As she gathered the last of her clothes, her mind ventured back to her dream the night before. When she usually had dreams, they were foggy and unmemorable, unlike the dreams she remembered suffering in her teenaged years. During that time, that horrible time when her reality had twisted so severely, her nightmares had been a regular event, as frightening as they were realistic. But it had been a long time, years really, since she had dreamed like that. However, the dream from last night had seemed to mimic some of that clarity. It was ironic that, for all the time she had lived in the apartment, an older building, singularly ugly and unremarkable, she had never dreamed of that building. But last night, she had plainly seen it in her nightmare, the very rooms she now inhabited. The figure in her dream had been a young man, his dress uniform neatly pressed. He had stood at the foot of Claire's bed, looking at her curiously with a mild frown creasing his brow. In her dream, she had opened her eyes to see him standing straight and tall, a faded picture from the past, but had not screamed or even cried out. She had just gazed back at him, cautious but unafraid. Finally, her dream-self had sat up and pulled her covers to her shoulders, leaning forward to study him more closely until he looked away. His eyes seemed to search the apartment, and he turned his head to scan the room before he moved into the hallway. As he turned back to face her, Claire saw his lips move silently, forming the words: *Where's my mother?* But there was no terror, no cold chills, no prickling sensation climbing her spine. Then he was gone, in his wake the lingering scent of something spicy and sweet, perhaps tobacco. As far as nightmares had been, it wasn't the worst she had suffered, but she knew from experience it could be so much worse.

Claire shook her head to clear it. *They couldn't be coming back! Those dreams, those hideous nightmares! The ones where someone, or worse, something not human, appeared to her out of nothing.* She couldn't be going crazy. *Stop!* Her conscious voice pushed her out of the thought. It would do no good to look back, or to dread the future. She knew the cause of the dream. As they were preparing to leave yesterday afternoon, they had been caught in conversation with their landlady. They were handing over their extra keys, and Noel had presented the older woman with the cake she had baked, the decadent lemony icing whipped in stiff peaks on the top. Mrs. Chambers had actually had tears in her eyes when she looked at the present and told them how much she would miss them. And hadn't she mentioned how much her Ted had loved that kind of cake. *Ted.* Claire frowned as she remembered Mrs. Chambers showing them the photo of her long dead son, killed during the Vietnam War. The photo had stood in a place of honor on the little table by the front door, framed in heavy wood and accented by a stiffly folded United States flag in its own frame, and a little faded prayer card, undoubtedly from his funeral. In the photo, he had been dressed in a full uniform, his young face so solemn, his posture stiff and formal. Claire smiled bitterly. Apparently, the story had more of an effect than she had thought. She suspected it had been that face she had seen in the dream last night. And that was why she had the dream. She felt her shoulders slump with relief. Mystery solved, no problem. *No problem!* Her mind insisted, and she deliberately directed her thoughts to her task at hand.

By 2:00 all their clothes were stuffed in bags and boxes, and the last of the dishes had been washed and packed. Amy was standing in the middle of the living room, taping up the last of the boxes. It reminded Claire of all the times she and Amy had packed all their belongings at the end of the school year when they had lived in the dorm. They had shared a room for two years, and the effort it had taken to dismantle their décor had been a challenge. But they had enjoyed their time together, eating at the cafeteria, dining on Pop-Tarts for breakfast, having all night study sessions, participating in the annual haunted dorm for Halloween, and silly girl discussions after lights out, dreaming dreams of futures full of potential. Dorm life had been fun, but they had both been ready to move to something off campus as they came closer to graduation. Amy had moved into a tiny house in the Highlands area for the last year of school, just blocks from Claire's old bookstore home. However, they still remained close since she came around the apartment frequently for movie nights and Chinese food. Her own house was stuffed to overflowing with people on any given night, her current roommates the social kind, and she liked to visit the relative peace in Claire's place. On other nights, Claire and Noel enjoyed heading out the Highlands to meet with Amy and visit one of dozens of fabulous restaurants. They had spent many carefree evenings walking the sidewalks, visiting the little shops, and grabbing hot strong coffee from the cozy coffee shops. Claire knew they would miss that part of their old life.

In the doorway, Claire saw Ben in the parking lot in front of the apartment and sighed with relief. Ben made the fourth of the moving group, a sturdy figure that could be trusted for lifting and additional muscle. He slammed the door closed on his battered truck and hurried up the stairs to the apartment, his face set and distracted. As the only one with a truck, he was the designated driver for most of the furnishings.

"Well, I'm parked illegally so we'd better get this going," he said, propping the door open, hurried and talking fast. Parking was usually street side, and a rare commodity in Old Louisville.

"We're ready and packed," Claire responded, shoving one of the boxes toward the door.

"Good, just let us know what stays and what goes," he responded, scooping up one of the biggest boxes.

"Most of the furniture can stay; it belongs here, but we'll take the things we brought," Claire assured him.

"I'll get the big ones, you all can start carrying out the smaller boxes once we've got these loaded," Ben declared.

Noel and Claire nodded obediently and dragged the few pieces of furniture they owned closer to the front door as Amy taped the final box of dishes and linens.

Claire watched from the doorway as Ben began loading the larger pieces in the truck and grinned as Noel hurried to help. Her constant flirting was a joke within their little group, but Claire firmly believed it was more. Noel might have tried to be tough, but Claire had known her long enough not to be fooled.

"He's my hubby-to-be," Noel often stated. "He just doesn't know it yet."

"You've known him for years and haven't been on a single date. How do you figure this romance is supposed to work?" Claire had asked pointedly.

"It just will." Noel insisted and laughed at herself. Despite the teasing tone, she had once admitted to Claire she had purposely consulted her palm reader and psychic, and she claimed they agreed with her supposition. "It will only be a matter of time," she said confidently, "and Ben will be mine."

Claire wasn't sure about how Ben felt about the situation, but he certainly never seemed put out when Noel smiled at him and gave him inviting glances. It wasn't any of her business either, so she dismissed it.

"I think you girls have almost as much stuff in this apartment as I do in my whole house," Ben complained as he took a third trip out to the truck.

Ben had just finished remodeling the little house he bought in Middletown, a suburb cozied up to the larger town of Louisville, and it was charming, especially for a single guy's lair. Claire and Noel had helped him with the painting and decorating and knew the place inside and out. It was a comfortable Cape Cod with two bedrooms upstairs and one down, a solid brick building that had suffered through two floods and one tornado in its almost 50-year history. When the threat of eviction had first come up, Ben had offered the house to the two girls as a place to stay temporarily.

Claire had flatly, but graciously, refused. "We can't do that to you," she had said, smiling to take away any sting. "You don't want a couple of girls cluttering up your new space, and besides, we're going to find something soon." And Claire had believed that at the time. It had just taken them longer to find their new home, but now that they were moving, it appears her prediction was coming true.

Noel hadn't been as happy with Claire's refusal. "We could just stay with Ben for a few weeks," she had argued while outside of Ben's earshot.

"Not a good idea," Claire had replied, and her expression told Noel her mind was made up. Noel had been disappointed, but Claire had known it would secretly kill Noel to be so close to Ben all the time and have no chance at a romance. It might have looked like casual flirting to someone who didn't know the people involved, but Claire knew better.

Sighing, Claire moved into her bedroom and picked up a box. It was time to finish loading the cars. Without their colorful decorations and homey touches, the apartment looked truly abandoned. The yellowed linoleum, the stained walls, the cracked ceilings were all shown in the brutal light of day. Claire wondered if they would eventually open the apartment back up to the rest of the house as it had originally been designed. They would need new flooring, new paint, new bathroom fixtures; who she was kidding, they would need to gut the entire thing to make it really livable. But the way it was now, it was just sad. The feeling of grief that welled up in Claire far out measured the lonely look of the apartment. It was as though she was soaking in the emotions of someone else. And perhaps she was. This had at one time been a home, but events – life – had turned it into more of a house, a business, a place to stay. Maybe what it needed was a heart again.

As the caravan pulled up to the house, Claire enjoyed watching Amy's eyes widen. The massive iron gates were opened before them, left by some curious host. The day had gone from balmy with misty sun to cloudy, the lawn stained with shadows. A chill had settled in the evening and the house looked huge and forbidding with the sun setting behind it. A few lights glowed in the second story where Charles had said the architect was staying for a few weeks.

As Noel guided their car in behind Amy's, Claire checked the rear-view mirror again. Amy and Claire had been in the first car, Noel in the second, and Ben driving his truck bringing up the rear. Noel had stopped on the way to pick up dinner because she was pretty sure she was the only one who could find her way to the house alone. Claire was surprised when she pulled in just after them.

"You all drive so slow!" Noel said, grinning. She held up bags of cheeseburgers and led the way up the front steps. Amy followed, helping Noel by carrying the drinks.

Amy stopped at the door and turned around, her dark curls blowing, and Claire could see that her rounded cheeks were not their usual rosy tone. Her warm brown eyes looked worried. "This is it?" she asked cautiously.

Claire followed her and dug in her purse for the key Charles had given them.

"Ta da. The grand opening. Welcome to 'Talitha,' the charm of the bluegrass," Noel said, dancing up beside them.

Claire felt a subtle hesitation. Her eyes went to the tall pines behind the stoned wall, the hedges framing the weedy lawn, and the fountain, the horses straining as though trying to flee.

"Claire, are you going to open that door or do we have to go through the window?" Ben groused, jolting her from her negative thoughts, and nodding toward his hands full of suitcases and bags.

Claire shoved the key in the lock and quickly twisted it in the lock. The knob seemed to vibrate under her hands as she turned it. She didn't realize she had been holding her breath until the door swung open and the draft of cold air made her gasp.

No one else seemed aware of her discomfort, and they hurriedly pushed into the house leaving her alone on the porch. She had to deliberately force her feet to move, to step over the threshold.

The entry looked as before, the marble floor dusty with boot prints and the walls appearing to molt with crumbling wallpaper. Without the morning sun, the room was cold and the shadows deeper. Amy shivered next to Claire.

"Creepy," she muttered under her breath. Catching Claire

watching her, she smiled apologetically. Claire was tempted to agree but held her tongue.

Ben broke the silence when he asked where he should drop the suitcases. "I don't know what you packed in here, but it sure doesn't feel like clothes," he complained, rolling his shoulders and wincing.

"Just put them here. While we can still see, we'll get the important stuff in the house, so we can just carry it all up the stairs later." Claire switched on a few lights, her hands now steady.

As Noel showed Amy where to take the drinks and food bags, Claire and Ben headed back out to the cars to unload. They knew they had to take advantage of the daylight while it lasted, and Claire dreaded the dark. She certainly didn't want to be outside, standing beneath the sharp hooves of the frozen horses, as the sun set. It was obvious the days were getting shorter, and the shadows were stretching over the lawn as they started to haul in the heavier items.

Almost an hour later, all the boxes and furniture had been carried up and dumped into the hallway. During the commotion, a thin figure emerged from the stairway to the second story.

"You must be the new roommates," the man greeted them cheerfully, approaching with hand outstretched.

"That's us," Noel replied, coming up behind Claire and dropping her load. "And you are?"

Claire was surprised at the edge in Noel's voice and realized her friend had been startled by his appearance.

"Sorry, John. John Fisk. I'm the architect for the renovation." He withdrew his hand when he saw theirs were full and smoothed his dark hair back in an unconscious gesture.

"Sure," Noel said, visibly relaxing. "Sorry, I was just a little jumpy."

"It's fine. I understand. We're working on the lighting in this place. It leaves a lot to be desired just yet." John's merry smile had reappeared.

"I didn't know architects lived where they worked," Amy interrupted, looking puzzled.

"I've been staying here for a couple of weeks, working on the final schematics." John shrugged. "It was my choice to stay here. It just seemed easier to oversee everything. The commute would have been a bitch." His smile came again, bright white in a tanned face. "Charles told me you were moving in soon. Do you need any extra help?"

Claire sighed in relief as she looked at John's open face. Charles had said they might have others living there with them, but she hadn't realized how much she had hoped for that until she had seen him there in the hall. John willingly helped carry up some of the remaining boxes, talking quickly all the while, easily lifting the boxes and loping up the stairs with practiced ease. On his way up, he briefly explained that he planned on staying for a few weeks to oversee some of the work and complete some recent drawings.

"Which rooms are you in?" Noel asked as they dropped their load in the hallway.

"Charles said he was in the old master bedroom," Claire reminded her.

John nodded his head back towards the central staircase. "I picked some rooms in the older section because they interested me. Here, I'll show you around." He made a sweeping gesture encompassing the wide hallway. "I wanted to be in the center of things, easier to keep track of the action."

"We went through a few of those when we first came here for the interview." Claire looked back down the shadowy hall. "They are very, um, formal."

"The carving and woodwork is definitely older, a little grim. But I like that the windows overlook the driveway. I can see when the workers get here, and if anyone else comes by, I can check them out before I go down."

It sounded like a good plan to Claire, especially if John had been living there alone. He would be able to keep track of anyone in the house as long as they came in the front door. And if they came in another door? She wondered how many entrances the house had. The house had the feel of such expansiveness, of hallways and rooms stretching out into the darkness.

"I like to know who's coming in and who's going out." John said, echoing her thoughts. "This place gets damn spooky at night." He suddenly looked embarrassed. "I really shouldn't have said that. It's not so bad once you get used to it, and I'll be here for a while if you need anything." He smiled a little weakly now, and Noel grinned back, clearly taking his statement as more of a challenge than an offer of protection.

"I ain't scared," she said playfully, leading the way into his grandiose chamber.

His room was amazing in itself. It was one of the few they hadn't toured the first time they had visited, and this one was fully outfitted for its occupant. The walls had been painted a stark white leaving the eye to focus on the elaborate carving of the fireplace, the huge canopied bed, and a built-in bookcase. The wood had a rich sheen and matched the waxed floor; although, John explained, the carvings had required only minimal touch ups.

The bed was the focus of the room with the wooden canopy hanging empty and a plain navy comforter on the mattress. Each post of the canopy was carved to resemble a forest animal including bears, wolves, and other fanged creatures. Pushed against the opposite wall was a huge library table covered with papers and an elaborate computer system. John smiled sheepishly as he explained the fax machine, scanner, plotter, and computer he used on all his various projects.

"I don't have a local office, so when I'm here I use this equipment. It all belongs to Edwards Incorporated." When he received confused looks he elaborated. "Mr. Edwards, the man that owns the building. He will be staying here sometimes but has business all over the country. Our firm has done a lot of work for him, office buildings, other jobs like that."

"What kind of business is he in?" Claire asked curiously.

"His main interests are in publications, but the company has diversified into other areas," John responded. He closed the door behind them and they descended the stairs. "I haven't worked personally with Cole Edwards that much. Once we got the job, he stepped back, and we've been consulting with his assistant and the other construction people in the company." He paused and began walking down the stairs, his hands lightly tracing the polished wood of the railing. "This is the first job Mr. Edwards has shown much interest in personally. That is, as far as I know, and I can't say I know a lot about his company. But rumor is..." John paused and gave them a sly, conspiratorial smile, "this place is his ancestral home. I don't know if he personally ever lived here, but apparently it's been in the family for years."

"So, did his family build this house?" Noel asked.

"No, at least not all of it. From what I understand, the main part of the house was built in the 1850s and lived in for a couple years." John appeared to be warming toward his subject, like a teacher lecturing on his favorite subject du jour. "At that time, Versailles and Lexington were bustling, and Louisville was one of the largest and wealthiest towns around. Louisville was going strong, linked with the rest of the country with the railroad going across land, and the steamboats traveling the Ohio River. Then the war broke out, and even though Kentucky tried to remain neutral, Louisville became a popular place for Union soldiers to gather and prepare for the fight. It was around that time the family abandoned the house, and with all the upheaval, we're not sure who might have stayed here, especially during those years when the soldiers were scrambling. Anyone could have broken in to camp out." He shrugged. "After the war was over, the place was vacant for a while. The Edwards family bought the place from the state for a steal. They later decided to add on the wings." He paused to glance at his audience. "That's why the place looks like it was put together without planning. It was designed by two different groups of people with very different taste in architecture and during different historic periods."

"And not all taste is good," Amy said dryly. Claire nodded her agreement, and looked back up the stairs nervously.

"And I'm boring you," John said, slightly embarrassed. "I'll tell you the rest of the sordid history of this place some other time."

Once in the kitchen, they all sat together, huddled over the chef grade kitchen counter, warming up their dinner. Noel had bought extra food, and John joined them in the harsh artificial light. Claire found him to be outgoing and engaging with a wicked since of humor. He told them several amusing stories about some of his other clients as well as his experience as a student in the College of Architecture at the University of Kentucky where the students ranged from brilliant to eccentric. She listened with halfhearted attention while he spoke, her mind on the silent dark spaces outside the window and just around the corner. But John seemed to know an awful lot about the history of the area. He also seemed to be content to work on the renovation because of his personal interest in historic preservation. Much of the structure of the house, he explained, had been sound, and they had tried their best to maintain the integrity of the original floor plan. Adding bathrooms and improving the kitchen had been the biggest jobs since serious changes in room sizes were required.

"The renovation is going to make this place a showcase," John stated enthusiastically. "It has been kept in good enough condition that we can keep most of the original finishes. It's just a matter of cleaning up what we have and finding replacements for what has been ruined by sitting here empty for so long."

"Why has it been empty?" Noel asked, delicately dipping a limp French fry in ketchup.

"Some bad history about this place," John said dismissively. "The Edwards family had a hard time while they lived here and apparently had enough money socked away they could literally walk away from the place. It's not exactly on a well-worn route, so the structure was mostly forgotten by the locals, except, of course vandals and the occasional teenager looking for a thrill. No one cared, and after a few more years, some family representative hired a caretaker to make sure it wasn't being completely destroyed. No squatters or druggies since then; it's just been empty."

"And now they have come back?" Noel's eyebrows winged up, and a half smile curved her lips.

"Not they. Just Cole Edwards. I think he is the last of the family." John quickly wiped his mouth with a paper napkin and crumpled it into a tight ball in his fist. "He came to our office and said he wanted to turn this place into something worthwhile. And frankly, we jumped at it. Ours isn't a big firm and this place is going to be a magnet for the rich and very rich, close enough for the horse crowd, but big enough to have special events, weddings, meetings, reunions." His voice has gotten more intense, his eyes glittering. "When we get done with it, this house is going to look as good as it ever did, better even. And it will take our reputation to new heights."

For some reason, his passion made Claire feel better about the house. In his eyes, she could see the halls crowded with wealthy people, a bridal party posing on the curved stairs, the busy shuffling of expensive soles on the marble floors.

"It sounds like a great job," Noel agreed. "You get to take something that looks like it's falling down and bring it back to life."

"It's just getting better, too," John agreed, a grin of satisfaction lighting his face. "The more people I see around here working on restoring this place, the happier I am."

When dinner was finished, they all pitched in and cleaned up the trash, gathering it into a takeout bag to drop in one of the huge trash cans around the side of the building. Darkness had settled on the house. Looking out the windows, Claire noticed that the blackness was complete with no stars or moon evident. The air seemed still and heavy around them, although the chill of the night was settling in her bones.

"We'd better get your things set up," Ben said, returning through the front door after getting rid of the trash. "It gets dark out here in the country."

The group returned upstairs to set up the beds, hurrying through their preparations. Tomorrow was a workday, and they knew the sun would rise soon enough.

John switched on the lights that lined the hallway, but the sconces, which had almost certainly been chosen due to their resemblance to the original fixtures, were still insufficient. Amy seemed especially nervous, and Claire noticed her glancing out the bedroom door over and over, as though watching for someone she expected to arrive. The boxes had blocked the top of the stairs, and it took time to lift them, one at a time, into the girls' chosen rooms. Both Noel and Claire had picked rooms at the anterior of the house and in the left wing. The bedrooms were mirror images of each other with tall ceilings and freshly papered walls. They were much airier and light compared to the gothic look of John's room, and in Claire's opinion, a million times better.

Noel's room was closer to the stairway and boasted a built-in wardrobe which reached the ceiling and opened wide enough to fit three full grown people. The wood was carved like the rest in the house, with ornate curves that blended into long stemmed lilies and slender foliage. On the opposite wall was a raised platform meant for one of the antique beds stored in the attic. Noel had stubbornly insisted on bringing her futon, so that no bed was necessary for her room. Behind the platform at the head of the bed was a carved panel of whimsical figures with cherubs and flowers entangled in a dance.

Kindly birds with wings outstretched looked down from the top of the panel.

To the left of the bed were double doors that opened onto a narrow balcony, one of the painstaking renovation for each room in the wings the owner had insisted on. This balcony was connected to an identical balcony outside Claire's room. Heavy brocade drapes shut out the dark night, and an Oriental rug covered the gleaming wooden floors. The only other furnishings from the house were a heavy armchair newly covered in a plain blue fabric with a matching footstool situated in front of the fireplace.

Claire's room was very similar, differing only in decorations and furnishings. Claire's platform held one of the antique bed frames, newly refurbished, and they only had to struggle to get her mattress in place. It didn't fit exactly because of the bed frame's dimensions, but it suited well enough. She wished then she had taken up on Charles offer to use one of the new mattresses they had acquired for the finished hotel. He had bragged about the top of the line amenities, and no doubt it would have been more comfortable than the mattress she had dragged from home to the apartment, and then transferred it here. The bed frame was obviously built for the room because the ornate carvings on the headboard and footboard matched those on the panel behind the bed. Flowers were again the subject but wound in the looping of their stems and leaves were tiny fairies peering from behind the foliage with pointed ears and lacy wings. Again, birds were a common subject with plump doves dotting the delicate trees.

Claire's wardrobe was similarly carved with flowers and reached the ceiling with only inches to spare. The doors to the balcony were covered with matching drapes and a stuffed chair with rose fabric was situated in front of the cold fireplace. The walls were papered with huge primroses, pink and raspberry, their leaves dark green with heavy stems. Overall, both rooms were large and comfortable, much nicer than any apartment they could have afforded.

Exhausted, Noel and Claire stood in the doorway after they had watched their friends leave. They were relieved to be moved in, but the house seemed cavernous when empty. John had retired to his room a half hour earlier, stating that he had to make some calls before it grew too late, but the sheer size of the house made it feel as though they were alone and far from the rest of the world.

Slowly, Claire closed the door behind their friends and locked it, leaving the light on as they walked up the stairs. Claire had looked around the foyer, the stairway winding up into the darkness. She had headed up silently, Noel following close behind. Their footsteps fell quietly on the threadbare carpet, the steps squeaking in protest as they ascended.

At the head of the stairs, they went to the left, ignoring the closed doors in the main section of the house. Claire had refused to choose one of those rooms, even though they were larger and closer to the functioning bathrooms.

When Noel had looked at her curiously, surprised by the vehemence of her refusal, Claire had only shrugged at her expression. How could she explain that she felt odd in the older part of the house? That standing in the foyer and gazing up the stairs made the back of her neck tingle like a ghostly hand was caressing the bare skin there? It had been years since those feelings of dread had disturbed her. That time, that slice of her life better erased from her memory. But as she grew older, the feelings became mere memories, and then fantasies of her imagination. She had fought to shake the image of a backward, mildly disturbed young girl, and she wasn't about to let the facade slip now.

Taking a few of the remaining boxes into their rooms, they left the bulk of them in the hall. Each girl had packed a suitcase with the most important necessities in it. They went together down the hall and took turns in the largest bathroom, located in the main section of the house.

The bathroom was a glorious mix of retrofit pieces, originals, and beautiful reproductions. It was not totally finished, but the potential was there. And the water was hot, the tile cool beneath their feet, and the unstained sinks and unmarred mirrors a perfect contrast from the sad little place they had left by the campus.

Their basic clean up completed, they went back down the hall to their rooms. Claire closed her door quietly behind her, listening to the soft click of the latch engaging. She looked around the room slowly, her eyes gritty with fatigue.

Her sheets were neatly tucked around the mattress, her yellow comforter glaring against all the antique wood. She picked it up and flipped it, the cream side up. That was better. Next, she rifled through the suitcase to find her nightclothes. She had purposely chosen a set that was modest with a short sleeve top and matching shorts. The temperature in the room was slightly cool, so she hurried to crawl under the covers. She took a paperback novel with her, a mystery romance to keep her mind off her situation. To be honest with herself, she was trying not to think about the house. Avoiding the odd feelings the room gave her, as though the clever fairies were watching her with their shiny brown eyes.

She straightened her sheet and pulled the comforter tighter around her legs. Her eyes wandered around the room. The lamp beside the bed cast shadows on the page in front of her. She could almost laugh. Her belongings looked obscene next to the room's lush furnishings. The table next to her had inlaid wood polished to a high sheen. Her yellow telephone sat atop it with a box of Kleenex next to it, her alarm clock sitting closest to the bed. Her Georgia O'Keefe poster, framed in yellow plastic, leaned against the wall beneath an oil portrait of a young woman in full formal dress.

Claire studied the portrait. The woman was attractive with a sharp nose and strong chin, which kept her from being a conventional beauty. Her dark brown hair was piled atop her head and secured with jeweled combs. A matching necklace was at her throat, the pearl locket glowing a soft pink. But most striking were her eyes, painted with such clarity she seemed to watch Claire with eerie directness from across the room.

Next to the portrait was the wardrobe and on the other side of the huge piece of furniture was an ornate mirror framed in heavy gold. The mirror was obviously old with lines and spots of black showing around the edges of the glass. It reflected the soft light and the wall behind the bed. When Claire moved she could see her shadow in the reflection. She wondered if she would ever get to sleep at this rate. But her eyes were getting heavy. She was almost nodding off when a tick tick sounded at the balcony doors.

"Is it raining?" she asked aloud, her voice swallowed up in the silence. She listened more closely, but realized it wasn't any rain. She could hear the wind shushing against the glass, but it was a dry sound, like a breath from a skeleton's mouth.

"Now that's a creepy thought," she said into the dimness. She slipped her legs out from under the blankets and tiptoes to the glass doors. She bent close, her eyes squinting with the effort to hear something.

The skittering clicking and clattering against the panes had her jumping back, her heart in her throat. She jerked open the heavy curtains to reveal a flutter of a shape outside the window.

"A bird," she breathed in relief, seeing its escape into the wind. "It's only a bird." She put her hand to her chest as though to still the beating of her heart. "Nothing but a bird in the wind. Lucky, it didn't kill itself against the glass."

She pulled the curtains closed against the night outside and walked more slowly back to her bed. For a moment, she just listened, but there were no more unexplained sounds. She took one more look around and sighed with fatigue. Slowly she sank back down, burying her head in her pillow.

CHAPTER FOUR

The early morning light seeped through the heavy curtains covering the French doors. It drew straight lines across the wood floor until it reached the fireplace on the opposite wall. The chubby faces of the fairies were highlighted; the clever grins of last night replaced by serene smiles frozen on innocent faces. As Claire sat up, the mirror reflected the top of her head as she leaned over to check her watch. It was 8:30, far later than she had thought. She slipped out of bed and went immediately to the window. The sun almost blinded her as it streaked though the glass, setting the room ablaze with light. There were no signs of her visitor last night, no feathers or tiny birdie prints on the concrete.

She gathered her shampoo and soap, filling her bucket with all her toiletries, and hurried down the hall to the shower. The bathroom was four doors down in the main part of the house. The plumbers hadn't completed all the pipes to the new bathrooms in the east or west wings so the only functioning ones were adjoining the master bedroom and the ones downstairs.

Claire ran into the nearest one, her feet chilled by the wooden floors. She immediately turned on the hot water in the tub and watched the steam rise in a sinuous cloud. As she dropped her clothes on the floor, she unbraided her hair and put her shower supplies in the tub.

Noel's were already in place. Claire decided she must have gotten up early and was downstairs getting breakfast since she hadn't heard any noise from her friend's room. Hopefully Noel had slept more comfortably than Claire had.

Once the water was warm, Claire stepped under the spray, letting it rinse away her fatigue. She stood there for a moment, basking in the heat and letting the water run through her long hair, pulling out the tangles. Next, she lathered her hair vigorously and rinsed it, breathing in the sweet scent of the shampoo. As she soaped her hands to wash her face, she noted she had been show-ering for longer than usual. As she finished rinsing, she felt the water steadily growing colder. It surprised her to think they would run out of hot water in a building that size. Charles had mentioned all the utilities, the plumbing and heating, had been replaced to handle the load of a full house. As the water temperature dropped, Claire hurriedly rinsed her hair of the remaining conditioner.

Hot, scalding water suddenly hit her back, sending her flailing forward. An involuntary scream choked her as she stumbled, hands grasping the curtain. She fell hard on her knees outside the tub, tears in her eyes. Her back screamed and her knees throbbed as she turned over, sitting naked on the cold tile floor. Breathing hard she looked up to the shower head. No steam rose from the water and when she stretched her hand out, letting the spray trickle through her fingers, the water was ice cold.

She dragged herself to her feet and stepped gingerly into the tub, her back burning with heat. The initial shock of the cold made her yelp, but the cold water gradually eased the pain from the burn.

After a few minutes, she finished rinsing her hair and turned off the water, trembling from the cold. Goose bumps pricked her skin and her back continued to ache, but the pain was less. She found her robe and towel. Carefully she dabbed her tender skin and pulled the robe over her still damp back. She stuck her head out of the door and seeing no one in the hallway, hurried back to her room. She dropped the robe from her shoulders to the crook of her arm and turned her back to the mirror, looking at herself over her shoulder. Her skin was an angry red but no blisters were evident.

A knock on her closed door made her jump and Noel peered around the door.

"My God, what happened to you?" she asked, looking at Claire's white face and red back.

"The damn shower. It almost took my skin off."

"What do you mean? It was fine this morning when I used it," Noel said, coming into the room and closing the door behind her.

Claire explained what had happened and let Noel have a closer look at her back. Noel immediately went to her room to get an aloe cream to ease the pain.

Together they went downstairs after Claire was dressed. They met John on the stairs as he was headed back up to his room. Noel indignantly told him about the accident as Claire stood silently at her side. He was surprised and told them he would immediately speak with the plumbers.

"That's so strange. The whole system is brand new and top of the line. As a matter of fact, the water heater's temperature is being kept very low so no one does get accidentally burned." He ran an agitated hand through his hair. "I'll get to the bottom of this. This is totally unacceptable," he declared. "One more thing going wrong," he muttered darkly more to himself than to the girls. He continued to look frustrated as he made his way up to his room, his feet heavier on the steps.

Breakfast was cold cereal and milk, and the rest of the morning was spent organizing their rooms waiting to be told further instructions. By the time they were finished, Noel had set up her futon on the platform with her new comforter in neon colors, and propped her funky beaded lamp on an old dresser they had found in the room next door. Colorful scarves of crimson and orange were draped on the wooden mantle above the fireplace, and candlesticks shaped like giraffes adorned a junky old bedside table Noel had painted yellow. Noel stepped back, satisfied by her decorating. It was an odd mix that expressed her personality perfectly.

Claire's room was next. With the bed made in soft cream, a desk procured from the room next door, and some pillows thrown in the chair and on the bed, her room was a reflection of how she wanted her life. Serene and controlled. Framed photos of her family with her collection of glass paperweights sat on the deep mantle above the huge fireplace.

Claire borrowed one of Noel's more conservative scarves with rose and cream stripes and wound it on the canapé frame. She stacked her books neatly on her desk and used her porcelain book-ends, delicate flowers sprouting from a heavy base, to hold them up. She dropped a braided rug in soft colors on the floor to protect her bare feet. Lastly, she checked out her framed poster propped it up under the portrait, waiting to hang it later. By the time the rooms were done, it was time for lunch.

John was below, eating a sandwich in the kitchen when they went down the stairs. He seemed to have calmed down since their meeting on the stairs that morning, and they talked with him as they ate. It appeared the architect was a font of interesting information. The renovation had been underway for almost a year with difficulties interrupting the work on several occasions. The snow of last winter had caused problems because of the drive, and continual freezing and melting had been hard on the old stone. Immediately after, the spring rain had arrived with a fury and seeped inside the house from badly sealed windows, doors, and a little from the storm damaged roof. The heat had gone out in the coldest weather, and the air conditioner, newly installed, had choked on the hottest day of the season. Work had stopped and started in sputtering attempts at consistency. Structural problems had been attended to first, although the house was stable considering the neglect, John explained, trying to add a happier ending on a string of bad luck.

"How long was this place empty?" Noel asked curiously.

"It was cared for by a small staff until the '60s. After that, the money ran out, and the house was boarded up. By then it had acquired such a reputation no one would touch it."

"Reputation," Claire said, looking closely at John's face.

He laughed slightly but avoided her eyes, looking down at his feet. "Nothing," he said quickly, "It's nothing really. Just rumors and ... well, old ghost stories."

Noel looked fascinated, "Tell us more about it."

John sighed and looked at them directly. "Look, we're not supposed to discuss this. Charles stated it at the start of this project, and apparently that comes from the top. Since this is supposed to be such a public attraction, Charles doesn't want any negative publicity."

"Oh," Noel looked deflated, but Claire suddenly felt relieved, then angry with herself for her own cowardice.

Slamming doors from outside drew their attention and they moved into the foyer in time to see a small convoy of trucks drive up. The workers moved quickly, nodding briefly to Claire and Noel as John performed a hurried introduction. They carried boxes of tools, extension cords, and materials. Soon, the building was alive with the noise of heavy boots and power tools.

Claire looked at John curiously. "Why are they starting so late?"

John looked surprised. "Charles asked them to wait. He wanted to make sure you had enough time to settle in. I thought he told you that."

"We haven't talked to Charles since Wednesday when we scheduled moving day," Noel explained. "It was nice of him to wait for us."

John nodded, distracted." I'm going to go up and check on Joe. He's working on remodeling for bathrooms. I need to talk to him about the water heater. Charles said he'd be in tomorrow to get you guys started." He grinned at them, suddenly looking boyish, "Better enjoy today while you have it easy."

By 6:00 the workers had cleared out, taking with them the incessant noise of power tools and conversation, but leaving some of their tools around to stub unsuspecting toes. The mess, if anything, had gotten worse with their presence. Bits of plaster and spatters of paint were generously spread throughout the hallway and down the stairs. The kitchen and bathrooms all bore the distinct handprints of the men, cast in dirt, concrete or dust, depending on what each person had worked on for the day. Claire began wiping up the bathrooms while Noel started dinner. By the time Claire had finished with two of them, Noel had a spaghetti dinner ready and was choosing a wine.

The sauce was canned, and the pasta dried, but eating in the dining room with the lights dimmed to lend it atmosphere and cover the wear and tear of time, made the food seem almost gourmet. Or maybe it was just the fact they were moved in and excited about the new job. And the wine was honestly good, dry with a hint of oak flavor.

John was out for the evening and the two girls sat in the comparative quiet, nursing their drinks and looking around the room.

"This place could be beautiful," Noel said softly, her eyes skimming the wood paneling.

Claire looked up to the ceiling. In the dim light, a painted pattern was barely visible. Her eyes dropped to the shrouded furniture against the walls. When they peeked beneath the sheets, they had been able to discern a tall china cabinet with glass doors and a long, low buffet. With some work, this room could easily be the central showplace of the house with seating for a good number of patrons. Claire had a sudden vision of the room as it once had been, the table buffed to a high gloss, matching carved chairs with rich red cushions, and the silver trays on the buffet mounded with rich food, the odor sweet and savory. Dishes and silver laid out artfully on the table glinted in the light of a huge crystal chandelier.

In a blink, it was gone and Claire was looking back at the scarred surface.

Her wine started to bubble.

Unaware, she looked slowly at her slender hands in her lap, devoid of rings with neatly trimmed, unpainted nails. Idly she thought of sketching the scene she had just imagined. What a rich and textured image it would make. Weird thought. Everyone knew she couldn't draw more than a stick figure.

The pop caused her head to jerk up as tiny pieces of glass and ripe red wine splattered her bare arms and white tee shirt.

Noel yelped as Claire jumped back.

"Oh my God, what was that? Are you all right?"

Claire stared at the shattered remains of her glass, sparkling like rubies in the dim light. Wine seeped into her napkin and dripped onto her light-colored pants like blood. She shoved away from the table, her chair scraping the wooden floor. "Yeah, yeah, I think I'm fine," she said slowly, sliding her fingers down her arms. Apart from a few scratches, she was unharmed. She stumbled to her feet and carefully used her napkin to stop the flow of liquid from reaching the center of the table. Slowly she wiped away the scarlet droplets, catching Noel's eyes on her.

"Are you sure you're fine?"

Claire crumpled the napkin in her hand and nodded. Clasping her hands over the red stained ball, she walked into the kitchen, trying to put some space between her and the table. "Let's just clean up. I think I'm ready to go back upstairs." She felt suddenly anxious to get out of the old section of the house.

"I'll get the glass; you take the dishes in." Noel gestured Claire further into the kitchen. In the bright light, it all seemed to make more sense. She must have tipped the glass over. She could have hit it with her hand without realizing it. The wood of the table, the thin glass, it was a pure accident.

"Okay, I've got it," Noel broke her reverie with her words. "No harm done, so I guess we're okay. It's not like any of the dishes here are the expensive type. I guess they'll add fine china later. They must have expected some accidents." Noel stopped talking and looked at Claire more closely. "Are you sure you feel alright?" she asked.

Claire forced a smile. "Sure," she responded. She swung open the door of the dishwasher and placed the few dishes in the rack with a light clatter, closing the door.

Noel dropped the garbage with the glass in the trash can and washed her hands. "Let's go on up," she said "We'll run the dish-washer when it's full. I'll wash the pans in the morning."

They walked up together, switching the lights off as they went.

Claire went in her room, exhausted and confused. There was an explanation about what had happened. She could picture it in her mind. But her mind screamed back that it was a lie. The glass hadn't fallen. The table wasn't tilted; her hand hadn't struck it. In fact, when she forced herself to truly focus, she realized when she had examined her place at the table after the incident, the base and stem of the glass stood intact and upright. So, what would make the glass just burst like that?

Now, tucked in her bed she left the light on. Her eyes drifted closed, and she felt herself began to dissociate. Her muscles eased as sleep took hold. She opened her eyes one last time, her gaze landing on the portrait by the mantle. The knowing eyes seemed to meet hers. Then she fell asleep.

CHAPTER FIVE

She woke up slowly, surprised to see the soft gray light of dawn fanning out across the floor. She felt as though she had slept only a moment, not all night long, so deep and dreamless was her rest. She knew the construction workers would arrive soon, so she unwillingly slid out of bed, warm feet touching the cold wooden floor.

Her eyes went automatically up to the portrait; the painted eyes following her appeared mildly amused. She felt herself smile back, feeling a strange kinship to the lady who may have once slept in the same bed she now used. Shaking her head to clear it, she stood up and walked toward the wardrobe, planning what she would wear for her first real day of work.

She caught her reflection in the mirror as she walked by and stopped short in front of the mirror. The middle of the glass appeared foggy, as though caressed by a soft, moist breath. Written in the haze, as though marked by a child's finger, were two words. GO HOME.

Her first instinct was to obey and flee the room. If that was what they wanted, she would be happy to oblige. But instead she stood still, torn between yelling for Noel to come see what she was seeing, to witness this, and running from the room hysterically. Instead, she decided that perhaps she wasn't seeing what she thought she saw. She blinked hard, her mind insisting, *wait for it, wait for it.*

As Claire stepped hesitantly closer to the mirror, the words appeared still visible on the surface. But when she reached the mirror, the fog began to dissipate. By the time she was close enough to touch, the glass was clear, and the words were gone.

Claire brought a single finger to the glass, watching as the reflection and her finger met. The glass was cool, but not cold, and the surface was unmarked except for the blacking age marks. It felt like, well, nothing unusual. It felt like glass, just glass. She looked at the frame and finally, gingerly, attempted to lift the mirror from the wall. Although it moved and would swing easily along the wall, when she tried to lift it off the hook, she realized it was too heavy for her to take down. Because of its age, she feared breaking it. With a grim look, she gave up her investigation of the mirror and looked around the room, still uneasy.

There was no doubt in her mind the words had been there. Someone had written the message; someone close by. She wasn't crazy or seeing things. The message had existed for such a short time, thought Claire, as though someone had breathed it to life as she had gotten out of bed.

She crossed her arms protectively over her chest, feeling a sudden chill of apprehension. If someone wanted to scare her away, they had chosen a good way of telling her. The message was destined not to last, at least not long enough for her to find a witness or snap a picture for proof.

And why would anyone want her to leave? She hadn't done anything destructive and hadn't made anyone angry. At least not to her knowledge. This had to be tied to something much larger, something about the house, about the renovation, perhaps.

Frowning, she turned away from the mirror and checked the French doors, finding them locked. The door to her room was also secure. The only person who had a key was Noel, and surely, she wouldn't play such a nasty joke.

Noel, she thought abruptly. *She was the only other person around just now. Could it be?*

She yanked her door open and went next door, knocking loudly. After a minute, Noel opened the door, her hair standing in tufts all over her head. Her eyes were heavy with sleep. Claire knew as soon as Noel answered she had not been the prankster.

"What?" Noel grumbled, her voice rough with sleep.

Claire thought furiously. If she told Noel about the incident, she would look idiotic. And frankly, she didn't want to bring up something new after her wineglass exploding the night before.

Noel continued to look at her curiously, her sleep forgotten as she watched the emotions pass on her friend's face.

"I was just checking to see if you were up yet. Sorry to wake you. I didn't realize how early it was," Claire lied weakly.

"Oh, well, I'll be up in about 30 minutes," Noel responded, running her hands through the shaggy hair, "if you're all right." With Claire's forced smile and nod, Noel waved and closed the door, choosing more sleep over her curiosity.

Claire stood in the silent hallway for a few more minutes. She glanced up and down the corridor, seeing rows of closed doors but little else. There were no footprints tracing up the worn carpet or suspicious sounds emanating from behind the closed doors. Pushing her hair behind her shoulder in an unconscious gesture of dismissal, Claire returned to her room. There she paced around the room for a few minutes, checking and rechecking the windows for loose catches or signs someone had crept in her room. With nervous energy, she made her bed and rearranged her pillows. Finally, she unplugged her cell phone and called her parents' house to soak in the reassuring voices from home. Her mother was naturally interested about Claire's new residence, so Claire spent an extra half-hour on the phone telling her details about the house and how the move went. When she hung up she felt an acute sense of loss, wishing she had been able to be honest with her family about her concerns. But no, they had enough just dealing with her father's illness. To even suggest that her "problems" were returning would send them into a panic.

Claire quickly straightened her bed covers again. Her braided rug seemed to have crept out from under the bed-frame as though it was slowly traversing the length of the room, so she tugged it back into place. Finally, she gathered her shower supplies and clothes. She went into the bathroom, feeling a little like she was playing Russian roulette with the shower. The water stayed warm but not hot, and by the time she was done, she felt much better. It was nice to scrub at the faded grime on her hands and she took a few extra minutes trying to remove some splotches of paint from her skin she must have gotten while passing through the active construction.

After quickly getting dressed, Claire jogged down the stairs in the morning sunlight. She was eating toast when Noel slipped downstairs, her hair still damp. As the coffee perked in the machine, they heard the rumble of the workers already busy in the other bedrooms upstairs. Charles arrived shortly after and got down to business, assigning each girl to a different room. He briefly outlined the tasks he wanted them to perform and was specific about the cleaning solutions he wanted used because of the possible chemical reactions with some of the more fragile finishes on the woodwork. Since the workers were still concentrating on the second and third floor bedrooms, the girls started work in the wings where the plaster and drywall had been completed.

"We want this done right and carefully, so take your time," Charles said cheerfully. "This place has to be close to perfect."

It was slow, painstaking work dusting and wiping the grim off the woodwork, cleaning and mopping the dusty floor. Each carving on the fireplace held numerous creaks and crevices, which had to be cleaned with precise care. The detail of the artwork, each minute fold of a figure's gown or twist of hair made the job an equal part fascinating and then with time, tedious. They were provided with small ladders to reach the higher surfaces of the mantles and the built-in wardrobes as well as some of the crown molding.

By noon, Claire felt filthy and tired, her eyes burned, and her throat ached. But she wasn't thinking of her problems, her classes and exams, or even the mysterious happenings at the house. And even though that was a small victory, it made the work seem a little more worthwhile, at least for her sanity since it had so thoroughly distracted her.

The girls met at lunch with some of the workers. They sat out on the lawn, leaves drifting to the ground in showers of golden green. They feasted on ham sandwiches, potato chips, brownies and ice-cold cokes, all provided by Charles. It gave both girls a chance to get familiar with some of the men they would be seeing day in and day out for the next several months. There was Paul, the best wood worker and refinisher in the business; Scott, the mechanical expert; and Brad, the electrician. All three men were sturdy and middle aged, appreciative that someone would be helping them clean up as they toiled in the old house. They had worked together on other jobs and were totally comfortable in their roles.

In the distance, Claire noticed the bent figure of a man wading through one of the overgrown gardens, plucking out plants at random in what seemed to be a monstrous job. She noted aloud that it would take forever to clean out the beds by hand.

"Who's that?" she asked.

Paul followed her gaze and answered, "Eddie."

"And?" Noel was less patient with the lack of response.

"Oh, Eddie's the caretaker. He's been working here forever." Paul nodded in his direction, "Eddie knows all there is to know about the outside of Talitha, but won't set a foot inside."

"Why?" Claire asked.

"Don't know. He won't say. Funny old guy," Paul replied and then climbed to his feet. "He's okay though." He balled up his trash in his fist. "Guess we'd better get going."

On cue, they all stood in the lawn and gathered their things. They dropped garbage in one of the outside bins and headed into the shade of the house. Claire had to admit she was a little disappointed in the men's lack of conversation. But they obviously weren't gossips and had they been more talkative, she suspected their preferred topic would have been sports rather than mysterious old gardeners.

Too soon, it was time to return to work. Claire scrubbed until 3:00, then got cleaned up for class in the evening. She had missed her Monday courses, so she planned to arrive early to get notes from some classmates. She just hoped she could stay awake through the long lecture.

It was approaching dark when she headed away from campus toward her new home. The center of campus had been brightly lit with friendly neon signs that advertised eateries and shops, and her eyes had difficulty adjusting as she traversed farther away from town following the interstate into the suburbs. In the Simpsonville area, the road was flanked by horse farms delineated by winding meadows framed by white and brown fences that sliced up the land into neat sections. Fewer lights out here and far fewer people. She had always enjoyed the scenery in the area in the past, but once she turned off the main road, her face became grim. The lane approaching the house was almost black in the shelter of the ancient trees, and the bridge glowed a pale pearly gray in the soft twilight. Claire had an eerie feeling of being watched and studied the bridge as she neared, suddenly seeing the vague shape of a person perched on the railing. Her heart leapt into her throat. She found herself glancing at the car door locks as though the figure might leap from the side of the road and tear into her car when she slowed. As she approached, she could see more clearly. It was an indeed a person, she realized, a man with longish hair and a sharply chiseled face with large deep-set eyes. He was still bathed in the gloom, indistinct in the shadows, but his features were strangely clear. His clothes were dark, his hair dark as well, but his skin pale. He appeared as solid and real as the structure itself, sitting on the broken edge of the bridge, one leg cast over the concrete rail that reached the height of the car door window. But as soon as she was in the middle of the bridge and glanced toward the railing, she realized she couldn't see him any longer.

A burst and flutter of movement on the opposite side of the arc made her gasp as a flock of birds, dark against the cool concrete, soared in their secret formation from beneath the arch of the bridge and toward the freedom of the sky. Her heart seemed to flutter along with them, but she forced herself to drive on. As she put more distance between her car and the bridge, she looked back into her rear-view mirror. There was no further movement there, no birds, no forest creatures, and no man. She braked slightly, staring into the reflection of the scene but then sped up again. She felt herself grow cold. He had been there. She was sure of that.

She muttered a curse under her breath. Now she needed to know where the man had gone. If for no reason than to prove she had seen him. She would have much preferred to see him walking casually back up the road, or even sitting back at the bridge, long legs crossed casually as he perched on the railing. But the road was dark ahead, and getting darker, so she tapped the accelerator slightly, feeling unsettled. She couldn't stop to go in search of some crazy guy trespassing on private property, she silently scolded to herself.

At the top of the incline, she had to stop because the gate was closed. She threw her car in park and sat in the heavy silence. The house looked dark and empty, its windows a dead black. She forced herself to open the car door and leaned out to look around her, frightened that if a figure who could disappear with such ease, he might be able to reappear just as simply.

The night was still and silent. Claire stepped out of her car and pulled at the gate, the air and twisted metal cool against her skin. It smelled of earth and age here. The gate opened with a stutter, and she left it propped wide. After driving through, she stopped her car again, leaving the engine running. She yanked hard on the cold black iron, hearing the sharp clang as the metal hit metal. Satisfied it was closed; she turned back towards her car and the massive house beyond.

Her eyes scanned the dark lawn and the shadowed facade of the house. From this angle, a dull glow could be seen through the front window, a reflection of a light in the dining room or kitchen. The second floor was dark. Then, as Claire watched, a light appeared in the left turret window several floors up. The glow was soft, like a candle or small shaded light bulb instead of the sharp beam of a flashlight. It hovered, still for a moment, and then drifted out of her line of vision. A second later, it was gone, as though extinguished by a breath.

Claire shivered, jerked her car door open, and climbed back in to pull it up in front of the house. She tried to mentally shake herself out of her mood. This was stupid! She was getting freaked out because of a light. Maybe John was checking out some of the upper floors? She smiled at the thought of John, candle in hand, creeping up the spiral staircase to the top of the turret. He had been neat as a pin when she had seen him in the halls earlier, the only one there unaffected by the dust and the heat. She would enjoy seeing him a little mussed after the ribbing he had delivered to her and Noel earlier.

She parked the little car at its place in the drive and switched off the engine. It died with a buzz and whir, leaving her in the silence of the trees. She glanced around her one final time and then hurried up the grand porch staircase. At the door, she yanked at the over-sized latch and felt it give easily. Thank goodness it hadn't been locked.

Inside the house, she hurried through the foyer and adjoining hallway to the kitchen, breathing a shade too heavily. There she dropped her books and purse on the counter and went looking for Noel. She found her in the back living room, a tray piled with Chinese food in cardboard boxes with little wire handles in front of her. There was a strong scent of cooked pork and the television cast a bluish hue over Noel's still form. The old set was blinking and rolling, the reception decreasing when Claire crossed in front of the bent antenna.

"Nice," Claire said, looking at the old TV, trying to appear cool and composed.

"Yeah," Noel agreed and nodded toward the light. "This is the one and only channel we get out here, so I hope you like it."

"So, no cable," Claire observed.

"Good guess," Noel agreed. "They'll have to figure something out if they want this place to be successful."

"Yep, but that won't help us. That's probably one of the last things they plan on adding."

Noel smiled and offered Claire a chair and a plate for the food. "We'll have to live with what we have." She sat back, holding up her soft drink can. "They don't deliver out here either, by the way."

Claire chuckled and dropped into her seat. The food smelled good, and she now realized she was starving. Aside from that, her nerves were frayed after the encounter at the bridge, her mind was alive with information she had digested during class, and her body was aching from all the bending and reaching she had done while cleaning.

Noel watched her for a minute, then turned back to the television, sitting in comfortable silence.

"Where's John?" Claire asked, her mouth full of sweet and sour pork. There would be plenty of food left to share if he wanted to join them.

"Oh, he's gone out. He got me this for dinner and went out with some friends that came into town. Said he'd be back tonight but late."

Claire looked up, surprised. "So, who was rooting around upstairs?" The words slipped out before she could think how it would sound.

"What do you mean?" Noel asked. Then, as Claire's words sunk in, she suddenly became more attentive. "No one's here but us, and I wouldn't dream of going upstairs. Not alone anyway."

Claire frowned thoughtfully, trying not to appear too worried. "There was a light in the window at the top of the turret. I'm sure someone was there; the light moved. "

Noel looked doubtful. "Claire, there's no one here, I swear. It was probably a reflection you saw on the window. The moon or something."

Claire thought about protesting. She had seen the movement; the way the light had been doused. It wasn't a reflection. But it would do no good to protest, so she nodded her agreement, "Probably." But she knew it wasn't. Just like the wineglass and the writing on the mirror. Something or someone was there. It wasn't in her head, please God let it not be her imagination. But she knew one thing. She wasn't about to go up those narrow stairs tonight. She'd wait until daylight and take someone with her to brave the dust and cobwebs.

The next several days were more of the same. Hard, sweaty work and mind-numbing classes. On days like that, Claire wondered what had ever given her the idea she wanted to get her master's in education. She wasn't even sure she liked teaching that much, what with the huge classes and poor salary. But she knew she needed to finish what she had started, so she sat through the classes and completed her exams and papers on time.

Charles had arrived and assigned them to very specific jobs, depending on the day. One day it was cleaning the kitchen and functioning bathrooms, the next day they cleaned up after the painters who left a tremendous mess of tarps and plastic, sticky brushes, and paint pans. Neither girl had the opportunity to do any extra exploration, nor had they set foot in the right wing or some of the upper floors. And by the time darkness had settled over the house on Friday, Claire had no desire to go looking for evidence of someone in the attic.

CHAPTER SIX

Claire stopped in front of the craft aisle and fingered the brightly colored yarn. She had always enjoyed using her hands, doing crafts or writing little stories. She had always claimed it was just a hobby although she had to admit to a desire to eventually write a children's book. It was a secret longing she had never been able to satisfy but planned to do after graduation. It wasn't a practical goal, and she had directed her life toward the practical, never the fanciful. She just wished she could do the illustrations that went with a picture book. Her lack of artistic talent grated. Now that she had moved into a much larger room, she wondered if she could set up her computer on the desk and again indulge in her hobby and try a little writing. Or perhaps some photography. The house would make a spectacular model for pictures.

"Claire, are you ready?"

Noel's voice pulled her out of her thoughts. "Sure," she replied, and stepped away from the shelves of beads and colored pencils.

She reluctantly left the store empty-handed, and they stopped for a quick meal on the way back to the house. They were taking the back way to get to the home. Shelbyville Road was a crowded commercial drive with not just one but two malls and dozens of other shops. As it snaked out of town, the road became a little less crowded, going from miles of shopping to neighborhoods and sloping fields. Even when they turned off the road, Claire continued to feel encouraged, and her mood didn't change as they pulled up the drive. With the sun glaring unmercifully, the house looked over-sized but peaceful. Claire couldn't understand her feelings of unease at times, the persistent feeling she was being watched, analyzed even. It was as though the house had a life of its own, a presence that was indefinable but very strong. She shook her head abruptly, trying to dismiss her doubts and retrieve her good feelings.

They quickly put away their scant purchases, mostly toiletries and basic groceries, eager to start what they considered a long overdue tour of the house. Dressed in torn jeans and tee shirts, the two girls started on the first floor. They passed through the now familiar entryway and went through the doorway to the right. Noel had been in this room before, but had said it was very disappointing. It was obviously a formal parlor, a small square room with low ceilings and a huge fireplace which dominated the far wall. The antique wall coverings were silky but gray with age. The furniture was either covered with sheets or had been sent out for repairs. One particularly large piece sat nestled in the corner. When Noel swept the sheet off, she saw an ancient piano, its keys so old they had yellowed and some were missing, leaving the piano looking like a smile with broken dentures.

Claire tentatively touched a key and listened to a soft note, surprisingly sweet considering the source. She wished briefly she had taken advantage of her parents' offer of piano lessons. There was little choice in entertainment in the house beyond the second-hand television in the living area and the multitudes of books in the library. Perhaps she would ask John if he played.

Slowly she crossed the room to pull gently on the heavy curtains. The windows were still cloudy with grime, and the original curtains expelled a cloud of dust with the smallest movement. The room had once boasted soft pastel greens and pinks, but now was yellowed with age. The floor was wooden like the adjoining rooms, an intricate pattern under the stain, with a large rug covering the majority of the surface, running almost to the walls. The color was impossible to discern because of the filth that had accumulated over time.

Claire approached the fireplace dubiously, surprised at the sheer size.

"That thing is big enough to roast a bull on a spit," Noel said dryly. "I can't say I like this room, too cotton candy girlish."

"I'd say it's a safe assumption to say the lady of the house decorated in here."

"And she must have been cold blooded," Noel added, gesturing to the fireplace. "That was made to generate serious heat."

Claire agreed with a nod and left through the far door, oddly uncomfortable in the room. The parlor appeared tiny in comparison to the chamber next door. The ballroom was part of the new wing; the windows considerably larger, and the rays of the sun cast a brilliant golden color on the marble floor.

The walls were painted, something light that reflected the sun, with gilded edging on the inlaid panels. The room was bare of furniture except for a few carved chairs with deep red cushions faded in places by the sun. The deterioration here was much less, and Claire had to admit with the huge chandeliers replaced, and some serious cleaning and painting, the room would be majestic.

A flash of light made her turn to see herself reflected, five then ten times, as she stepped away from the back wall and nearer to the windows. Mirrors in gold frames lined the interior wall, making the room look twice its size. All were freshly polished and no chips or cracks showed on the slick surfaces. She stopped to study her own reflection, her angular face shown plainly in the bright light. She looked like a hag, she thought grimly. Her hair pulled severely back from her face, a gray shadow of dust under her sharp cheekbone, and her oldest clothing hanging loosely from her slender frame.

Noel, in contrast, grinned and danced in delight, watching her reflection twist and spin. "Oh, I'd love to have a party here!" she exclaimed.

"Or a wedding reception. Wouldn't it be lovely?" Claire said, her mind blanking out her own reflection and replacing it with the image of a bride, her expression verging on dreamy.

Noel made a face. "You're such a romantic. Imagine, hot lights, loud music, and some jamming moves."

Claire ignored her and looked down the long room. For a moment her vision blurred, and she could see them. Women in loose sheaths with feathered hats glittering as they spun in smooth moves with handsome partners guiding their steps. Claire could almost smell the rich perfume of bouquets of flowers and womanly scents. The music would be sweet, the strains of a string quartet or the livelier beats of a piano.

Claire sighed and looked back toward the mirror. From the corner of her eye she saw a figure, gowned in a long dark blue dress moving swiftly through the far door. She had the impression of dark hair, piled high, and smooth pale skin. Claire spun around, eyes skimming the windows behind her, but no one was there.

Claire knew there would be no sign of her. No sound of a closing door or light footsteps on the wooden floors. There would be no footprints or even the lingering scent of her perfume. Much like the visions, those sick visions of before, when the figures left, they could rarely be found again.

Because they're not real. They never have been, and they never were. She rubbed her eyes gently, feeling a light headache coming on. Why did it have to start again now? She was so close to finishing school. And she finally had a job that would provide her enough money to save for a real home, somewhere she could settle down once she had found a teaching position.

She gave her forehead a last stroke and turned to Noel who was still looking in the mirrors. She was grateful her friend hadn't noticed her little lapse. "Let's move on. We've got a lot more exploring to do and the light is giving me a headache." She hoped her voice didn't sound too strained.

After stopping in the kitchen for an aspirin and a soft drink, the girls next ventured into the library on the opposite side of the foyer directly across from the parlor. The apparently untouched volumes that lined three walls from floor to ceiling delighted Claire. Many tomes were locked behind glass fronted cabinets; some with pages still bound and unread. Someone had taken more care in preservation here, for the books had escaped most of the mold and mildew. There had also been some visitors because footprints were plain upon the dusty carpet and a layer of dust had been removed from some of the furniture. A large desk dominated the room, but it also held several cushioned chairs, newly recovered, and the fireplace was full of ashes. The room had been inhabited recently, but the renovation had not been completed.

The next room, as they moved into the newer wing, was long and narrow with bare walls stripped of the wallpaper and unconcealed windows with newly polished glass. The only hint of its past use were the sheeted instruments pushed up against the wall. The one thing that had been left uncovered was a sizable table, plain and utilitarian, that stood by the windows, flanked by two equally functional chairs. As Noel peeked under sheets, Claire walked over to the largest piece. It was a second piano, much newer and in much better condition.

"A baby grand!" Noel exclaimed.

"It sure doesn't belong here," Claire replied, running her hands on the cool, glossy surface.

"I wonder where it came from."

Claire pulled the sheet back in place. "They must have brought it here recently. I wonder if it was bought specifically for this place, for all the rich visitors to use, or if it is Mr. Edwards', and he had it moved here."

"If that's true, he must plan on spending some time here. Funny that we haven't seen or heard from him."

"Well, John said he hadn't seen him much either. I got the impression John considers him pretty remote, not very involved in the project just yet."

Noel ran her fingers down the sheet thoughtfully. "Maybe he was wrong. If I wasn't interested in a place, I sure wouldn't move a valuable piece like this one into the house until I knew all the construction was finished."

Claire had to agree, and took one last glance at the room. It held none of the unpleasant sensations the rooms in the older part of the building evoked.

"I think I like this room. It has potential."

Noel shrugged and went through the next door, following the simple layout of the house. As soon as the door was cracked, a hot, sticky breath of air leaked through, carrying with it the smell of rich soil.

"A greenhouse! Look at this!" Noel walked in first, pulling the door wide. One wall of clear glass let in a glare of pure sunlight while the opposite wall was lined with heavy shelves full of gardening supplies. Basking in the rays of the sun were trays upon trays of delicate seedlings, their pale yellow-green shoots just peeking out of the rich black soil. In front of them were several large pots with huge tropical plants and lining the floor were more pots with rose bushes and ornamental trees being nursed back to life.

The steady spray of water in pipes filled the room with sound so that Claire had to speak loudly in order to be heard.

"We have a gardener and a musician. Do you think all of this is for the house or do you think it just belongs to Mr. Edwards?"

"I don't know, but he spent some money in here. I'll bet he had to replace every pane of glass at least. I wonder if he has any fresh herbs in here."

"I don't see any, but I wouldn't know parsley if it came up and bit me. Let's get out of here, the heat's making me melt." Claire turned back toward the door.

As they sat together at the table, Claire looked carefully at the meal set before her. Noel had gone to great trouble, slicing and baking for the rest of the afternoon. The kitchen and dining room smelled strongly of garlic and Italian spices, bubbling pots of pasta and deep red sauces splattering a variety of colors on the once pristine appliances. The clean-up was going to be a pain, but the food was wonderful, Claire had to admit.

"You promise you didn't put any mystery plants from the greenhouse in here?"

Noel laughed and dropped her fork in her empty plate. "Yes, I swear. That doesn't mean I may not eventually grow some of my own herbs, but I'm not going to use things that aren't mine."

"Just checking." Claire leaned back in her chair, her hands resting lightly on her full belly. "Okay, let's see what we learned today."

"This place is huge and a long way from finished. I'm so glad we don't have to clean the whole thing. Can you imagine?"

Claire laughed at her friend, feeling comfortable after a long day. "And what about our mystery employer? He's rich, he plays or appreciates music..."

"Or just likes shiny furniture. And he hopes his guests like music."

"Whatever. He has an interest in botany or at least amateur gardening..."

"Or he's hired a gardener who we haven't met yet. Or maybe it's meant for Eddie! You can't assume just because he equipped the place like that that he automatically is working in there himself."

Claire looked sheepish. "I guess seeing all those plants made me jealous. It gave me the urge to start digging myself, so I projected those feelings on him."

"I didn't know you liked to garden."

"I don't all the time. I just like to plant things and see how they turn out. I'm not crazy about the pulling weeds or watering every day."

Noel grinned. "Well, that's more than I would want to do."

"And what else have we discovered?"

"I don't know. I wonder if he's related to the lady whose portrait is in my room."

"This place is full or portraits," Noel said grimly. "And some of them are pretty ghoulish looking. I hope he isn't taking after those guys in the third-floor hall. Way too serious for me."

Claire grinned. She had grown accustomed to the portrait in her room casting a watchful eye on her movements. Much easier to have a painted observer than some of the spiritual ones she had feared in the past. *Imagined,* she amended to herself.

The door was thrown open and John pushed through, his hands full of fast food containers. He looked surprised to see them and seemed faintly embarrassed. "I can't cook," he said shortly, and dropped the bags on the table.

Noel laughed teasingly at his discomfort and pushed an empty plate in front of him. "Eat some of ours. We'll never eat all of this. I love to cook, but I always make too much."

John looked back dolefully at his bagged meal and took it into the kitchen where he dropped it unceremoniously into the trashcan.

"Can't refuse, thanks."

He loaded up his plate in the kitchen and returned to the dining room, plate and drink in hand. He sat quickly, stuffing food into his mouth with the enthusiasm of a very hungry man. As he spoke, he talked between mouthfuls. "We got some news today. The big man is coming in next week or so. Going to finally grace us with his presence."

"Mr. Edwards?" Claire asked.

"None other. Wants to check on our progress, I'm sure. But I think he'll appreciate it. He hasn't been here for over a month, and we've gotten a lot done." His voice trailed off as he considered the room. "Well, at least the kitchen is done, and it turned out perfect."

"You eat while we clean up," Claire said briskly. "If Mr. Edwards is coming, I want everything to look perfect." She paused, looking at the layers of dust and dirt on the floor. "Well, at least it can look decent."

The evening left them feeling tired, but Claire still felt uneasy since the morning's events and sat up in bed, a book in her lap. She had borrowed a new romance novel from Amy but was having difficulty sympathizing with the heroine who seemed determined to make every man aboard the pirate ship angry. Claire thought darkly that the idiot might as well walk the plank now and get it over with.

Claire glanced up and her eyes seemed to settle on the mirror. The glass reflected the room with each tiny detail, but no messages had been forth coming, and the glass had remained blank for the day. But now the eyes of the portrait seemed to be watching her. Just like she had felt all day. Someone watching and measuring, judging and warning. She wondered briefly if the figure in the ball-room had anything to do with the lady in the portrait. Her mind may well have recorded the appearance of the woman in the painting and projected it on the mirror, a shift of light, a shadow from a window, and like magic, she was seeing a fleeing shape. She had a great imagination. Not that it was a good quality to have all the time, and just now, she wished she wasn't quite as creative.

Claire got up, frustrated and confused. She walked determinedly to the painting, muttering to herself.

"If you're just going to watch me then I'll find something else to do with you." She grasped the portrait by the ornate frame and lifted it down. It was heavy, far heavier than it looked, and she struggled to set it down gently with a frown on her smooth brow as she turned the painted face to the wall and brushed off her hands. In the portrait's place, she hung her cheaply framed poster and stepped back. She had dust on her shirt and a splinter in her thumb but at least she would sleep with some privacy.

Satisfied at her redecorating, sleep came quickly, and she slipped into peaceful dreams.

An hour later, a subtle tap, tap roused her out of her drowse. It was a cautious sound at the French doors with none of the flurry she had heard the other night. She tugged back the blanket and slid out of bed. Her feet were noiseless against the wooden floor as she stepped to the balcony doors. She carefully pulled back the curtain, gingerly peering through the gap.

A pale shape, a bird, was perched on the railing. From that distance, she wouldn't have heard its movements, but she felt sure this was what had woken her. She carefully released the latch on the door and cracked it open, letting in a breath of wind, damp from the overhanging leaves.

The bird stood very still. A low murmuring sound caught her attention, a coo. It was some kind of dove, creamy brown shade flecking its smooth feathers. It gave an impatient fluff and resettled its wings close to its body.

"What are you doing out here?" Claire's voice was soft, meant to be soothing.

The bird seemed to look directly at her as thought considering the question. Then without a sound, it spread its wings and seemed to catch a breeze, the movement throwing its body into an arc that swooped toward her. She stepped back from the door quickly, the wind causing the glass and wood panels to swing wide, allowing the bird to flutter into the room with a dry rustle of wing.

Claire had only scant experience with birds. She hadn't ever had one as a pet, but the errant house wren had habitually built their nests in the planters on her mother's front porch, and she had spent many hours of her childhood watching the birds gorging at the feeders when the snow blanketed the backyard at her home. She had photographed her more colorful visitors, and as a college student, had enjoyed feeding the fat strutting pigeons that ruled over the campus grounds.

This bird had drifted to a graceful perch on the footboard of her bed and was eyeing her with surprising calm. The low coo hinted at contentment over its current circumstances.

"I don't remember asking you in," Claire said wryly. Her heartbeat was finally slowing. The bird was unexpected, but considering the other creepy things that had occurred in the house, this late-night visitor was almost normal.

The bird cocked its head and shuffled its wing feathers with a puff and soft rustle. Whatever its reason for coming in, it now seemed disinclined to leave.

Claire looked toward the doors, now flung wide and offering a panoramic view of the night. What to do? If she closed up the room, she would be left with an overnight guest who might, despite the dignified demeanor, poop on Claire's belongings. But she couldn't leave the doors open to the air all night, the wind felt damp and the rain might come again. If she tried to corral her guest to force it to leave, she might end up scaring the thing, and she would hate to see it hurt itself.

She sat on the side of her bed and looked at the bird as it observed her. Its feathers were scalloped in a lovely pattern, its eyes dark and somehow wise, its beak slender and sharp. It wasn't frightening; not in the least. Claire crawled a little further into the bed and tucked the blankets around her. She was so tired. To her surprise, she was feeling sleepy again, which she couldn't believe considering she was currently being watched by her uninvited guest. She felt her eyes blur and her lids drop as she leaned against the headboard, the hard knobs of the carving pressing into the back of her skull. How would she get the bird out? How would she deal with all the weirdness in the house? How would she...

She wasn't aware of falling asleep or her continued watcher as the bird settled in for the night, a silent observer as she slept.

On Sunday morning, Claire rose slowly, feeling an odd feeling of loss. The doors to the balcony were shut tight, the curtain dropped over the glass although she could swear she hadn't done it herself. Besides that, she couldn't recall how the bird had gotten out of her room either. Curiouser and curiouser.

Added to that, she was feeling a heavy loneliness. She yearned for the familiar Sunday breakfast with her family after going to the 8:00 mass at their local parish. She longed for the bustle of the family, the sounds of other lives being lived around her, the familiar routine of life. She checked the clock. Maybe she would go to church. Although her family was a couple hours away, the familiarity and reassurance of church was just what she needed.

She sat up and put her feet on the chilly floor. Her braided rug had been pushed away from the bed again. Claire frowned, not remembering ever moving the thing. Then her eyes moved up.

"Oh, no way," she exclaimed aloud. Her framed poster sat on the floor; leaned up against the wall as it had been just the day before. And on the wall in its place was the portrait, the eyes again boring into hers.

Fighting the urge to panic, Claire got up slowly and straightened her shirt hem over the shorts she wore to bed. Her hands were chilled. She checked the French doors first, then the hall door, knowing before she touched the knobs that both would be locked. She looked down at her hands, reassured when she saw the red place where the splinter had been thrust in her skin. Her hands looked a little dirty too, with a line of color, probably from the frame when she lifted it. It hadn't been a dream. She had moved the painting. She muttered an expletive under her breath and turned away from the painting. She wasn't going to talk about this to anyone. No one. If the dreams were coming back, she wanted to handle it. And hopefully, she could.

Briskly, she gathered her clothes and set out towards the bathroom. What she needed was a little sanity, and getting out of the house would be the best thing for her.

Two days later, Claire was jarred out of her trance of scrubbing and wiping in one of the newly renovated bathrooms by John.

"Hey, um, I have a question for you. You don't paint, you know, paintings, do you?"

Claire looked at him blankly for a moment. "Paint?" She had the sudden fear he had learned she had moved the painting in her room and was upset by it. But no, he wasn't asking about that.

"Yeah, we've found a painting someone has been working on. It's not that it's bad, it's just," his pause was somehow meaningful, "unusual. None of the other workers have 'fessed up to painting it, so we thought..."

"You thought I painted it?"

"You or Noel," he replied, one brow raised.

"Not me and not Noel. We don't paint." She looked at him curiously.

There was the clatter of shoes on the floor and Noel slipped in. "I heard my name. And I heard painting. What's up?"

"Someone has been painting a picture," Claire began.

"No one has admitted to it, none of the other workers, no one working in or around the house." John left the words hanging as though he thought one of them would suddenly admit they were secretly dabbling in a new hobby.

"Really?" Noel asked, clearly intrigued by the thought. "Why do you look like that? Is the painting scary or something?"

"No, not at all. It's just the fact someone has decided to start a painting project in the middle of the construction, and in a really strange place, and won't say who they are." John shrugged. "We have some kind of secret artist, looks like."

"Where is it?" Claire asked, interested but feeling a bit of unease.

"Down in the basement," John replied. "Another weird thing. Have you been down there? The basement is basically an unfinished storage area. Very rough. It has the old coal furnace and the fuse boxes, the heating and air stuff, some plumbing, the hot water heater. There's no reason to go there unless you needed to look at some of the mechanicals. And you certainly wouldn't want to go there to hang around."

"We've never been down there," Claire said thoughtfully. There was no reason for them to ever venture to that area. They didn't have any interest in the guts of the house, the inner workings of the electrical or heating system.

"We've had a lot of structural guys down there, and the heating and air guys. But the place where the painting is," he paused and pursed his lips, looking thoughtful again, "it's pretty out of the way. You wouldn't go there unless you had a reason to."

"Can we see it?" Noel was smiling, totally enjoying John's obvious discomfort now that they were off the hook.

"Well," he hesitated. "Sure. I don't see why not. I'll get Joe, and he can walk us through." He turned slowly. "Do you want to see it now?"

"Sure," Noel exclaimed, and grinned crazily when he turned his back.

They followed him down the stairs to the main floor and waited as John went in search of Joe. Some of the other workers filled him in, explaining that Joe was already downstairs working on repairing some of the stonework in the basement.

"Come on down here." John led the way through a narrow hall that ended with a plain wooden door. "The basement, or cellar," he explained, gesturing to the closed door. "It's locked up during the weekends and when people aren't down there. Not a good place to go wandering. Not particularly safe."

As they ventured down the unfinished stairway made from wooden planks, some obviously newly laid, the smell of damp rose from the depths of the lower level. At the foot of the stairs was a wide room, long shelves lining the walls. In the back, Joe was standing with another worker, buckets of gray goo, trowels, and other tools Claire couldn't name lay on the stone floor.

"Hey Joe!" John called. "We came to look at the new art."

"Yeah?" Joe responded. "Who's goin'?"

"Just us." John gestured to the little group.

"Okay, sure. Let me just get him started," he cocked his head toward the young guy kneeling on the floor. He took a moment to give some instructions, bending down to point out something unseen on the wall. He rose with a grimace, one hand to his back. " 'kay, you ready?"

John nodded moving behind Joe, and Noel and Claire nodded along like bobble head dolls. Joe put a weathered hand to his face and mopped away some invisible sweat. They moved in silence to the other end of the room.

The two men led the girls into a tight hallway that ended in a thick rough hewn door. It wasn't like the rest of the house. The finishes were nowhere near so fine. It was a door meant to keep things out... *or hold things in,* Claire thought gravely. She peered at Noel, but her friend appeared to be enjoying herself. This little adventure, this little mystery, was a good diversion from the manual labor.

The key for the door was typical for the period, but again, it was a much more utilitarian piece than some of the other keys that fit the locks in this fantastic house.

The lock turned with ease, surprisingly quiet, and the door swung open with just a draft of chilled air.

"These are mostly cellars," Joe explained. "Good for keepin' wine but not much else." He hit a switch on the wall and a bare bulb blinked on, hanging from a wire above their heads. "We rarely come down here," he continued. "There's no need for us to be unless we're workin' on plumbing or the furnace."

They followed him further into the big room, their steps oddly muffled. The light seemed to spread only to the center of the room, and the corners were shrouded with shadows. It was not a comfortable place.

"So, who found it?" Noel asked, peering over Joe's shoulder.

"We heard some sounds comin' from down here late last night. Workin' late," he shrugged casually as though to say this wasn't an unusual event. "A couple of us came down to check it out."

Claire wondered if that was deliberate. Were they uncomfortable in the house? Did they instinctively want to travel in groups?

"We found this door open and went on in. It seemed like it was left open on purpose like someone wanted the painting to be seen. Most of these doors are kept closed on a regular day when we're not workin' in those rooms."

They had entered a hallway with cool crumbing brick floors. On three of the walls were doors, just blank planks of wood with knobs, no locks. One was open.

"No lights in these yet, " Joe explained, holding his flashlight high. "We've been usin' these battery lanterns when we have work to do." The harsh glare of a work lamp almost blinded them as the dark was wiped away in one great sweep of illumination.

"Wow," Noel breathed, standing in the doorway.

The painting was huge. It covered half the length of the wall. They stepped just inside the door and spread in an arch for better viewing.

"It's painted on a piece of subflooring we were usin' upstairs. The pieces are more awkward than heavy, but it wouldn't have been easy to get down here. "

Noel stepped into the room and Claire followed.

"The paint is ours too. Looks like someone helped themselves. "

"It is!" Noel agreed. "Look at the cans."

Claire followed her gaze. The cans were the small sample pots the painters were using for touch ups. She recognized a few colors from the upstairs bathrooms and bedrooms and even a few new ones that were just opened. The original colors, however, had been mixed and toned so that a million shades seemed to blend into the painting.

"What is it?" Noel asked, tilting her head to the side and angling closer.

"It's a woman at the window," Claire responded in a faint voice. The words seemed to slip out without conscious thought. But she could see it, the square of the window, the outlines blurred by the blowing curtains. And in front of it, her back to the painter, was the willowy form of a woman.

"Oh, I see it now," Noel agreed. "There's the window, her arm raised here, her hand..." she gestured to where the woman's fingers seemed to brush the glass.

"If you say so," Joe agreed. John, their silent companion, had circled around the room, looking at the other walls, the floor, like a detective looking for clues.

"But why here?" Noel gestured to the damp room, the light only serving to emphasize the grubby walls and mud stained floors. "Why would you want to paint down here?"

"They didn't want it found?" Claire guessed.

"It's just weird," Noel said firmly.

But Claire was looking at the painting. It seemed so familiar to her. Was it a copy if a more famous work she had seen elsewhere or studied in school? Or was it similar to something she had seen in the house? Her mind catalogued the pieces she had seen in rooms she had cleaned.

"I feel like I have seen this before," she murmured. "Does it look familiar to you?" Noel shook her head but remained thoughtful. "It's good," Claire said. "Whoever painted this has a lot of talent. But I don't think I have seen the painting here before." She approached and put her hand out, her fingers brushing the sweep of the woman's skirt. "It's tacky!" she exclaimed. "It's not even fully dry yet! How long does it take for this to dry? "

"Overnight," John finally spoke up from where he stood at the opposite side of the room. "This must have been painted last night. Or at least someone worked on it."

Claire drew closer to the painting, amazed by the details on the wood. The wood itself was sitting on the dirty floor and leaned casually against the wall. Around it was the small pots of paint including a larger pint of white that had been used for mixing. There was a second piece of wood to the side where dabs of paint had been mixed, darkened, or lightened. Claire knew very little about painting, about art in general since her talents definitely didn't lie in that area, but the method looked right.

"So, what are you going to do with it?" Noel asked.

"Do?" John looked a little surprised. "I guess we hadn't thought that far ahead. No one is using this space. It's not like they are destroying property." He thoughtfully gazed at the picture. "We didn't need the subflooring, but the paint is going to cost us." He ran a frustrated hand through his hair. "I don't know if there is much we can do about it right now. Until we know who the painter is, we probably will just let it be."

"Too many other things to do than to worry about this," Joe agreed. "I'll just have the boys bring up the paint they need. We can clean up the place later."

John nodded. "Yeah, let's do that. No reason to mess with this until we have to."

Both men seemed satisfied and turned to go back down the hall. Noel exchanged a look with Claire, and they headed out of the room.

"Grab the light, will you?" John asked, glancing back over his shoulder.

Claire went back into the room. The high-powered lantern was propped on a stool. She wrapped her hand around the handle and hefted its bulk, looking back toward the painting. The figure in the picture seemed to sway in the unsteady light, the light of the painted moon subtly changing, dimming, brightening beneath sketched clouds. *Stranger and stranger,* she thought, and followed the rest out the door.

CHAPTER SEVEN

The next week progressed smoothly with Claire spending an extra amount of time writing reports and completing projects for classes while work at the house continued at an increased rate with men working after dark most weeknights. Noel took care of most of the cooking for the household, and the number of diners varied from just the girls and John, to up to ten men when Charles called one of his meetings. Noel had grown in confidence and was using much of her free time to look up new recipes to try out on her new victims, or diners.

Preparation for Mr. Edwards' arrival continued, and Claire was given the job of caring for his room. He was staying in the newer, right wing where the previous owners had built the updated master suite. His room was in the same style as her own, comfortable with a large fireplace and balcony, however, it was almost twice the size of Claire's room. The colors were neutral earth tones that only served to accent the gorgeous woodwork and finishes. It had an adjoining sitting room as well, with a new walk-in closet and the only other functioning bathroom on the second floor.

As Claire opened the door, she was happy to note the room had been left in neat order after Mr. Edwards' last visit, and she had only dusting and sweeping to finish. She put fresh linens in the bathroom and changed the bed, noting the beautiful carving on this bed as well. She worked quickly and finished in only an hour. Later she would add a vase of fresh flowers from the market if they had any warning of Mr. Edwards' arrival, just like they might in a high-end hotel.

She stopped at the fireplace, turning back toward the room to take one last look around. She was interested to see the furniture he had chosen for himself. An extra desk, bookcases, and the abundance of books that filled the bookcases showed Mr. Cole Edwards to be a kindred spirit. The room was otherwise bare of other personal effects except for two portraits hanging side by side. Claire hesitated and then stepped closer. One was a woman, fine boned with light brown hair and rosy skin. She looked young and innocent, with a half-smile on her face, as her eyes, a bright sapphire blue, seemed to gaze somewhere beyond the observer's shoulder.

The second was a portrait of a man. His face was more arresting with large dark eyes, a sharp blade of a nose and strong chin. Although not conventionally handsome, he had a strong face, and his eyes shown with an eerie light. His hands were long fingered and rested on the arm of the chair, his positioning and posture somehow conveying a certain tension. On the ring finger of his right and was a large band, gold and wrought in such detail Claire could almost read the inscription on the side.

She felt a niggling doubt. Had she seen him before? Something in his face was so familiar. She brought a tentative finger up to the painting, running her fingertip over the ridges of the painted surface.

Noel, rushing in like child caught in a game of hide and seek, jerked her from her revere.

"Okay, you ready? I want to eat lunch before I go meet Ben."

Claire gathered her supplies and left, closing the door firmly behind her.

"Meeting Ben again? That's twice this week. Is he still helping you with classes or is this a more casual meeting?"

Noel had the grace to blush. "It wasn't all my doing. I said I had some studying to do, and he just invited me over. I think it's finally working; he's finally noticing me."

Claire looked at Noel's hot pink shirt and skintight jeans. "I can't imagine him not noticing you. Did you paint those jeans on?" Claire said, eyes alight with amusement.

"No, but I did lie on the bed to get them zipped. I really hope I don't have to pee while I'm at his house. I don't want him catching me lying on his bed sucking in my stomach and yanking on the zipper of these things."

With Noel out for the evening, the house seemed strangely empty. Claire went into the library and browsed through the books, fingers lightly skimming the spines as she walked. Leather bound classics butted up against paperback thrillers. She pulled a few from the shelves and looked inside the front covers for clues to who owned them. But most of the new texts were blank while the bookplates on the older ones held names such as Horace, Frances, and Abraham. A few were written in a feminine hand, and two of the older historical books held the name Caroline, a change from the rest of the masculine scrawls.

The lights flickered, and Claire looked up. Dusk had settled outside and shadows blanketed the room. She slowly approached the desk and turned on the lamp there, throwing a circular glow on the dusty desktop. She cast one last look around the room and walked out into the foyer.

"John, are you here?" she called softly, her voice sounding

hoarse to her ears. She looked around the foyer, the light overhead casting long shadows on the tiles. The house was deathly quiet, and ever so softly a tiny squeal sounded from above. She looked up quickly to see the ancient chandelier swing slowly, just inches at first, but the arch increasing with each sway. The thing was horrid, a mere skeleton of its former glory with most of the crystals gone, long since smashed on the tiles below. Only a few of the bulbs still worked, and those were flickering dangerously. The workers hadn't touched the fixture yet and it dripped with dust covered spider webs that swayed with the motion. Claire backed away, imagining the thing coming loose from its moorings and falling to the floor, taking her down with it as she stood frozen in its path.

A thunderclap of a noise sounded with a huge rattle from above, and Claire's heart leaped to her throat. She looked up the staircase and heard a second noise, a steady thump and drag. She backed quickly against the front door, her fingers curled in tight fists by her sides. It would have been funny if it was happening on the movies. The failing lights, the boom, then the pathetic pacing of a thing, some unknown creature exploring the upper floors.

"John!" she called out, her voice still diminished in the empty room. If this was his idea of a joke, she would kill him. She tried to imagine him upstairs, stomping against the scuffed hardwood floors. *Please let it be him. If only it was him!* But she knew it wasn't John and strongly suspected it wasn't anyone. Not anyone real or human. She had felt the shiver of dread, and the urge to run was almost insurmountable. She knew it was coming, it was happening, and it would be soon be coming for her. The noise continued, gradually increasing in volume while Claire stood frozen at the front door.

Closer and closer, a low roar began to build, and she turned in panic to unlock the front door, trying to escape what was surely racing down the stairs. But the key, conveniently left in the lock, refused to budge in her sweat slicked fingers, so with a backward glance she fled, running straight into the parlor. The pastel room was muffled in darkness and the dark maw of the fireplace opened like a giant mouth at the opposite end of the room. The air rippled and an acrid stench seemed to emanate from the dead fire, from beneath the shrouded forms, from the walls themselves. A flutter of a movement beneath the pale sheets stirred the air and the shapes seemed to breathe.

Her heart was pounding in her ears, the sound so loud she could think of little else. But she could still hear it; the roar escalating into a high keening sound that now seemed to rip down the chimney in the room with her, and with a huge burst, a deathly black cloud of ashes and smoke exploded out into the parlor.

Claire felt the thrust of heated air strike her and she stumbled, almost falling. The dark mass blanked out the room, filled her vision until everything was darkly distorted. She doubled over, her arm thrown protectively over her face. Crouching, she turned and staggered out, her lungs burning as she tried to breathe the tainted air.

The foyer was completely black, the light extinguished from above, and she had no idea if the chandelier was still swaying in the darkness. The door of the library straight across from the parlor was cracked open, a sliver of light from the fireplace barely visible. Claire pushed the library door ajar and stood shaking, her lungs aching with each breath. She grabbed the edge of the heavy wooden door and slammed it closed, shutting out the darkness and the smell from the foyer.

The firelight cast a warm glow over the room, the flames blazing from a hearth that had been stone cold just moments before. *Fire? Who set the fire?* She raised a trembling hand to her head. Was she finally losing her mind? Her eyes slid from the bright flames. The fireplace wasn't the only thing that had changed. The books in the shelves had shifted as well, several pulled free and dumped to the floor. Papers were scattered on the rug as though struck by a hand. She couldn't swear to the position of the furniture, but she felt like some of the pieces had been moved as well, scooted out of place by an invisible body. Her head jerked around as another boom sounded from outside the door. There was a painful crack on the wooden door, and a hot gust from behind her pushed her forward while the protective door slammed open behind her with a booming echo allowing thin plumes of smoke and ashes to swirl from the foyer into the room with her. Her hands reached out to the nearest chair, clutching desperately and avoiding the heat from the yawning doorway, trying vainly to keep on her feet.

"What the hell is going on here?" A voice roared and a figure rose, standing impossibly tall and dark before her blocking the opposite doorway into the empty music room.

Claire had a moment to register that familiar face, the man from the portrait in the upstairs bedroom. A face from the painting, a ghost from the past. With a stifled cry, her fingers slipped on the smooth fabric of the chair, and she went forward, her numbed limbs no longer obeying her, her head filled with darkness. She sunk into blessed oblivion. The man in the doorway had barely reached out from his place at the threshold of the library before the door slammed closed on his astonished face.

She coughed weakly, feeling as though she had been swimming underwater for a long time. She put a hesitant hand to her aching chest. Her head was pounding a steady rhythm of pain, radiating likes snakes around her skull. Her eyes squinted, and she blinked rapidly.

"Claire, Claire. Wake up now."

Noel's concerned face hovered above her. Her hair with mussed from running her fingers through it, and her eyes were wide. Claire had seen her friend mildly frightened before, but she had never looked as scared as she did now.

"Where am I?"

"We're back in the library. Don't you remember? Ben is here too."

His pale face came into view over Noel's shoulder. "You scared the crap out of us! Are you hurting somewhere? Do you need an ambulance?" His eyes went to Noel where she was squeezed in close next to him. "Maybe we should call an ambulance." His eyes went back to Claire. "Do you think you passed out or did you fall? Did you hit your head?" Again, he looked toward Noel. "Maybe she has a concussion."

Claire shook her head slowly. "I don't know." Her voice was hoarse, low with an unfamiliar rasp. Then the memories starting flooding back and panic overtook the pain in her head. "No, no ambulance. I think I just passed out. It was so hot," her mind was still trying to process the moments before her fall. Then she remembered, and her hand caught Noels', squeezing tight enough to feel the bones beneath the skin. "The house. There's something here. There was someone here. And there was a fire! In the parlor, Ben, there's something in the fireplace! I can't remember but..." she closed her eyes, feeling hysterical. She realized she had been reaching out toward Ben, fingers hooked like claws. She lay back, feeling helpless tears fill her eyes and leak beneath her closed lids. Nightmare pictures flashed through her brain, the ashes gritty on her skin. How could she explain something that no one else had experienced? How could she sound rational when she didn't feel sane at all? She tried to gather her thoughts, swallow panic, keeping her eyes shut for a moment longer.

"Ok, ok. Calm down now." Ben sounded as though he was comforting a child. "You're all right, and we're here." He paused. "It's just us here now," he said forcing calm into his voice. "We haven't seen anyone else here, and I haven't see any fire or smoke."

Ben was leaning down, one hand on Noel's shoulder, the other catching Claire's grasping fingers.

"There was someone here." Claire's voice was harsh and painful.

"Yes, Mr. Edwards, Cole Edwards, is here. We didn't know he had arrived. He probably unintentionally scared you. We know he was here when you fell."

"But I saw someone else. And I saw a fire, and smoke, the ashes," Claire's voice trailed off.

Noel's cool fingers caressed her brow. "Don't worry. Ben said Mr. Edwards has checked the house and didn't find anyone. The house is fine, no fire. It was probably a dream. No stranger was here, and no one broke in the house. There was no fire, but we think something happened in the chimney, maybe something broke loose and made a noise. You were alone and may have gotten freaked out. Then you just ran into Mr. Edwards unexpectedly, and that was enough to panic you. You maybe tried to run and fell and hit your head. You've got a pretty good lump here on the side." Her fingers fluttered over Claire's icy ones. "You've just been working too hard. Maybe you're not eating enough..."

"But the fireplace. The ashes. Didn't anyone see the explosion?" Claire's eyes opened wide and panic laced her voice. She sat up quickly, the movement making her voice rise uncomfortably. "Didn't anybody see him?"

"See who?" Noel knelt next to Claire. "Claire, Ben checked all over. There wasn't anyone in the library except Mr. Edwards, and he certainly didn't break in or mean to scare you."

"No, not a man. It couldn't have been just a man. It was a ghost. I saw him. He was a ghost."

"What do you mean a ghost? There were no ghosts, sweetie. Just Edwards. He was in the library when you ran in. That's all." Noel's voice became soothing and she took Claire's hand firmly in her own. "Here, lie back down, we'll talk about this later. Let me get you a drink." Noel stood with quick efficiency, and Ben took her place beside Claire.

"There was no one else?" she asked him faintly.

"No," he said, rubbing his hand over his face as though trying to wake up. "We found you collapsed on the floor in here with Edwards. He said you must have hit your head when you fell. He saw you standing in here and heard a loud noise. Then there was a draft and the door closed in his face." He gave her a slight smile. "I think you must have freaked him out too."

Claire raised a shaking hand to her face, pausing to look at the dark stains on her fingers. "But the fire," she said softly, pleading. She turned her head and looked into the open fireplace set between the bookcases. There were no flames cheerfully burning. It was empty. Dead.

"We saw your hands," he agreed. "You were pretty dirty, but Noel said you had been going through some of the books in the library. And with the crap that came from the chimney, it's no wonder the room is so messed up."

"That's impossible," she replied, her voice gaining strength. She was looking between the fireplace and Ben as he stood over her. "I saw something. It came from the fireplace, not the one in here but the one in the parlor. And it wasn't just something falling down the chimney. I swear!"

"I know what you think you saw," Ben said, his voice softening. "But we've gone over everything. There was no explosion, no ghosts, no fires." He forced a smile and said wryly, "Although I have to admit, this place would make a good haunted house."

Claire considered his serious face. "Did you go in the parlor? Did you see the fireplace?"

"It's fine structurally. Looks like a big clot of stuff fell and crumbled when it hit the floor. There was a mess of ashes in the parlor around the fireplace, but just that. Some ashes on the hearth and some dragged through the foyer and in here that might have been on your shoes and clothes as you walked. It's not much. And it's just there in that one room. There was nothing unusual in any of the other rooms down here. Mr. Edwards has gone to check on the upstairs rooms himself."

Claire closed her eyes again. She knew what she had seen. And she knew it had been real. She could tell the difference between a flesh and blood person and a spirit. Couldn't she? And since when did she believe in ghosts or things that go bump in the night? She felt a little sick and closed her eyes again. How could it be happening again? She had thought she was done, over all that craziness. But here she was, swearing something had flown out of the chimney and blown up the parlor. And better yet, she was sure she had seen a real ghost. Not some foggy impression wafting through the air.

Why, she thought desperately*? Why me? Why now?* She opened her eyes and looked up toward the ceiling. Ben was still studying her, leaning back in his chair. The expression on his face was a mixture of fear and concern, not for the house, but for her. She couldn't let that happen again. She couldn't let her friends and family down like that. She couldn't look crazy.

"Okay," she said softly and pushed her hair from her face, still feeling the grit on her cheeks. "Maybe you're right. Maybe I did just hit my head. Maybe I dreamed the whole thing." She tried to keep her voice steady. She was determined to appear sane, to talk herself into thinking she was sane. She gathered her tattered dignity and silently counted to 10, aware of Ben's scrutiny. Feeling calmer, she beaconed him closer and let him help her ease up into a sitting position. "I'm fine. Really, my head just hurts." A forced smile seemed to calm him because his expression relaxed. He sighed and stepped back as Noel returned with a huge glass of ice water and pain reliever. Claire took the pill and downed it quickly hoping that when her head cleared, she could convince herself it had been a dream. Of course, she knew that was a lie.

CHAPTER EIGHT

Claire sat at the kitchen table, her head resting in her hands as she wearily considered her full plate. Noel was sitting opposite her friend, her eyes concerned as she attempted to fill the silence with meaningless small talk. Ben sat next to Noel, fingers nervously drumming the tabletop. Noel had insisted they sit down then and busied herself making food no one wanted to eat. Now the table was set, and the food was cooling in the uncomfortable silence.

The tension was broken when Charles walked in, John following him through the back door.

"What smells so good?" Charles asked, looking cool and comfortable in tan slacks and a striped shirt.

John went immediately to the stove and took the top off the pan, dipping a spoon in even before Noel could respond.

"We're having dinner. Do you want any?" Noel offered, holding up a bowl full of salad.

"No thanks," Charles responded, "I was just dropping John off and came in to have a meeting with Mr. Edwards at 8:00. I'm a little early yet, but I've still got some paperwork to go through. Have you seen him?"

Ben and Noel exchanged glances and Ben slowly got to his feet, moving to stand behind Claire's chair as a silent sign of support.

"We saw him a little while ago, but he said he had some phone calls to make," Noel supplied, turning concerned eyes in Claire's direction. Claire maintained her composure, concentrating on moving a piece of lettuce around her bowl. "When did Mr. Edwards arrive?" Noel asked casually, her eyes once again drifting to her silent friend and back to Ben's serious face.

"I dropped him off a few hours ago. He said he needed to get settled in, maybe take a rest. I got back into town to meet John around 3:00."

Claire was silent, watching Noel's face. Noel looked frankly relieved. Claire could almost read her thoughts as she pondered Charles' statement. If Mr. Edwards had come in during the after-noon and had indeed closed himself in his room for a few hours, then when he emerged in the evening, Claire would have been surprised since they hadn't been told about his arrival. That and the mess in the chimney were certainly enough to scare Claire if she had thought she was in the house alone.

But Claire knew there had been so much more to it. The ques-tion was, while she had been hearing the noises from above, had Edwards heard them too? Had he been the source? And why hadn't he responded when she had called upstairs to John? And after that, when the noises fairly shook the house, where was he then? Obvi-ously, he must have been close to the library in order to slip in there unseen while she was in the parlor. But the house was a maze of staircases and back entrances, not to mention any of the possible hidden tunnels or passageways that often characterized houses of this age. It made her feel a little sick. If someone wanted to fool her, they certainly had enough opportunities. But what reason was there for anyone to pretend, to orchestrate, a haunting in the house?

Charles continued to look from one, then another, trying to read their expressions. John had paused from his search for food and was also watching them with interest.

"When I dropped Mr. Edwards off the house was quiet, so I assumed you were all out for the afternoon. He said he was going straight up to his room, so I just left. He didn't look particularly well, so I guessed he was going to lie down." He paused and looked at Claire. "You haven't seen him?"

"No," Noel interrupted. "Claire was resting. She had a little fall earlier today and bumped her head."

"We were out at my house," Ben volunteered, referring to himself and Noel.

"Well, if you happen to see him, can you let him know I'm here?" Charles turned away to leave the kitchen and then turned back, suddenly recalling his manners. "Oh, Claire, are you all right? It was rude of me not to ask."

"I'm fine. Really. And we'll let Mr. Edwards know you're here as soon as he shows up."

Charles looked like he might ask more questions, but seemed preoccupied. Claire guessed he was thinking of the upcoming meeting. He disappeared into the office, and Claire lowered her head to hide her expression. It seemed evident that if Cole Edwards wasn't the man in the library, he had to have seen or heard something. Perhaps he would even have an explanation for some of the noises from second floor. Claire only wished he had admitted that much to her friends. Instead, she felt like everyone was watching her, wondering. Well, she thought grimly, he's going to admit what he knows to me even if he doesn't say a word to another person. She was determined to find him, and to face him, even if she may put her job in jeopardy. It was ridiculous, cruel even, that he hadn't spoken out to confirm her experience.

While Noel was busy cleaning up after dinner, Ben reluctantly left for home. Charles was busy ensconced in his office to prepare some paperwork for Edwards, the sound of the computer keyboard like background music. John stayed on in the kitchen with Noel, snacking on leftovers and offering her an occasional helping hand.

Seeing that everyone was occupied, Claire excused herself, unobtrusively slipping out the door. She quietly crossed the foyer by herself, feeling a cold queasy feeling in the pit of her stomach as she looked up the stairway. The parlor was empty and didn't appear very different from how it had looked the first day she had seen it. A few faded soot stains marred the white sheets blanketing the furniture and the rug laid out on the floor. But the room was in poor condition anyway, so the marks could have been overlooked easily. Claire looked down at her shirt and pants. Streaks of gray and black traced down her front, ground in as though some invisible weight had been applied. Her hands still held traces of the stains even though she had scrubbed at them before dinner. She had been appalled at how dirty her skin was, her nails filthy. Dropping her hands in frustration, she retraced her steps and headed for the library.

The door was open as before, but the floor showed signs of dust, but no, it was the gray black of ash. On the bookcases, several books were still shuffled out of place and more had been scattered on the desk. Whether this was the work of spectral hands or human, she wasn't certain, but she was determined to find out.

The fireplace remained sadly empty. She had a flashback of the inexplicable flames burning in the grate just before her world had exploded. It wasn't cold in here now, but despite this, she was freezing still. Even her face felt frozen, as though the shock had set in to her very bones. Although she was eager to find the mysterious owner, she doubted she would be brave enough to seek him out in his room. She felt suddenly cowardly and decided if she didn't find him in the next few rooms, she would wait to see if he would seek her out. She saw the door to the music room was again closed, and she knocked lightly. When she received no response, she opened the door quietly and stepped in. On the table was a briefcase and flung over a chair was a suit coat with a tie dropped carelessly on the floor. The far door to the greenhouse was ajar, letting out a warm draft of moist air. She opened the door wider and looked in, pausing when she spotted the figure at the far end of the room.

He was hunched over the plants as she came in, his long fingers black with soil. When he straightened and looked at her, she was struck again at his resemblance to the portrait. But up close, she could see differences as well. His hair was a shade lighter, his eyes almost green rather than blue, and he must have weighed thirty pounds less than the man depicted in the portrait because his skin appeared tightly stretched over bone.

When he turned to face her directly, she had to tip her head back to look him fully in the eyes. He moved slowly and deliberately toward her, a slight limp in his step. Without preamble, and almost as though he was continuing a conversation they had begun earlier, he spoke.

"I apologize for this evening's events. I had no idea you were in the house until I heard the noise upstairs." he halted, looking awkward. "Are you feeling better?"

"Yes, thank you," she ran her fingers nervously through her hair, some of the long strands escaping the ponytail down her back. She had been determined to speak to him and to be frank. But seeing him face to face had an unexpected effect on her. She was at a loss for words, her anger drained. He didn't look like he would manipulate anyone. He wasn't the cocky spoiled snob she had expected. He was calm, steady, and sad.

Abruptly she wondered what he might be thinking of her. The wild hair, the dirty face and hands, and the poorly fitting clothes, stained now with ashes and soot. Maybe this wasn't such a good idea. She should have waited until she was cleaned up, until she had calmed down.

Get a grip on yourself, she thought grimly. He wasn't exactly comfortable himself. Although his clothing was clean, it was rumpled and creased. A dusting of soil marked his sleeve, and his expensive shoes were covered with the stuff.

"Mr. Edwards, right?"

He moved closer, "Yes, sorry. And you're Claire. Noel made introductions." He appeared to be watching her curiously. "You're sure you feel better? I saw you fall and..."

"I'm fine, a little headache is all." She touched the tender spot at the side of her head.

"I'm sorry you got hurt. I tried to catch you before you hit the floor, but I couldn't move fast enough." He paused for a moment.

"I'm fine. Really." She replied quickly, feeling embarrassed and flustered in his presence.

"I still don't understand what was going on," he said, turning and glancing behind him. "I've stayed in this house before. I've never had any problems like this." He gestured toward the rear of the long room where a door stood slightly ajar. "I was out back bringing in some supplies. I thought I heard something when I was out there, but I just ignored it. It can be noisy out here." He gestured toward a palate stacked with pots and seedlings. "When I heard the crashing sound, I dropped everything. I thought we had had a wall collapse. With all this construction, I worry about people getting hurt. Then I saw the soot on your clothes, so I went looking for a fire..." he paused to put a hand casually on the nearest shelf shifting his weight to his other foot. "After your friends get to us, I went through the other rooms, but didn't find anything out of the ordinary. This old house, well, you never know what surprises it has in store for you."

She noticed he was shifting uncomfortably. She could tell he was in some pain, but did not remark on it.

"So, you didn't see any signs of a fire?"

"No, and I checked in every room. With that loud of a crash, I was sure something had fallen." He seemed to be eyeing her closely. "But that's not what you were thinking of, is it?"

She felt vulnerable under his scrutiny, as though he could see more than she wanted him to. His eyes were an even clearer green up close, the light catching reflections and giving them a strange glow. With his thin, prematurely lined face, he seemed to somehow match the house, the genteel deterioration.

"I was just wondering, no, I need to know what you saw before my friends got here." She kept her voice surprisingly even. "Did you hear the voices coming from upstairs? Did you hear me calling for John?"

He looked confused for a moment, then his face seeming to tighten under the harsh lighting.

"I thought that the worst of the noises were coming from upstairs, but it's hard to pinpoint sounds in here because of the water pipes. The spray can be quite noisy at full force." He paused and turned away, his eyes seeking the tranquility of the plants around him. "When I went out into the library, I heard a ruckus upstairs, but thought it was John or you and your friend. Charles said you probably would be home soon. I just didn't think much about it until the loudest sounds started. The crashing and breaking."

"But didn't you see the lights blink? Or smell anything?"

"The lights blink constantly around here. It's the price of construction, I'm afraid. I wasn't concerned." His gaze sharpened, "Where were you when the lights acted up?"

"I was in the library. I went into the foyer looking for John, thinking that maybe he had done something. Then I heard the noise. I guess it was several noises, actually. They came from the floors above and seemed to get louder and louder." She felt her hands shake and clenched them in tight fists. She looked away from his curious gaze, wishing that he wasn't so focused on her. She cleared her throat and swallowed, trying to search for words that wouldn't make her look like a raving lunatic. "I admit I got pretty scared," she said stiffly. "I didn't see anything in there, except the chandelier. It was swinging." She bit her lip in a nervous gesture and looked behind her where the door led into the library. "I didn't know if it was going to fall, if the ceiling was going to come down, or what was happening, so I ran into the parlor." She knew her attempt at sounding factual and calm about the situation was failing miserably. She could see he wasn't convinced, but he said nothing about her obvious discomfort.

He nodded slowly. "I heard you earlier in the library but didn't want to disturb you. I stayed in the music room until you had left." She felt a stab of awkwardness. Despite what he had said, he had been avoiding her, and she wasn't sure how she felt about that. He went on. "When I went into the library later, some of the books had been rearranged, dropped on the floor, so I assumed you were coming back." His look was purposefully blank, and she found herself looking intently at him to read the truth in his eyes.

"I didn't rearrange all those books, and I certainly drop them on the floor. I only had two or three out, and I put them back just where I found them." Now she felt like she was defending herself.

"I don't care if you borrow books..."

"But I didn't. And I didn't leave the mess in the room. I was gone for just a few minutes before you came in." She paused, weighing her next words. "So, who did move the books?"

"What are you implying?"

"I just know when I went back to the library it looked different..."

"That's when I scared you into a faint?" He interrupted wryly.

She felt her face heat but shook her head. "No, you didn't scare me at all. There was something in the parlor. Maybe it was some-one, and it's an awful joke they're pulling..." her voice trailed off, unwilling to add any incriminating information.

"A ghost?" He asked, his lips curving into a half smile.

"I didn't say that!" She corrected him quickly.

"You didn't have to. You looked so panicked when you came in, I thought you were being chased by the devil himself."

Claire felt her temper rise, a familiar sensation this evening. She could tell he didn't believe her, and that was reasonable. But to mock her was not.

"So, what was in your house making all that noise? You admitted you heard that yourself!" she asked, her tone angry and a little too loud.

"I can't say for sure but..."

"Claire, God, I've been looking everywhere for you. I thought you were going to sleep or something. Charles said after his meeting we could go out for drinks..." Noel's eyes went from Claire's red face the Mr. Edwards' pale one. Her voice trailed off and she hesitantly put her hand on Claire's arm. "I'm sorry. I didn't mean to interrupt anything."

"You weren't," Claire said bluntly. "Our discussion was finished." At that moment, she didn't care he was their employer. She didn't care about anything except the fact that he was denying seeing anything. And he was the only other possible witness.

Noel glanced back to Edwards, her indecision evident on her face. She could see the angry red abrasion on Claire's temple and felt a sudden concern for her friend.

"Claire?"

Claire moved as though jerked by a string and turned to her friend.

"I think I will go up and lie down for a while."

Claire left the room silently, her face expressionless as Noel stared silently at her retreating figure.

Noel came up to Claire's room an hour later. Darkness had blanketed the windows, and Claire had left her light on beside the bed. She was sleeping lightly and woke immediately with Noel's knock.

Noel had changed into more conservative jeans and a bright fuchsia sweater. She had three bracelets on one arm and two on the other. They clattered softly when she moved. Her hair had been combed sleekly back from her face, and huge hoop earrings dangled almost to her shoulders.

"How are you feeling?"

Claire sat up and rubbed her eyes, noting her hands were steady and warm.

"Charles said Mr. Edwards has asked us all out for drinks and dessert since we already ate dinner. I guess they want to have a little meeting."

Claire leaned back against the headboard. She recalled with vivid detail her confrontation with Mr. Edwards only a few hours before. She'd be lucky to keep her job, much less get a free cocktail from him.

"Do we all have to go?"

"Yeah, I think we should. Look, what's up with you and Edwards?" She dropped to the side of Claire's bed and frowned. "You were pretty, um, heated, and that's not your style at all." Noel forced a smile, "That's usually my thing. You sure you didn't hit your head too hard?"

"It's a long story." Claire wanted to avoid the conversation. Any conversation really, but this one especially now she would be facing the man himself very soon. "I'll tell you later," Claire responded wearily and slid off the bed. "Help me find something to wear."

––––––––––––

They chose to go to the Bristol Bar and Grill, a nice restaurant in the Middletown area noted for its varied menu and some hometown favorites like the Hot Brown, a delicious Louisville recipe. Claire and Noel had ridden with Charles and John while Mr. Edwards had driven separately in a sleek, expensive sedan. Claire had been silent most of the ride, her mind tracing the events of the day, culminating in the argument with her employer. She knew now that confronting her employer on his own property had been a huge mistake. Of all the people she wanted to impress with her level head and responsible nature, he should have been at the top of the list, but no, she had to hysterically accuse him of seeing things that weren't there and admit that ghosts were lighting fires in his ancestral home. Her distracted mind barely registered the passing scenery, but she was jerked to attention when Charles stopped the car at John's insistence, still on the property.

"There was someone on the bridge. Someone was just standing there, in the middle of the lane," John said anxiously, peering out the passenger window. "Didn't you see him? He was almost on top of us!"

"No, I didn't see anyone." Charles seemed a little short himself. "These damn trees are too close. They make it hard to see, even in broad daylight." He blew out a breath. "I'm surprised this hasn't been taken care of before now. I'll have a word with Cole about it later."

"I saw, look, I still see him," John's voice was urgent. "Don't you?" he asked, looking from Claire to Noel. They both turned around, seeing the glare of the oncoming headlights as Cole Edwards' massive car tailed them in the darkness.

"I don't see," Noel said softly, "no, I don't see anyone."

Claire had turned as well and was watching closely as they moved away from the bridge. When the headlights turned to spear the darkness of the woods to the side of the drive as the big sedan took the curve, she silently caught her breath. In the momentary dim, it did indeed look like someone was standing in the center of the bridge. As she watched, wide eyed, the figure seemed to move, raising one arm in a casual salute as the expensive car glided across the bridge. But the car neither slowed nor stopped, and the figure melted away.

Claire felt sick and turned back around, looking toward the front of the car, the dash's lights dancing in the dark. She focused on that, on the numbers rising, the mileage, fuel, radio stations, all the flickering reminders of the world outside her head. She barely registered the conversation around her, the drone of the voices comforting as they sped away from the house.

As they entered town, the traffic slowed to a crawl. Charles deftly pulled the sedan into a space between a late model Mercedes Benz and a Lexus. Claire looked nervously at the patterned fabric of her dress. She wasn't dressed up; she had basically thrown on the clothes Noel had pulled from her wardrobe. She stepped out of the car and smoothed her skirt. It might not matter. She might not have to worry about impressing her employer if he decided to fire her here. She huffed out a sigh. Time to face the music.

The restaurant was decorated with warm colors and the glint of glass, and the lighting was dimmed to provide atmosphere. Claire wondered just how she could force anything down. She took her seat at the table, trying to place as many people between her and Cole Edwards as she could. She was nervous everyone was watching her, waiting for another sign of a troubled mind, of a breakdown. She took a deep breath and looked down the table, ignoring Noel's troubled looks. She had fought hard to cultivate her poker face, and she would use it tonight. She sat tensely as everyone ordered their drinks, choosing a few appetizers to share even though they had just recently had dinner. Claire kept her eyes averted, sipping on the crisp white wine and concentrating on keeping her face expressionless. Gradually she relaxed, aware that despite her worries, no one seemed to be paying any unusual attention to her. Surprisingly, the atmosphere was of easy camaraderie with the wine and conversations flowing.

John was in rare form, amusing them all with stories about his adolescent pranks. He punctuated his stories with long swallows of beer and waved an artistic hand when he wanted to illustrate a point. His attempts at making everyone comfortable were much appreciated, and Noel appeared to be making a distinct effort to egg him on and laugh at all the appropriate places.

Charles was quieter, but steady and reassuring. He casually added his own opinions about tee ball and high school dances. He spoke often of his wife whom he had met in high school, and soon had them all laughing when he described his first meeting with her dad, "the coach". His gentle smile and humor were welcome reminders of one of Claire's brothers, and she felt herself relax slightly.

When John brought up the subject of basketball, Charles began to show some of his competitive edge, and they debated about the University of Kentucky's basketball team versus the University of Louisville's. Claire kept silent but Noel dove into the subject with her usual vigor and soon had them laying down money for the next tournament games. Claire enjoyed watching the relationship Charles and John shared, and was unsurprised when John mentioned he had been an honorary member of Charles' family for years. It certainly explained a lot.

In contrast to his noisy companions, Cole Edwards sat back quietly, smiling at appropriate times but eating and drinking very little. His face still looked pale, even in the dim lighting, and his long hair was slightly ruffled, as though he had run his fingers through it while deep in thought. He had changed out of his dress clothes into some casual slacks and a soft sweater for the evening out, but Claire could tell he wasn't the sort of man that relaxed easily. He appeared distracted during much of the conversation, his eyes wandering to the windows when he thought no one was watching, and Claire noticed he frowned when they mentioned seeing shadows on the bridge. Claire knew he had purposely driven by himself, claiming he needed to run an errand on the way to town, but had arrived only 15 minutes after the rest of the group. She wondered what the true reason was for his traveling alone.

"Okay, so maybe I did cheat a little at poker, but you lost, fair and square," John's voice interrupted her thoughts, as he and Charles argued genially about a past game.

"So, you play cards?" Noel asked, her eyes alight with mischief.

"Do we play cards?" John said boastfully. "We have the hottest game going in the area every Thursday night when Charles' wife lets him out to play."

"Now, now," Charles interjected mildly.

Noel grinned back; "Can we play next time?"

"You got any money?"

"A little. How rich is your game?"

Claire listened as Noel and John discussed the details, her eyes going back to Cole Edwards. To her surprise, he was looking directly at her and frowning. When he caught her gaze she looked down again, avoiding the eye contact.

She felt the blood seep into her cheeks. He knew. He had to know something was in that house. Something that was not meant to be there. It certainly wasn't all in her mind. With John claiming to see the figure on the bridge, and the frequent allusions to mysterious stories about the house, she knew for sure there was something real, and something not natural about the house. And now Cole Edwards knew she was somehow involved. Well, if he knew so much about it, and now she was sure he did, she might just have to look into his background. Whatever was going on in the house was not just in her head. She was sure of that now. And Mr. Edwards was going to help her prove that.

CHAPTER NINE

The days blended together as the renovation became more intense. With Mr. Edwards home, the workers were called in earlier and left later. He was a perfectionist, going through each room with a fine-tooth comb, noting problems with plaster, floor refinishing, and painting. The workers responded with appropriate respect, although a little grumbling could be heard during the lunch hours. But all were pleased with the generous over-time checks including Noel and Claire when they were called upon to do extra jobs on the weekend. Noel was concerned with Claire's extra work load, but Claire insisted she felt fine. Since her fall, she had tried to rest more and study less, making a concerted effort to care for herself more consciously.

All of these efforts were only minimally successful. Claire found she was often overly fatigued in the mornings, struggling to rise from bed. Her nights tended to take one of two distinct routines. Some nights she would sleep so deeply she would wake in the morning with no memory of the night at all. It would seem as though the time had passed in just a flash, and she would have to drag herself upright to meet the day.

On other nights, sleep was an elusive creature she could not catch no matter what methods she used. She tried to read, to play little games on her cell phone, to practice relaxation methods she recalled from her long ago difficult times. But they did not appear to help her at all. She had waited in vain for the visiting bird as well, but had not seen a single feather to remind her of what she now thought of as a friend. Now, as the house settled into slumber, she alone remained on watch to hear the other things waking. There was the sigh of the wind, the scuttle of little creatures in the attic or eaves, the old wood groaning as it settled, and then there were the other sounds. And those were the ones she hated the most. The soft footfalls, the scrape of weight against wooden floors, the hollow howl of a voice, the high tinkle of a toddler's cry.

They weren't real, these sounds that seemed to fill the night around her, but she surely felt like she could hear them. Like a child, she would curl up in her bed, covers pulled close; a light left on to scare away the worst of the shadows. Her eyes would probe the darkness, watching the door for any sign of movement, glancing toward the heavy curtains shielding the blank windows, and then the massive armoire that would hold more than one full grown man.

But despite her lack of rest, she felt like she was putting on a pretty good act of normality. She ignored the sore muscles from overexertion, the paint spattered hands, the persistent headaches. She was doing this for her parents, for herself, for her friend. She was going to see the project through.

Another change for her was when Mr. Edwards became a familiar face around the house, eating with them at dinnertime and sitting in the library during the day, his laptop computer open and the cell phone constantly ringing. In the late evening, Claire had come upon him twice sitting at the piano in the music room and playing, his fingers deft on the keys. He seemed to prefer somber pieces, which he played with skill and passion. His eyes were dark and intense, his face pale and set. She wondered what he thought of as he played, a past love, a tragic event, or maybe it was just a reflection of his personality. Claire had found herself momentarily entranced while he played and both times had hovered outside the door to listen to his music. When the music stopped, she had quietly crept out of the room, hoping he had been unaware of her presence.

Despite his frequent appearances in the Talitha house, Edwards' past remained a mystery to all of the inhabitants. Although no one had discussed it, it was obvious he had been injured in some way, and the injury had been recent. He walked slowly and deliberately, with a slight limp that became more pronounced at the end of the day, and winced at times when climbing stairs or walking on uneven terrain. His skin showed signs of injury as well, and Noel had remarked upon a particularly vivid scar that traced from his left wrist, beneath the sleeve of his dress shirt, to emerge at the collar and end at his throat.

Claire quickly realized Cole Edwards' arrival had changed her life in other ways as well. Claire had often enjoyed borrowing books from the library in the house but found she was uncomfortable going into his territory. Now she made herself scarce, avoiding him when possible. After their confrontation, he had been studiously polite, greeting her and addressing her at times, but she knew it was forced. When he found her alone in a room, he often paused to ask about her health, but found a reason to leave almost immediately. She wasn't sure if the avoidance was because he had decided he just didn't want to be in her company and was uncomfortable with her, or if he was hiding something. She was sure he knew something about the house but was equally as certain he wasn't going to share it with her.

And Claire knew she had her own problems to be worried about.

Monday was almost a relief. There was a joy in routine, and Claire was happy to return to her classes in downtown Louisville. Her morning went by quickly, and as she rushed to her car, she tried to reorganize her mind. Class work, paper due Friday, scrub the antique tub in the bath on the second floor, call her mom, study for the test on Thursday evening, sand the fireplace in the bedroom by the turret. She almost missed the insistent buzz from her purse and had to fumble her phone out. Noel. Good, she wanted to make sure she wasn't missing anything from her calendar.

"Hey," she said, her tone distracted.

"Oh, Claire, where are you!" Noel's voice caught, and she sounded like she was fading.

"Noel? What's wrong? Are you okay?"

"It's not me," Noel sobbed, "It's John. He fell. He fell off the ladder, and he's really hurt."

"Where is he?" Claire asked, standing still in the middle of the parking lot, her keys forgotten in her hand.

"They are putting him in the ambulance now. He's not breathing. I don't think they can get him awake. He won't open his eyes." Noel's pitch was rising with hysteria, and Claire felt her stomach drop.

"I'm on my way. I'll be there in a few minutes. You just stay there, and we will head to the hospital as soon as I get there."

Claire ended the call and ran to her car, throwing her bags in the back seat. She drove fast, faster than her usual pace, but with a close eye on the road. It seemed to take way too much time to get to the driveway, and the narrow single lane felt like it was pressing in around her. When she passed through the open gate, she saw few cars remained. Leaving her bags in her car, she rushed up the porch stairs to where the heavy wooden door was hanging ajar.

"Noel! What happened?"

Noel immediately got up and ran to her, throwing her arms around her. "Oh, Claire, I can't believe it. John! He was looking at some of the woodwork in the foyer. The ladder collapsed. He fell. God, he just fell like a rag doll. They said he just hit the floor, that there was nothing to catch him."

Claire felt the blood drain from her face. Her mind was full of pictures of John. John at dinner balancing a spoon on his nose, in the restaurant daring them to a poker game, in the kitchen snatching bites from the pots on the stove, and cutting up to make everyone laugh. Although they had only known him for a short time, she felt as close to him as she was to many of her childhood friends.

"Why was he up on a ladder to begin with?" Random questions swept through her mind.

Noel looked down at her hands, her fingers lacing and unlacing with nervous energy. "I'm not sure. Something about the banisters they were working on. He wanted to check something on the carvings, I think. He was only up there for a few seconds before he fell. I was in the kitchen, looking for something for dinner when I heard the commotion and saw him." Her voice weakened and she paused to wipe her nose with her sleeve, looking like a child. "We have to stay here and catch Charles," she added in a muffled voice.

Claire felt tears in her eyes as she turned. The door from the office opened, and Cole stood in the doorway. He looked even paler and more rigid; his face set with harsh lines bracketing his mouth, his lips compressed in a thin line on his expressionless face. He had his cell phone pressed to his ear and was dropping keys into his pocket as he moved quickly to the door. He glanced to Claire and nodded in their direction as he left through the back door. Claire and Noel sat on the overstuffed couches, the television buzzing mindlessly in the background.

After a few minutes, the front door burst open and they could hear Charles calling from the foyer. Both girls quickly stood, and when he caught sight of them, he immediately stopped.

"I was hoping the message was a mistake, or a prank. Where is

Edwards? Has anyone called John's family? Which hospital are they taking him to? Where's his damn phone?"

Claire put a hand on his sleeve. "Wait a minute. Cole went out a few minutes ago..."

"He was going to John's apartment to get his address book. He didn't have any numbers for John's family, and the police said he could meet them there." Noel was wiping her eyes with one hand, and sniffed loudly. "He wanted to be the one to call. I think he feels responsible," she explained. "He wanted us to bring you to the hospital."

"Well, maybe he should feel guilty. This damn place has been nothing but trouble since we started work on it," Charles interrupted bitterly.

"You know that's not true. This is just one of those flukes. An accident. I'm sure it was no one's fault. John knew how to climb the ladder, and it was secure on the floor." Noel stopped and looked at Charles, her expression earnest. "There wasn't anyone around to disturb him; I guess he just lost his footing. It could have happened anywhere." Noel still looked pale, but was beginning to regain her composure.

Charles put his head in his hands. His voice was tight with grief when he spoke. "I've known John for years. We met through my wife; she was a friend of his long before I met him. Oh, she's going to freak out. John's always been such a great guy to her, to both of us. When we lost our first child to a miscarriage, John was the first to come over and brought Annie a huge container of ice cream..." Charles stopped, his breath coming fast.

Claire felt frozen in the face of his grief. She watched Noel put her arms around Charles and looked listlessly out the window to the tangled garden. She wished she were brave enough to grieve with them, but she felt the protective facade she had built rising around her. She knew it wasn't right for her to control everything, but she tried, twisting her fingers in her lap as she fought off tears. A light rain had begun to fall, and the glass was streaked as though the house itself was crying.

"I'm going to the hospital now." Charles said abruptly, pulling away. He pulled his keys from his pocket, disregarding Noel's protest they were going to drive him. "If you hear from anyone," he objected, cutting her off. You can give them my number. I need to be there now." Charles was at the door, turning to look back at the two girls.

Claire felt a strange stirring. A prickle seemed to rise from her spine and creep up her scalp. "Charles, wait," she said softly.

He froze for a second, her tone catching him. The house phone began to wail at his side, the landline they seldom used, and they all stared at it, a slice of time that would change all of them forever. When Charles finally moved and raised the phone to his ear, Claire knew John was gone.

The funeral was held two days later. Noel and Claire rode with Charles' wife in his sedan as he rode with the other pallbearers in the second car, following the hearse. Claire watched as a tearful older woman emerged from the first car, supported by a younger girl with dark hair, John's mother and his sister. The rest of the family followed, a fluttering group in black and dark gray, their handkerchiefs in hand as they walked up the steps and into St. Joseph's Catholic Church. Although he would be taken home to Florida for burial with the rest of his family, John's mother had requested to have his funeral at the church where he had first worked as an architect. His family had flown in from Florida the previous day, and it had taken Noel and Claire nearly an hour to finally get to the funeral home. Cole was last to arrive, his limp more pronounced as though his grief was weighing him down. His suit was finely made, but seemed to hang from his emaciated frame.

They all had only weathered the storm, but not unscathed. She shivered despite the heat in the car feeling the ghosts of those left behind dancing on her bones.

The funeral was long, but Claire was comforted by the familiar words of the Catholic mass. The scent of the candle wax and incense surrounded her, the soft drone of the speaker's voice buzzed in her ear, and she leaned back against the slick wood of the pew to rest her aching head. When it was over and the last strains of music were echoing in the high plaster ceilings, the pallbearers wheeled the casket out and the family followed. Claire watched as Cole walked out in front of them, pausing to genuflect at the center aisle.

Noel and Claire left for Talitha immediately following the funeral, with Cole driving them since Charles and Annie, his wife, had decided to stay in a nearby hotel. Claire could tell the ordeal was affecting Annie; she looked as though she had aged years in the day they had been with her.

The ride was a long and silent one. Noel drifted to sleep in the back seat while Claire watched the cars pass out the side window. She felt sick at the prospect of returning to the house. Nothing good seemed to come of that place. And she couldn't get it out of her mind that John's death wasn't just an accident. Noel had said no one was around to cause the fall. The ladder was sound. What would make a man who was familiar with manual labor of that type suddenly lose his balance and fall? And the way he had fallen was strange in itself. One of the workers claimed it looked as though he was trying to turn away from something because he had landed, not on his back, but face down, arms outstretched instead of beneath him. Claire suppressed a shudder as this vision ran through her mind. All she knew was that something strange was going on in that house, and she was no longer sure it was a safe place for her or anyone else to be.

Cole maneuvered the car confidently into the drive and parked in the back. He helped them gather their purses and jackets, and then unlocked the door, holding it open for them. The house seemed emptier than ever without John. Cole excused himself and disappeared into the library while Noel and Claire went upstairs to bed. Noel's eyes were still red-rimmed and her face was pale with fatigue. When she asked if she could stay with Claire, Claire gratefully agreed and helped her as she made a cot on the floor. Claire went down the hall slowly, her eyes gritty with exhaustion and pent up tears. It had been a long and dreadful day, and she prayed she would never have to repeat it.

Claire pulled on her shorts and tee shirt to sleep in, bundling her clothes into an untidy ball. She quickly finished cleaning up, bathing her face and hands and brushing out her hair while gazing blankly in the mirror. She looked years older. Her face was white, and her hair was pulled loosely back from her thin features, revealing fine lines that bracketed her mouth and eyes. She frowned at her reflection and pressed cool fingers to her temples. It was going to get better. It just had to.

She quickly pulled the door open and stepped out into the hallway, jumping when she brushed against another figure in the gloom.

"Sorry. I didn't see you." Cole looked even more tired than she.

"It's alright. I was just heading for bed," she murmured, acutely aware of her dishabille.

"Are you all right?"

She smiled solemnly. "We're as good as can be expected. Thanks for asking."

With that, she retreated down the hallway to her room, pausing at the doorway to watch him as he stood, head bent as though in prayer. She felt a sudden urge to go to him, to hold him for a moment and was shocked by these feelings. Shaking her head in confusion, she slipped in her room and closed the door quietly, resting her head on the panel for a moment. Behind her, she could hear the soft breaths of her best friend as she escaped into sleep. Claire doubted the same sleep would come to her.

Later that night as she huddled in bed, she thought she heard the sounds of wings against glass. With an almost unhealthy eagerness, she flew to the window and pulled wide the curtains. And it was there, the little mournful dove in a fluffy ball of feathers perched on invisible feet atop the railing. She silently pulled the doors wide, hoping ridiculously the bird would take the invitation to come in. Why? She couldn't say why she felt that way. She just knew she wanted it, the presence of another soul in the room. But she didn't want to disturb Noel who no doubt would be startled to see the animal in the room.

With an eerie understanding, the bird took to the wind, its wings emitting a shrill whistle as it moved in a speedy glide into the high-ceilinged space. It took a few turns in the room narrowly but effort-lessly avoiding the furniture in its way and landing unerringly on the foot of the bed.

When Claire cuddled back in bed, she pulled the covers around her shoulders. She looked towards the cot on the floor, but Noel had not stirred. She looked toward the open door that led to the balcony, but didn't move to close it. She didn't want to close the door and trap the bird. But she hated to leave allow the night to seep into her room.

"I'm doing this for you, Leta," Claire whispered. The name had snuck into her mind without thought, so she accepted it.

Upon hearing her words, the bird glided onto the bedcovers and hopped up to Claire, pausing to cuddle in the pool of blankets in her lap.

Claire lifted a slightly trembling hand and cupped it ever so gently over the creature's back. Leta did not move, but stayed in the shelter of her hand. When Claire rested her head back against the headboard, the bird emitted a sad coo and settled still and warm.

The next day dawned dim and already filled with shadows. As before, the dove was gone like a ghost, and the doors were closed, latched, and smothered by the heavy curtains. Claire and Noel got up late and ate cereal in the kitchen, sitting at the counter. The house was quiet and empty, the only sign of life the soft clicking of the keyboard in the library. There would be no more work done in the house for the rest of the week, and the girls decided to skip classes for the day. Noel planned on taking a long tub bath and dying her hair bright red to make herself feel better. Claire wanted to look in the library for some reference books about the house. She needed to keep busy, and research was a soothing way of distracting her mind. She didn't know if any books existed that would tell about the history of the house or the family that had built it, but she speculated if something did, it would be in the library. She also was curious to see what other books might be there. Anything about the history of the Bluegrass area or the local flavor. She pondered the idea that there may be less factual tomes among the books in the library, maybe even some juicy ghost stories about historical sites in Louisville, Shelbyville, or the outlying counties. But was that healthy for her to read? With John's accident on her mind, she wasn't sure what her reasoning was for wanting to find that kind of information. To make her feel better? To make her feel there was a real reason for her to be afraid?

She went to the doorway and knocked lightly on the doorframe. Cole was sitting at his desk; several binders open in front of him. He glanced up when she knocked and waved her in.

"Can I help you with something?"

"I just wanted to look at some of the books. Is that all right or will I be in the way?"

"No, it's fine. Let me know if I can help you find something. I've been through most of these myself."

She nodded and went to the shelf. The books were loosely arranged according to sections with fiction in one area, biographies in another, plays and poetry on the highest shelves, and reference and history books on the far wall. Claire looked at the array of titles including a set of encyclopedias that was over 40 years old. She quickly became absorbed in her search, stopping to pick out several titles with the promise of historical information. She sat on the floor; her legs crossed beneath her and books spread out around her. When she found a pertinent chapter or reference, she marked with a sticky note and moved on to the next book. She decided to take the best ones up to her room to read at her leisure later.

She didn't even hear as Cole approached and squatted down next to her. She looked up quickly, blinking as he looked over her shoulder at the book.

"Interested in history all of the sudden?"

"No, just looking for some information."

"Anything I can help you with?"

"I don't think so," she said evasively.

"Did you see this one?" He handed her a small volume; its cover worn at the corners. When she flipped it open she saw the title was just an address. 110 Talitha Heights.

"Is it about this place?" she asked.

"It is supposed to be a history of my family, but it does cover some of the construction of the original house. I can't say it's the best book ever written, or the most truthful, but it does have some interesting information. Is that what you were looking for?"

She felt embarrassed but nodded. "I just was curious about the previous owners. Do you mind if I borrow it for a little while?"

"Of course not. I've read most of these myself."

She smiled her thanks and put the slender book on top of her stack. Then she climbed to her feet, gathered her books, and slipped out the door, closing it behind her.

CHAPTER TEN

The house was empty for once, and the silence was almost deafening. Claire prowled nervously around the well-lit kitchen, her hair hanging loose around her face. She was dressed in her usual jeans with a well-worn sweater, her face pale with little makeup to add color. She wore small gold studs in her ears and her usual crucifix around her neck, which she caressed when she was nervous. Like now. She was expecting Noel to return any minute, and she had to admit she was anxious for her friend to return. The evening was falling, and Noel had gone out this afternoon with Ben to look at some property he was thinking of buying. He had plans to eventually build a house, and was always looking for the next real estate deal. But time was flying. Surely, she would return soon before the steadily setting sun made it too difficult to see.

Shaking herself, she sat at the table a moment, resting her fingers on the cold wooden surface. She knew she could go upstairs and get the book to read. She had left it sitting on the table, a tempting reminder of what she could be doing instead of homework when her studies got too hectic. But she didn't move, letting her mind wonder. She glanced at the closed door, feeling slightly abandoned. She had noticed the increased frequency Noel and Ben were together. Neither seemed as interested in her company as they had once been, and Claire was happy for them. The night before, Noel had visited Claire in her room for a little girl talk. Both had pointedly avoided the topic of the house or any of the inhabitants, although both agreed they were going to miss John. After dabbing tears, they had retrieved chocolate chip cookies from the kitchen, and began discussing their usual topics of school, romance, and friendships. Although Noel had admitted Ben hadn't "made his move" as she termed it, she was confident it was just a matter of time.

Claire smiled to herself but quickly sobered. She didn't like to be alone here, not anymore. Since John's death, she felt as though a line had been broken. Something was going on in this house. Something was wrong here. She knew it wasn't just in her mind either. There were too many times when someone else had experienced a disturbance, a vision, an unexplainable happening. Whatever had held the house in its control for all this time seemed to be growing stronger. She knew she wasn't the only one who knew it either. And although she was not superstitious, it was Halloween, and she had seen enough scary movies to be a little wary of that particular date.

She tugged the crucifix from under her sweater again and straightened the chain. She had worn it for years, since her mother had given it to her on her twenty-first birthday. It had always been meaningful for her, but now it seemed vital to her sanity and her spirit, and she wore it constantly, even while she bathed and went to bed.

The lock turned on the side door and Claire heard the welcome sound of footsteps, real and solid, coming through the short hall.

"Oh, I didn't realize anyone was here." Cole looked uncomfortable and stiff, with lines of fatigue tracing grooves around his eyes and mouth. He was dressed in one of his many well-tailored suits, a dark charcoal ensemble with a burgundy tie and soft leather shoes. His hair had been recently trimmed but still fell on his forehead, accentuating his pallor. Claire felt an odd and surprising urge to reach out and touch the soft waves of his hair and stuffed her hands into her pockets. That had certainly come from nowhere.

"Noel and Ben will be back in a little while. Some of our friends are coming over to stay the evening. We checked with Charles..."

He smiled without humor. "This place is supposed to be a hotel one day. I don't think a couple extra people will matter much. By the way, the bathroom adjoining Noel's room is working now. Yours should be soon."

"Great, thanks." She paused, ill at ease. Still there was something very vulnerable about him. Something she found engaging that made her want to continue the discussion when all her instincts told her to turn and run. "We're having pizza tonight. You're welcome to join us."

He nodded and glanced at his watch. "Maybe. Thanks for asking." He stood very still for a moment as though reluctant to leave, and she found herself studying him more closely.

"Are you feeling alright? I know all this has got to be wearing on you. Trying to run a business while all of this has happened at the house..." She swallowed suddenly thinking of John once again.

"Yes, well, the job has been a little more difficult than I anticipated, but I never figured it would be easy. Nothing worth your lifeblood ever is. And this project has definitely taken its pound of flesh." He turned, his eyes seeming to catch memories. "And John's death." He seemed like he couldn't speak of it anymore, and Claire dropped her eyes.

She was silent for a moment, considering his words. A pound of flesh, an old-fashioned sentiment, but seeing him standing there, it was also suitable. She couldn't help feeling a well of sympathy for this man. He seemed so alone. He never spoke of family, or friends for that matter, and existed only for his business. What a sad way to live one's life.

"So, your classes, they are going well?" he asked politely as though realizing there was a ceremony for conversation, a script that must be followed.

"Yes. Yes, they're going fine. I'll be glad when I'm done."

He nodded. "I finished my degree several years ago, but I remember the challenge."

She felt a mix of unease and interest. She wanted to ask him more. Where had he gone to college? What had he majored in? What was his life like when he wasn't ensconced in the family estate? For that matter, how old was he? A chime interrupted her thoughts, and she watched him pull his cell phone from his pocket. He glanced at the display.

"I have to get this," he said quickly.

"Sure," she nodded, and turned away as he slipped from the room. She felt a mixture of disappointment and relief. But almost immediately her eyes went to the darkening windows. No trick-or-treaters here, she thought grimly.

After he had left, she retreated to her room to wait. She felt safer under the watchful eye of the woman in the portrait than downstairs in the main part of the house. She carefully parted the curtains and looked out into the dimming night. She didn't see the bird, her mystery dove, but the other night birds were active and she could hear plainly the cry of the crows against the black branches of the overhanging trees. Finally, she pulled the curtains closed and gave up on her avian friend. Maybe later. She glanced around the room, and ignoring the book about the house, she instead chose the mystery novel she had started to read. She tried to become involved in the plot, but found her mind wandering far too often.

When her friends arrived, they had several pizzas with beer and soft drinks. They had picked out a few classic horror films to celebrate the holiday. Claire wasn't sure she was in the mood to be scared, and said so, but Ben assured her all the films were well chosen.

She had to laugh when she read the titles: Bride of Frankenstein, Swamp Thing, and Godzilla.

"Let's eat. I'm starving," Noel said, yanking open cardboard boxes. The steamy tomato, garlic, and spice smell permeated the kitchen as they all started to divvy out pieces.

Amy was in a rare mood because her fiancé, Bill, was off for the weekend and able to come home for a few days. She showed him into the kitchen with a flourish and busied herself filling his plate. He smiled ruefully and let her wait on him.

"I may as well enjoy this while it lasts. When we're married I doubt I'll get this much tender loving care."

She laughed at him and handed him his plate.

"You're right about that. I'll expect to be waited on; clean my car, take out the garbage, paint my house."

Claire laughed and watched them, feeling a tug of envy. They knew each other so well they often finished one another's sentences. They had dated for so many years, they seemed married already.

"Claire, are you going to eat?" Noel asked pushing a plate in her direction. Claire had recently lost weight and although she also gained muscle, her appetite had been poor since John's death. At times, she just didn't feel like eating and found her stomach in nervous knots. She didn't want to admit her suspicions, even to herself, much less to Noel. It preyed on her mind often, the image of John's fall to the cold tile floor. Had he fallen or was he pushed? And pushed by what? Or whom? And if it was murder, was it committed by the spirits that held Talitha in their power? Or some human hands? She wanted to deny it. She told herself she didn't believe in ghosts or things that go bump in the night. But yet, there had been that time. That horrible time when she had seen, no, she corrected herself, she had thought she had seen something. She shook her head briskly. The fact remained that something had happened to John, and there had been plenty of witnesses who claimed no human hand had moved him away from the safety of the railing.

Noel called her name one more time, and she took two pieces of pizza and grabbed a soft drink, following the rest of the group into the living room. It was dimly lit, already prepared for the movie to start. Despite the recent renovation, Claire still felt uneasy in the room at times. The space had once been a roofed back porch, which was framed in during the 1940's. The more recent renovation had been completed at the same time as the office; the floor covered in Berber carpeting and the walls painted a soothing taupe. The furnishings were modern sectional pieces, bought for comfort more than appearance. The television was used; an old set brought in by one of the construction workers who wanted to watch the news during his lunch hour. The DVD player was another of the workers' contributions. In the dim light, the sickly blue glow flickered against the pale walls.

Bill entered first and led Amy to one couch, and they collapsed against the thick padding, leaning back against the over-stuffed arms. Noel and Ben followed and sat on the floor, scooted up close to the coffee table where they placed their dinner and soft drinks. Claire took one of the cushioned chairs, placing her plate on the table next to her and cradled her chilled drink in her hands.

Noel got up after a moment and held up the movies. A lively vote followed, and they settled on "Bride of Frankenstein". The room quieted as the movie began, and they finished their dinner. Claire found herself again distracted, her eyes skimming over the faces around her and worrying which of them might be next. She looked at her friends, all dear and special to her in different ways, and felt a cold chill ripple down her back. No, she thought angrily. She couldn't think that way! It was crazy, and she would not be pulled into that insane path. She would not allow that. She forced herself to ease her grip on her soft drink can and take a deep breath. Relax, she reminded herself.

Almost an hour later, Claire heard a movement in the kitchen and looked up in surprise as the adjoining door opened. Cole stood in the doorway, plate and glass balanced as he let the door swing closed behind him. He had changed out of his formal clothes and looked years younger in his jeans and sweater. Claire realized his position and wealth had always given her the impression he was much older than she. Now, watching him sit in the chair next to hers and carefully set his plate down, Claire could study him a little more closely. He was a little older, but not more than five years, and although his face had lines etched around his eyes and mouth, she doubted he was much over 30.

Why would a man as successful as he obviously was choose to leave his company, even for a few weeks, to pour money into a venture like this one? The location wasn't ideal, the house was not renowned for any characteristic architecture or any historical value, and already disasters had plagued the project. What had made him want to see the job completed? So much so that he had moved to live in the unfinished building suffering the unpredictable plumbing, heat, and constant noise of construction.

"So what movie are we watching, anyway?" Cole asked in a whispered tone.

"I'm not sure anymore. It's gotten a little ridiculous. Is the pizza still good?"

"Better than any I ever make. I'm a terrible cook at best. What about you?"

She smiled at the question, knowing full well he had already heard of her mistakes in the kitchen.

"Why, I'm quite a gourmet myself. I can make a mean grilled cheese."

The television unexpectedly made a loud popping noise and blinked off.

"What the?" Ben asked, going up to the old set.

Cole got up as well and walked over to the set. Ben grasped the set and rotated it. A thin plume of smoke drizzled from a seam in the plastic at the back of the set, and the sharp smell of hot plastic spoiled the air.

"The thing's shot." Ben said frowning, waving away the smoke in a careless gesture. "Better to pitch it and buy a new one. I think it would cost more to get it fixed than replace it. I don't think they even make this kind anymore."

Noel frowned, and rose from the couch to bend over his shoulder. "No more movies, I guess."

"No, it doesn't look like it. At least we got to see one. I really wanted to see "Godzilla". Haven't seen one of those since I was a kid," Ben replied.

Bill laughed. "I don't think you're missing much."

Claire silently agreed as Noel took out the movie and put the disk in its case.

"Claire, why don't you get your cards? We'll play a few games of poker if anyone's up for it."

"I'm up for it, but I can guarantee I'll win. You have a terrible game face," Ben said, giving Noel a sly grin.

"Fine! Claire and I will be on a team. We'll skunk you," Noel retorted.

"Bill and I had better be getting home," Amy interrupted. "We have to go shopping for china patterns tomorrow."

Bill rolled his eyes but followed her to the door. Claire was smiling at the exchange until she got a closer look at Amy's face. She looked tense, her color a shade paler than usual. Her hands betrayed her as well; the slight trembling revealing how much unease she was feeling. Claire remembered what she had said the first time she had come to Talitha and was not surprised. To see her normally even-tempered friend so distraught made Claire more concerned for all her friends' safety. The house was having an impact on all of them, it seemed.

Claire went obediently up the stairs while Noel walked Amy and Bill to the door. Claire paused on the landing to watch the car lights disappear behind the massive hedges, the stained-glass casting blood red tinting across the stair steps.

A shiver ran up her spine. It was so isolated out here. No lights from the city touched the sky and while others were waiting with porch lights bright for hungry little costumed ghouls, they were locked up in this massive fun house with its own kind of spirits.

She tucked the cards into the loose pocket of her pants and headed back down the hall. She had hit the switches as she passed and the stairway was bathed in light. The foyer below looked even grimmer since the workers had begun scraping off layers upon layers of wallpaper; the colorful swatches scattered like dying leaves upon the tiled floor.

She ran her hand along the banister as she walked, picking her way down the stairs. At the curve she paused, a sound above her causing her to turn quickly for the source. As she turned, the lights blinked out and she yelped, momentarily blinded as her eyes adjusted to the dark. A chilled gust struck her from behind, like a draft from a freezer, but stronger, stirring the loose strands of her hair, washing over her. Just as suddenly she felt a pain, sharp and hot on her shoulder, and her feet slipped on the thin carpeting as though the threadbare runner had been replaced with a paper-thin sheet of ice. Her hand which had been lightly resting on the wooden support grew numb, and she lost her grip, her body tumbling forward. She hit the curve of the railing once with her ribs before falling to the side. Then she struck something else, no someone, and they fell together, stopping at the landing with a resounding thud. The arm around her was tight and strong, and she gripped it for a moment before they drew apart.

Her eyes had not quite adjusted to the dim light filtering from the dining room, but knew it was Cole. Even without light she would have known from the faint scent of his soap or aftershave.

He leaned over, wincing. "Are you all right? Don't move until I can get a light on out here. Damnit! What happened to those lights?"

He fumbled up the stairs, the switch clicking loudly in the silence with no corresponding light.

Finally, the lights came on from one of the bedrooms, and he gingerly picked his way down the steps.

The pain in her back dulled into an ache, and she slowly stood. She felt herself sway, and lowered back to the step, nausea rising in her throat.

"You are hurt. Just hold on." He sat next to her. "Hey, Ben, get a light in here!"

Ben and Noel came into the foyer, their faces flushed in the dim light. Ben hit the switch in the library and carried out the table lamp from the desk. Noel looked guilty as if caught with her hand in the cookie jar, and if Claire hadn't ached so much, she would have been amused.

"What happened? Jesus, we heard noises but thought you were looking for something. Are you all right?"

Claire looked at Cole's face, pale and serious, down to his hand which shown wetly in the yellow light.

"She's bleeding. Help me get her down."

Ben ran up the stairs and picked Claire up easily in his arms. She held him tightly around the neck and watched over his shoulder as Cole limped behind them, wincing as he put weight on his weaker leg.

"Noel, find the first aid kit in the pantry. It should be on the top shelf. Ben, take her to the bathroom."

He went in front of them, switching on lights, pausing to get a clean washcloth from the kitchen.

Claire was faintly embarrassed as Noel pulled her sweater over her head, but grateful her bra was a modest one. She felt her face flush as Cole leaned in close, and she breathed in the scent of soap and shampoo from his beautiful hair. Beautiful! Now she actually was losing her mind.

The sting of the alcohol was almost a relief when it pulled her from her embarrassing thoughts. Cole quickly cleaned the wound with before bandaging it securely with a small piece of gauze and tape.

"It's long but shallow. Shouldn't leave a scar."

Ben looked sick in the bright lights. Claire knew he had a weak stomach and now that the emergency was over, she watched as he excused himself hastily and ducked out of the room.

"You're awfully good at that," Noel observed, watching Cole's deft fingers.

Cole grinned. "I've had a lot of practice. My friends in college had more scrapes, stitches, and bruises than anyone I've ever known. They played a rough game of football."

"Well, they certainly taught you good techniques."

Claire leaned against the sink, the warmth starting to creep back into her face. It was bad enough she had been attacked on the stairway and had collapsed in the arms of her employer, but now they were speaking around her as though she were a child.

Cole finished the dressing and washed his hands. "Do you want to go see a doctor? Just to have it looked at?"

Claire shook her head and pushed a stray lock of hair out of her face.

"What did you cut yourself on?"

"I don't know. I just felt a pain on my back as I was coming down the stairs. That's when I fell. That's what caused me to lose my balance." She frowned at his disbelieving expression. "Well, something obviously hit me! What else could have cut me like that? And through my shirt to," she said, pulling the offending garment over her head. "What were you doing on the stairs?" She knew her voice had the shade of suspicion in it, and she felt a mild sense of shame because she knew for a fact he had nothing to do with her fall.

He seemed to catch her implication but his voice was mild when he responded. "I came into the foyer, and the lights went out. I tried the switch, but nothing happened. I was going upstairs to turn on the lights up there when you fell."

"I didn't really fall," she said, her voice more unsteady than she would have liked. "Someone hit me from behind. I don't know with what, but it left that." Her fingers touched the bandage beneath her shirt lightly, feeling the sting still.

His expression was unreadable, his eyes dark and unsmiling. She felt a sudden urge to shake him. To force him to admit the truth.

"You know something is going on in this house. Something isn't normal here." Her voice was sharp.

His response was almost inaudible. "Yes."

CHAPTER ELEVEN

When Claire got home from class on Monday, Noel was waiting for her in her bedroom. She had laid out Claire's favorite sweats and had two cartons of Ben and Jerry's ice cream, spoons ready.

"How was class?"

Claire sighed and dropped her bags. She had avoided any chances of being alone with Noel for the last three days. She knew uncomfortable questions would be raised after the events on Halloween, and she knew Noel would be doubly curious about her relationship with Cole.

"Class was fine." She peeled off her damp clothes and slipped on the others relishing the warmth of the fleece against her skin. The damp from the recent rain showers had made the day seem like one endless walk in the fog, and she was relieved to be inside, even if it had to be inside the dreaded walls of Talitha. She sat on her bed, crossing her long legs under her and took the offered carton of ice cream.

"I'm going to be so glad to graduate. I'm sick of exams. I've got two next week." Noel stopped and took a bite.

"Yeah, I've got one. My head is so full of all that meaningless information. I'm trying to get this paper done by tomorrow. I think I've just got to proof it tonight and write out the bibliography..." her voice trailed off as Noel pinned her with a sharp glare.

"Let's cut the B.S. What's going on, Claire? You've had me worried these last few weeks. You're losing weight, you're distracted, tired all the time, and won't talk about any of it! You keep acting like you're just clumsy, or not paying attention, which isn't like you." She sighed in frustration. "And then you fell down those stairs! I just don't know what's going on anymore." She gestured broadly. "And Cole! What the heck is that deal? You seem to have something going with him, and we hardly even know the guy."

Claire said quickly, "Wait," holding up her hands in a gesture of consolation. "Okay, okay. I know you've been worried, and I appreciate it. I really do. I'm sorry I haven't said anything earlier, but I just didn't want you to think I was losing it." She paused and took a deep breath. "I'll tell you what's been happening, but I know it's going to be almost impossible for you to believe. I haven't talked about this with anyone for years. I don't want you to make any comments until you've heard me out." She pulled her crucifix out of her sweatshirt and rubbed it absently. "When I was a kid, before I met you, my parents always said I had a lot of imagination. But more than that, I had imaginary friends I would see." When Noel looked like she would speak, Claire rushed on. "Wait! I'm serious. No one would believe me then; I was so little. But I told my mom, my dad, sometimes even my brothers about it. They always listened, but pretty much ignored it as my imagination. They thought it was funny or cute." She glanced down into her lap, frowning. "When I got older, and they saw that I was serious, I wasn't giving up the idea that I was seeing these people, they kind of got worried. It wasn't cute anymore. It was scary." She found herself wringing her hands, and tucked them under her legs. "So, they did what they thought was best. When I didn't drop it, they took me to a child psychologist to try to figure out if something was actually wrong with me." She was silent for a moment and smiled with no humor. "Needless to say, it didn't work." Noticing her friend's confused expression, she tried to clarify. "See, I started out by saying they were imaginary friends. But they weren't pretend, not from my imagination, they were just," she took a deep breath and shrugged, "people."

"People," Noel said slowly. "What kind of people?"

"You know what I mean," Claire responded, not wanting to say the word.

"Those kind of people," Noel said, her eyes subtly widening. "And you're not joking with me?"

"No," Claire said slowly. "Noel, do you remember that time? The time in the abandoned house?"

Noel's eyes darted to the window, and Claire could see the subject bothered her. "You mean when we were in middle school." Noel's voice was flat. It was a topic they didn't discuss. Despite their closeness in later years, at that time they had just been part of a wider group of seventh graders that hung out after school in the park just across from the campus, playing basketball and tossing Frisbees in the sunshine. They were cocky and sure of themselves, foolish in their ignorance. They had started branching out when boredom had set in, separating into groups to wander the adjoining neighborhood, some of the more adventurous kids causing a little trouble as they went. Claire's chosen friends had been a little edgier. One Friday, shortly after Halloween when the moon had hung in the sky like a chiseled pumpkin, they had broken into an already dilapidated house, determined to stay the night for the thrill of it. It had been a ridiculous "I dare you" prank that had changed their lives.

"I know you didn't see it." Claire looked at her calmly. "I didn't expect you to believe me then, you didn't know me well. But Noel, you know me now. And it wasn't a dream. It wasn't a panic. It wasn't my imagination, or illusions, or hallucinations." Her voice grew tight with emotion. "It was real, what I saw was real."

"Claire, you said you saw…"

"I know what I said, and I know what I saw." Claire bent her head, eyes on her now clinched fists. "And I know what I have seen here, and I can't deny it anymore."

Noel looked wide eyed at her friend. "You think it's a ghost. You think this place is haunted."

"I know it is."

———

Claire retold her stories, her experiences in the house of Talitha. The mirrored words, the dancing figure in the ballroom, the bursting glass of wine, the attack in the parlor, and the horror of the final encounter on the stairs. She couldn't read her friend's face well enough to gauge whether or not she believed the stories, but just telling of her experiences let her analyze them more thoroughly.

"I'm not a kid anymore. I didn't imagine the glass exploding. You saw it too. And you saw the ash in the parlor, the books tossed around in the library."

"Claire, there's got to be some explanation," Noel began.

"I'm giving you one. I think it started early. I think it started with the shower that burned me. And there have been other things. The painting in my room, I took it down one night, and it was rehung the next morning." She stood and paced a few steps to look out the window. "If it were just that, some things being moved around, noises at night, I wouldn't mess with this. I can handle those things. But when I got hurt, it really scared me. And with John…" she let her words die.

"So, if what you're saying is true," Noel's voice was little more than a whisper, "what do we do about it?"

They agreed she would have to go to Cole with the information, but Claire did not feel even close to being ready for that confrontation. She knew she wasn't having a breakdown, but she had no way of proving that to him. And unlike Noel, he had no prior knowledge of her, no history to fall back on.

Although she still harbored suspicions about him and firmly believed he had some knowledge of the hauntings, she wasn't ready to stand up to him. She had tried on several occasions to get him to open up to her, and he had resisted at every turn. And to make matters even more complicated, she found her feelings for him to be increasingly difficult to define. He made her so angry with so little effort, yet she couldn't help but want to be with him. She had to admit a physical attraction. She liked to watch him when he was unaware of her, and she loved to listen to the deep warmth of his voice. She found herself blushing in his presence and feeling frustrated at her own behavior. It aggravated her that her fickle heart would decide now would be a good time for her to develop feelings for someone. Like a school girl, she had a crush on her employer, the same man who was not only the owner of the haunted house she lived in, but might be involved in whatever had caused the ghostly occurrences to start.

As evening descended, she, Noel, and Cole ate a quiet dinner. Noel tried to carry the conversation, but Claire was distracted, and Cole seemed content to spend most of the evening listening to them talking.

They finally retired upstairs, Claire going across the ballroom and taking the stairs at the far end of the hall to avoid the main staircase. If she had to go out of her way to avoid the resident ghosts, she would. Neither of her companions commented on it, and she hadn't honestly expected them to.

She took a late-night shower in her bathroom, dressed in her nightclothes, and settled down in bed with a book. The history text about the house mocked her from its place on the desk, but she wasn't about to begin that project now. The last thing she needed now was to find names to fit the ghosts in her dreams.

She didn't know what woke her, perhaps just the draft of cold air coming from the French doors that stood slightly ajar. As she sat up, she became aware of a visitor.

Oh, God, but it was not her bird, not her little dove.

A woman hovered at the foot of her bed, pale as the moonlight, her figure wavering like a candle softly blown by a draft. She appeared unnaturally still, with features blurred like a character from an old black and white movie. Her dress was plain and dark, falling in stiff folds to sweep the floor. Colors were indistinguishable in the pale light, but she seemed young with unlined translucent skin and delicate light-colored curls escaping a modest cap to frame her face. She seemed completely unaware of Claire as she walked quickly to the wardrobe and pulling up a ghostly chair, as faded and transparent as she, stood upon the seat and deposited something on top of the big piece of furniture. She climbed back down and slowly turned in Claire's direction, her gaze seeming to light upon Claire's frozen face. But under the loose cap, her eyes were blank, and Claire felt only intense relief turned away from the bed again and moved toward the door to the hallway. In the moonlight, her figure seemed to flicker and then fade like a dissipating puff of smoke leaving nothing in her wake.

Claire lay back down against her pillow, eyes wide, concentrating on breathing. She waited in complete stillness for any other visitors as her mind raced about what she had just witnessed. A ghost. She had seen a ghost.

She deliberately tried to replay the little scene in her mind, tracing the path the specter had taken as she had moved about the room. This was not the owner of the room; she felt sure of that. Her dress had been too plain to have been anything but a servant on the estate. Doubtless, her rooms would have been on one of the floors above, far smaller than these chambers. But she had known her way around and had come for a definite reason. She had carried something. Something she had placed on the top of the wardrobe many years ago, and she wanted Claire to know that.

The idea that the apparition had come to essentially communicate with her was shocking, but then again, perhaps it shouldn't have been. Long ago, she had seen these spirits, had talked with them, had lived with them. It was only with disbelief and fear of being ridiculed Claire had forced them to fade with time. Like fairies, it seemed when she had ceased acknowledging them, they had fallen away.

But had they gone away? And who had been the fool? She had gone along with her family, her doctors, her psychologist, and buried away the spirits with facts and realities. And when the crack in her reality had broken, that night at the abandoned house, she had cracked with it and it had taken months to put her back together again.

She shook her head and looked ruefully around the room. Reality had definitely taken a turn to the weird side. And she didn't even feel afraid this time. When it seemed apparent no other apparitions were going to show themselves, she rose and turned on the small bedside light. Another mystery to solve, on top of all the other mysterious happenings. She couldn't say it would surprise her to know there was more than one spirit inhabiting the house. It was large enough to contain a whole legion of them, and the atmosphere was gloomy enough to make any of them feel at home.

But to have one visit her room made her nervous. She had grown used to the sensation of being watched, and the message on the mirror hadn't been too disturbing, at least upon retrospect. But to see them moving around in the room was disconcerting. Her little guardian Leta was one thing, an earthly being, but this was something completely different, not of this time or place.

She stood and went to the French doors, closing them with a little too much force and pulling the curtains closed. She hadn't opened them. She knew for sure of that. So who had? She double checked the door to the hallway, glanced back at the French doors to see if they remained securely locked, and then tugged at the doors of the massive wardrobe. Nothing but her clothes, including the pitiful black skirt and white blouse she reserved for funerals. No other entrances, no visible means of access besides what she could see clearly in front of her.

Rubbing her eyes, she slipped back in bed. She propped herself up with some of her extra pillows and opened a book in her lap, deliberately leaving all the lights burning. Sleep was not going to come visiting, she was afraid, but she feared more what else might show up in the night. Even though she remained attentive, she heard nothing more in the night, not even the flutter of wings. She sat in silent vigilance and didn't nod off until the sun was streaking the sky with slices of color.

When Claire heard movements, she swung her legs over the edge of her bed. She blinked her tired eyes and wiped her face with her chilled hands. Forcing herself to wake up, she dressed quickly, choosing fitted blue jeans faded to a soft gray/blue and a light weight purple sweater that fell down below her hips. She yanked a brush through her silky hair and braided it in a long rope down her back. When she was finished, she immediately took her heavy chair from in front of the fireplace and dragged it next to the wardrobe. Gripping the side of the piece for support, she reached up and ran her fingers along the top. The dust had accumulated into a thick felt that crumpled as she dragged her fingers along it. She wasn't surprised when she felt the hard object beneath the dust and picked it up gingerly.

"A key," she said softly, holding it up to the light. It was large, big enough to fit any one of the doors in the house, with an ornately carved top. The metal was blackened, tarnished from years of disuse.

Someone wanted her to have this key and had gone to quite a bit of trouble to point it out to her.

Stuffing it awkwardly in her pocket, she headed downstairs, going the long way to avoid the main staircase and foyer.

When she got to the kitchen she discovered Noel had already left for class. The note she had placed on the table, weighted down with the salt shaker was brief, something about being back as soon as she could, and warning Claire to be very careful. No workers were inside, no staff buzzing around, no Cole Edwards shadowing her, so she ate a solitary breakfast. She decided to spend the rest of the morning cleaning up all the bathrooms before sitting down to read the book about the house. Although the library would have been the more suitable place to settle in with a book, she instead chose a kitchen chair with all the harsh lights of modern day. After a few minutes, she retrieved a spare notebook from the little table next to the telephone and hunted for a pen. Taking notes was something school had drilled into her, but she knew that with all the recent events, she was likely to get some of the names and dates confused she had found in the little book. Almost two hours later, she marked her page with scrap of paper and jogged upstairs.

She was surprised when she reached her room to find it slightly rearranged. The crystal cap had been taken off the top of her perfume bottle, and the subtle floral scent greeted her at the doorway. Her powder was also opened and a light layer of it dusted the top of the dresser where it sat. One of her lipsticks was uncapped and a nail polish lay toppled on its side.

But most noticeable was the bed which had been neatly made. Lying atop the spread was an old church dress taken from the wardrobe, the pale-yellow chiffon skirt spread out against the cover. It was something she rarely wore; finding dresses uncomfortable and impractical. But there was just a glimmer of the girl she had once been who had ached for a princess dress and a prince charming to go with it, and so she had kept it. The ultra-feminine concoction was the result of this impulse buy, and no one was more surprised to see it out off its hanger than her.

She paused in the doorway, fingers tapping on the doorframe. Who would have done this? True, the house was now alive with workers and had been for the last two hours, but most of them were strangers to her. The majority of them had returned to the third floor in the afternoon to work on the bedrooms now that the second floor was completed. But all of them were men who would not have shown the slightest interest in her belongings.

On the other hand, just that night a possible ladies' maid had been prowling around her room. Had the specter returned in the light of day to get a better look at the occupant? Or had she simply resumed her duties in the room she had once cared for? Claire had seen other ghostly effects at times in her life. Chairs rocking, doors closed, locks turned, and objects moved about. Had she inherited a ghostly caretaker who would continue to care for this particular room even years after death?

She shook her head briskly and rehung the dress. As shocking a sight as it was, she found she was becoming somewhat immune to some of the occurrences in the house. She found she was slipping easily into her old role she held as a child. She was the sensitive one. The one whose imagination had run away with her, causing her to live on an edge between this world and the one beyond. The difference was, now she knew a little more about that world and she wasn't so sure she was ready for it anymore.

Slowly she went around the room, picking up mislaid objects and putting away her cosmetics. Her clothes she had thrown on the floor that morning she found in her wardrobe, neatly folded. She pulled them back out and dropped them into the laundry hamper in the bathroom. That completed, she ran downstairs to drag up her cleaning supplies that had come to feel almost like an extension of her arm. She carefully dusted the furniture and cleaned the glass on the windows, doors, and mirrors. She took an extra few minutes to climb on the chair and check the tops of the wardrobe, bookcase, and ledges over the doorway. Nothing but dust. Next, she dust mopped the floor and finished up by cleaning stray cobwebs from the ceiling. Her chore completed; she sat down at her desk with the book and began reading, not stopping until she heard Noel return from her classes.

"So, what did you find out?" Noel asked, gesturing to the book as she sat on Claire's bed.

"A lot. This thing goes into detail about how the house was built, at least from Cole's family's perspective. But it doesn't mention anything about the former owners or what happened to them."

"Have you talked to Cole?"

"No. I know," she held up her hand to stop Noel's complaints. "I will talk to him tonight, but I just haven't had the time."

"The time?" Noel said incredulously. "Claire, this place may be hazardous to your health, or your sanity, and you're saying you couldn't fit it in your schedule?"

Claire sighed, irritated by her own cowardice. "I know. And I have a feeling it won't be a huge surprise for Cole either. But things just seem to be happening so fast..."

Noel got up and sat next to Claire on the footstool. She looked seriously at her friend, noting the tired eyes and small creases between her brows.

"We should move. You know we should. It can't be good for

someone as sensitive as you to be living in a place like this. I talked to Ben and he said anytime..."

Claire held up her hand, her chin raising an inch.

"Now wait. It's only a week and a few days until Thanksgiving break, and I'm going home for that. It should give us some time to cool down. By then maybe we can find an alternative place to stay. We could still come here and clean and just sleep elsewhere."

"Do you hear what you're saying? You want to keep coming here even after everything that's happened? Look at you. You were pushed down the stairs, you passed out from one ghost, and I hate to remind you, but John DIED here. I think you should run away from here as fast as you can and never look back!"

"No!"

"But, Claire?"

"No. Look. I've lived with this, this thing for a long time." Claire's hands were making unconscious gestures like flattening her doubts with a push. "And now for the first time, I'm really accepting that I'm not crazy." Claire's voice was intense, strained with emotion. "I have to get over it, or figure out how to deal with it. I'm not running away because I hear things, or see things. I have to learn to live with this, and now is as good a time as any to figure out how."

Noel sighed and looked down at her hands, tensely clasped in her lap. "Okay, so I can understand that you don't want to just run away. And I know you won't give up. It's not in your nature to do that. But have you said anything to your parents?"

"No," Claire hesitated. "I stopped telling them about all of this a long time ago. I certainly don't want to spring it on them now. They're trying to put their lives back in order, and I won't mess that up. You can tell Ben if you want, and I'll speak to Cole later, I promise."

Noel nodded but didn't look happy.

After dinner, during which Cole was conspicuously absent, Noel said she would finish the dishes while Claire went looking for him. Noel was being insistent now that the decision to stay was made.

Claire ran up to her room first, telling herself it was just to straighten her hair. She cautiously opened her door, but found it in perfect order just as she left it. She slowly brushed her hair, pushing it back off her face but letting it fall in a loose sheet down her back. Her jeans were stained from cleaning, so she quickly changed into a better fitting pair and a light grayish green top that complimented her eyes. She hastily checked the mirror a second time and slicked a light pink gloss on her lips. Studying herself in the mirror, she was satisfied she didn't look like a woman who was hallucinating or worse yet, making up some story to destroy a man's dream.

With one last glance back into her room, she headed down the hall to the far stairway. She hurried through the ballroom, looking neither right nor left, fearing she might be accompanied on the dance floor by ghostly dancers swirling to their own music. The soft tinkling of the piano led her though to the music room. She paused in the doorway, listening intently and frowning in confusion. The sound seemed to be coming from the parlor.

"What now?" she murmured aloud. She had followed the music on other evenings, tiptoeing into the library and sitting quietly as the unseen player in the music room next door serenaded her. Cole seldom played the calm or comforting, but he always played well. The music was often passionate, sobbing pieces, which varied from classical to blues. She was always impressed by his playing.

This music was classical but poorly played with halting rhythm and missed notes. As Claire listened, she realized it was also not being played on Cole's piano. Someone else was playing music, and she strongly suspected it wasn't anyone who still lived.

CHAPTER TWELVE

The room sat empty, the piano covered except for heavy clawed feet. But the air hung heavy and the odor, ripe and putrid, greeted Claire so strongly she took a staggered step backwards. She stood a moment longer, knowing instinctively she was not alone. Her eyes skimmed the shrouded furniture and the gaping fireplace. The smell persisted, familiar now, the same as she had smelled the first day she had seen something shadowy in the house. She stiffened her spine, standing stubbornly. They were not going to run her off, not yet. As she watched, the empty air seemed to distort, then ripple. Like smoke from a chimney, a form developed, dark and dense, blocking the pale evening light from the windows. The figure grew and spread, its height reaching well above Claire's 5'4", and widened until two separate forms could be detected. Like a whisper of shuffling leaves, a voice seemed to emanate from the walls of the room.

LET ME GO. LET ME GO.

The two figures remained twined, wound into each other in an intricate braid.

Claire felt her heart pound, the fragile bones of her chest vibrating like thin reeds, the beat of her own blood rushing so loudly in her ears it almost managed to drown out the external sounds. Then the whisper rose to a roar and the figures grew, losing all human form and growing into something indecipherable.

Claire stood transfixed, unable to move or speak, her throat closed tight, painful. The heat of them was there, fighting with the chill of death, freezing her, burning her to the core. Her muscles felt like water, her stomach churning, her eyes burning. She felt the overwhelming fear, the knowledge that they could get her, take her.

Claire found her voice then, as the stench rose around her and the heat hit her in the face.

"No."

She felt herself grabbed from behind by some very real, very solid arms. Her voice sobbed into nothing as she sagged back, her legs giving away beneath her.

She was shaking and crying all at once. Never had they touched her, invaded her. She had never felt as though they could harm her, not until she came to the house.

She knew it was Cole again who had held her, even before he turned her, easing her to the floor as her knees buckled. Her hands clutched at his shirtfront, pressing her wet, stinging face against the smooth material.

"Easy, easy, you're all right. I'm here," he chanted, his hands easing up and down her back.

She laid against him, giving up, for once, the control she had tried so hard to maintain. She realized gradually that the odor had cleared. Her ears buzzed with the silence.

He continued to hold her until she pushed away, carelessly wiping her face with her sleeve. He pulled her arm down, his fingers following the curve of her cheek.

"I think they burned you," he said softly.

Her fingers felt like ice as she touched her hot forehead and cheeks. Then she looked at him; really looked closely into his eyes.

"You saw them. You know."

He paused and slowly stood up. He looked into the empty parlor, his hand going warily over his face.

"Yes, I know. But I've never seen them." He leaned down and caught her hands in his. "Come on. Let's get a drink."

She allowed him to pull her to her feet and followed him as he kept her hand securely in his. They stopped in the library long enough to get a bottle of dark whiskey and went into the heated green house. He hit the light switch, flooding the room with hot house lights.

"I've got clippings from most of the original plants in the garden," he said softly, as his eyes unconsciously followed the line of the shelf. He stopped at the far side of the room and pulled up two stools. He carefully set the decanter down. From under the shelf he found two paper cups and filled them to the brim. He handed one to Claire and drank the other in one long swallow.

She followed suit, choking on the fiery liquid. But it settled warmly in her belly, and she felt her shaking cease.

"I've been working on the house for a long time, but I just started the garden about six months ago. I had help finding the original plants to get clippings from, but most were too overgrown to be saved. I wanted to start it all over, but use the original plants and design." He paused, running his hand through his hair in a nervous gesture.

Claire pulled her stool closer to the shelf and leaned against it weakly. She listened as he talked, knowing he was just skirting the subject.

"This house has potential, but frankly I just wanted to get the damn thing finished. I want it to be used, to be functioning again instead of hanging around my neck like some albatross. What a disaster." He turned away, disgusted.

"But you knew this place was..."

"Haunted? Possessed?" He laughed dryly. "There have been rumors for years, but no one believes them. And our luck has been so awful when dealing with this place I just figured it was a lot of imagination and bad blood."

"You said..."

"I said I knew about them. It takes some time and experience to lend credence to what you can't see. What you smell, feel, hear, but never see. I could never prove anything and neither could anyone else."

"I could."

He looked at her gravely. He raised his hand to smooth a strand of hair from her brow. "Yes, I guess you could."

Claire felt herself blush at his touch, her feelings tangled with confusion, fear, and desire. She couldn't deny she found him attractive. Her eyes had betrayed her often enough, seeking him when he wasn't in the room. She had constantly found herself listening for him, for his footsteps, his music.

She turned away from his steady gaze and looked down at her empty cup, her pale fingers indenting the soft sides.

"What did you see?" He asked softly.

"Are you sure you want to know?" She smiled, trying to sound as though it was a joke, but knowing it wasn't. "There have been a lot of small things, little signs that have seemed to build up. Like they're trying to tell me something, and I just can't get it."

He caught her hand lightly. "What was the first thing you saw?"

She sighed, her mind quickly reviewing the last weeks. If she told him the sum total of her experiences, he would think her mad. She carefully began recounting her story, describing the wineglass, the mirror writing, and the occurrence in the parlor when she had first run into him.

"You thought I looked like the portrait, and that's why you fainted?"

"Maybe at first, but not later, when I really got to see you." she paused and took a deep breath. "No, I thought you looked like the ghost on the bridge."

His face visibly paled and he drew back. "What do you mean?" His voice dropped to a hoarse whisper.

She felt her face redden in response. She hadn't meant to mention the bridge; it sounded too insane. How could she have seen him on the bridge when he was out of town? She had never seen the spirit of someone still alive and well. She had convinced herself that for once it was her imagination, a mixture of anxiety about the new job, and suggestion from the many portraits in the house. But now he was staring at her as though he were seeing a ghost.

"Nothing, no, I think it was just my imagination..."

"No, it wasn't. You said you saw a ghost on the bridge. He looked like me."

"He was you," she responded softly.

He sat back, rubbing his eyes. "He was my father."

She stared at him, trying to digest the obvious look of pain on his face. She knew then what had happened, and perhaps his reason for being there at the house. His father had died there and was like the other shades in her life. A visitor just watching, checking on her and the life going on around them after their lives were lost.

"When did he die?" she asked softly.

"Almost 20 years ago. He loved this place; he was almost obsessed with it. He dragged me here all the time. Camping in the woods, climbing to the turrets to look out over the grounds; he loved it all. It was his dream. To take this old place and restore it. Fill it with life. He even had plans drawn out for the renovation, the gardens, the fountain, the grounds with a swimming pool out back and golf course." He turned and looked bitterly out the window. "We had come to visit in the winter. It had been empty for years, but he just couldn't give it up. He needed to make sure it was holding up against the snow and ice, and I think he had a hard time staying away. We were coming up the drive. I don't know what he saw: why he veered. But the next thing I knew, I was in the hospital like this," he paused and looked at his weak leg, "and he was gone."

"I'm so sorry," she said softly, responding to the naked grief in his eyes. "You must have been close."

"Yes. He was a fine man. We had our differences, but I thought the sun rose and set on him." He pulled the wallet out of his back pocket and flipped it open, extracting a bent photo. "He was a special kind of person." As he showed her the picture, she felt a second tremor of shock. The two figures, standing side by side and leaning against the hood of a bright red Firebird, were very similar. But the man could have been Cole in a different decade, longer hair, dusty jeans, a white tee shirt, and tattered tennis shoes. The boy at his side was the younger carbon copy, struggling to stand up next to his father, to match him in stance.

"You could have been twins," she said softly.

He smiled, looking more amused than sad.

"Dad loved this place. It was a long time before I had the money and the ability to help. But I decided this was the time. I wanted to do this for him. To keep his dream going when he couldn't."

Claire nodded. With her own father's recent illness, she had felt a shadow of what could have been. What would she have done if her father hadn't made it through the heart attack and surgery? She felt sure she would have been haunted by his death, by all the unfinished business he had left behind.

"So, you're going to renovate the house for your father? And then what?"

He sighed. "I hadn't gotten that far in the plans. If the place made any money, I could keep it in the family for the investment. But that's a big if. Right now, I'm wondering if we'll ever get the place finished. And if we do, I'm not so sure it's a safe place for people to visit."

She watched as he visually shook of the memories, and looked again at her, changing the subject. "You've never been hurt by these spirits before?"

"No, not really." She said evasively. She didn't want to delve into her history. Not now, and maybe not ever. "I wasn't sure what was happening, and I didn't want to blow this all out of proportion. I guess I still wanted to believe it was someone, some person trying to scare me."

"And now you don't think so."

"No, these things are different. They're malevolent," she searched for a stronger word, "evil. I've had the impression of other ghosts before, but I've never been touched by them. This house is the strongest place I've ever been. It's too strong, and it's changing, growing all the time."

"We've got to get you out of here."

"I don't know if it will do any good now. They're trying to talk to me, to communicate. If they don't get to me, I think they're going to find someone else. You can't just get rid of me and assume the problem will be gone."

"I'll just tear the whole thing down," he said abruptly, standing up to pace the room. "It was a bad idea to start this project. I think my best alternative is to just destroy the house and whatever is in it. Leave it back here in the woods. Finish this."

"No," she said quickly, suddenly sure that that was the worst idea. "There is something incomplete here. There is something wrong, and it can't just be swept under the rug. Something happened here, something bad, and you've got to help me figure out what it was."

He turned back quickly. "I'm not going to risk you getting hurt."

She couldn't deny she was touched, even flattered by his expression of concern, but she forced herself to reason with him.

"I won't. I'll be more careful. I won't go anywhere alone. I'll take someone with me everywhere, as long as I'm in the house. I've never had one of the ghosts show up unless I was alone."

He frowned. "All this happened in the foyer, the parlor, the steps. All in the main part of the house. What about the wings? Your bedroom?"

She looked uncomfortable. She didn't want to seem naive, but she also felt like she was safe with the ghosts in her room.

"Let me show you something."

He looked puzzled but followed her up as she left the green house and headed for the side stairs. As with the rest of the wing, the side stairs had been built later than the front staircase and were almost half the size with bare wooden treads and a sharp angled bend that made them double back on themselves. They were also poorly lit and poorly tended with cracked and bent slats and a handrail that abruptly ended before reaching the second floor. Claire could feel Cole's body hovering close behind hers, and she wondered if he were concerned about her previous falls.

When she reached the head of the stairs she went quickly down the hall to her room where she could hear the radio droning behind Noel's door and guessed she was studying.

She quickly opened her door and looked in, standing in the doorway. She was almost happy to see the results of her visitor.

Once again, a perfume bottle was open, this time a spicy floral filled the room. Lipstick was open on the dresser and her cleanser and moisturizer were both uncapped. In contrast, her shoes were lined up precisely at the foot of her bed and again her clothes had been disturbed. This time a nightgown, a deep green satin with ribbon straps, was laid out on her bed with the matching robe next to it as though waiting for the owner to return.

"I have my own ladies' maid," she said lightly, stepping inside. "She lays out my clothes, checks my cosmetics..." She picked up the lipstick and replaced the cap.

"What are you talking about?"

"When I left my room, none of this was out," she said gesturing to the cosmetics. "And my clothes were all in my drawers. I didn't do any of this."

"You mean they move your things?"

"She does. She seems interested in my belongings, but she always does her job. She made my bed this morning and picked up some of my clothes."

"You've seen her?" His face was a mixture of disbelief and awe.

Claire told him briefly about her experience the night before and then pulled the key from her pocket. Cole took it from her palm, the brush of his fingers causing a slight flutter in her chest. He turned the key over, holding it gingerly in his fingers.

"This could go to any door here."

"I wondered if all the keys would look alike. But I'm betting it's the key to her door. Or at least one important to her. Why else would she hide it?"

He nodded his agreement and sat down warily by the fire. "This is a lot to digest."

Claire prowled around the room, her hands gesturing as she talked.

"I've read some of the book, the one you lent me. And there's definitely enough tragedy to account for a few ghosts. But I just haven't figured out the specifics. There are some pretty powerful beings here and they are hell bent, if you'll excuse the expression, to speak to me."

"Claire, I think that's even more reason for you to leave here. I can't have you risking yourself..." He stood and strolled toward her as she leaned against the fireplace, taking her hand tightly in his own. "Look, I'm not your family, and I haven't known you for long, but I like to think we have something of a relationship here. I wouldn't want to presume where I'm not wanted, but I can't just stand by and let you throw yourself into something dangerous like this."

She stared into his handsome face, momentarily overcome by his proximity and the sheer power she felt in his grasp.

The door burst open and Noel came in, freezing in the doorway.

Claire felt herself color as Noel looked from Cole standing uncomfortably a few feet back from the chair, to her, as she stood next to the cold fireplace.

"Oh, sorry. I didn't mean to interrupt," Noel said, backing back out of the doorway.

"No, Noel, come in. This involves you too," Cole responded, waving her in the door. He turned quickly, moving with rare grace considering his recent injury, to close the door behind her.

"We were talking about the house," Claire said slowly.

"The ghosts," Cole clarified.

Noel looked from one to the other and sat slowly down on the bed. "Has something else happened?"

Claire walked to the bed and sat next to her. "Just more of the same. It was in the parlor again. I feel like it's really trying to contact me. They know me, and they're after me for something."

Cole stood at the closed door. He leaned against the panel, his face sober. Abruptly he swung the door open again and stepped into the doorway, glancing down the empty halls.

"Let's get out of here. Pack a bag, we'll spend the night in town. I'm not sure I want to have this conversation with the extra audience."

Noel stared at him as he left and turned her surprised gaze to Claire. "He's spooked."

Claire nodded and got up, running her fingers through her hair. "Let's get going. We have a long night ahead of us."

CHAPTER THIRTEEN

The streetlights seemed unusually bright as they pulled into the lot at the Danbury Inn. It was located close to Louisville off I-64 on Blankenbaker Parkway. It was conveniently flanked by two newly built fast food restaurants with a Cracker Barrel close by. The parking lot was easy to maneuver in since it wasn't a particularly busy night for travelers.

Claire's head ached dully and her stomach was queasy. The ride in from the house was anything but soothing. Cole had driven slowly; eyes riveted on the road as his headlights pierced the deep country darkness. As the bridge loomed ahead, his speed dropped even more, and she knew he was thinking of his father. But as she scanned the scarred stone and rutted pavement, she saw no extra shadows in the broken moonlight.

Once on the familiar road leading to the city, his speed increased, the engine going from a purr to a roar, as if they were being chased from the darkness. Although horse farms mostly dominated that stretch of road, a few gas stations stood in stark contrast to the unending black of the night road, beacons of civiliza-

tion. It was with great relief she watched him merge onto the interstate and closer to civilization. At the hotel, he went inside alone to
get the keys, leaving the girls huddled in the car, a sense of unreality
pervading the almost pedantic scene. The contrast between the
monstrous house and its other worldly occupants and the neon lit
inn with station wagons and mini vans almost brought tears to
Claire's eyes. She watched anxiously as Cole reappeared with the
keys and almost smiled as he brushed off their offer to pay for their
rooms. Since they were being run out of the house by the remains of
his ancestors, he insisted he would pay for the rooms, and the girls
were in no position to object.

They walked into the dimly lit atrium that opened on both sides
in five floors of rooms. The center of the atrium boasted an indoor
garden area, which gave the whole room warmth and life. Their
rooms were on the ground floor, two adjoining rooms for Noel and
Claire, Cole's room just next to theirs.

Claire dropped her hastily packed bag on the bed, leaving the
adjoining door to Noel's room open. Noel came in almost immediately. She looked the same, shedding only her jacket and shoes in
her own room before coming over. She sat comfortably on one of
the twin beds curling her long legs beneath the voluminous skirt of
her peasant dress.

"I'm so bushed. I know you must be tired too. Are you going to
class tomorrow?"

Claire took off her shoes and dropped on the opposite bed,
leaning back against the pillows. "I need to. I can't miss many more
classes no matter what happens. Maybe Cole will drop me off
before he takes you back." She paused. "You are going back,
aren't you?"

Noel looked undecided. "Claire, you know I want to help you,
but I'm thinking we both need to get away from that place. I told
you we can stay with Ben."

"No, I'm sticking it out until Thanksgiving. I'm going to be a lot more careful and avoid the worst spots in the house, but I can't just leave now." She felt her eyes fill and rubbed them with the back of her hand, looking away from her friend. "Noel, I'm not so sure they wouldn't follow me. I just have this feeling I'm stuck in a nightmare with these people now, these lost souls, and I must see this through. I've lived with this for so long, maybe I'm getting tired of it. I want this to stop, but I feel like they are stronger than I am, and they're not going to let me get away so easily." Her voice dropped to a whisper. "I think they could find me, no matter where I went."

Noel looked stricken. "Claire, I'm worried about you, girl. I know you've been under a lot of pressure and I'm trying to understand this ESP stuff, but you've never seemed this...You just seem like you're getting out of touch. It's reminding me too much of before."

Claire sighed. "It's hard to be the serious college student with exams and term papers when you have a ghost maid making your bed. Maybe by fighting it for all these years, I've done myself a disservice. Maybe if I had faced this when I was younger, I would know what to do to get away, or make them go away. But I didn't. I've run from this all my life, and it's time I faced up to it."

Cole interrupted their discussion, easing the door open with a spare elbow and closing it behind him with a swift kick. He carried three cans of soft drinks and an equal number of candy bars from the vending machine.

"It isn't gourmet, but it's sugar," he said dropping the supplies on the little table.

They busied themselves for a few minutes, rummaging through the candy and settling back to their places. Noel had brought a pen and paper to take notes while Claire had brought the book about the house. By unanimous agreement, they were figuring out what was behind these hauntings. Claire opened the little book to the front and frowned as she read the beginning chapter aloud. Stopping, she looked up at Cole.

"This talks about your family, how they brought their money over from England and when they bought the house. But it never mentions who they bought it from or when."

Cole settled himself in the chair and propped his feet up on the bed Claire was sitting on. "I can tell you what little I know, but it isn't much. John looked up some of the information for me when we started with the construction. The house was started in 1853; that's on the corner stone. It was built by a man for his wife; they had no children. He meant to enlarge it eventually, I think. I've always had the impression he was a pretty wealthy man at that time. Anyway, they only lived in it for a year or so when his wife ran away with her, um, paramour. The man remained in the house and became something of a hermit, but was eventually assumed dead when the natives braved the house and found it empty. I don't think anyone knew what happened to either of them, and I haven't got any real history of their family, or how they ended up in the area. The house had been vacant for a few years when my relatives bought it."

"The book said they bought it from the state."

"Yes, as far as I know, the original owners had no heirs, and the property reverted back to the local government."

"And after your family bought it they decided to add on to the original building. It looks like it took several years to complete."

"There were problems in the building," he said, looking grimly amused. "I can understand that completely. There were a few workers who died or disappeared, I don't know which. And the house acquired something of a reputation, so some of the locals refused to work. Then, of course, the Civil War had its effects as well. The Confederate sympathizers actually attempted to attack Shelbyville, but the Federals soon ran them out. There was only minor damage done to the house at that time."

Noel was writing furiously as she listened and looked up when he paused. "When was it completed?"

Cole pulled a small notebook from a jacket pocket and flipped it open. "Sometime in 1866 after the war had ended. But my relatives moved in before that, in 1857, I think. Yes, here it is. The first family was a couple with three small children. The parents' names were Matthew and Mary, pretty traditional. They also brought Mary's aunt with them; she was from Germany." He paused. "There's no name for the aunt." He flipped to another page. "The area was known for its agriculture, but they didn't stay long enough to try their hand at farming. In fact, one of the kids died there at a fairly young age. The mother apparently became a little, I don't know, unstable, and claimed the house had something to do with the death. She insisted they move, and they did. I seem to recall they were there for almost 10 years."

"Yes, that's about right," Claire said, looking up from the book. "It mentions the house being completed, and when they moved out, but it told nothing about why. I guess that's not the sort of thing you wanted spread around back then."

"Or now," Cole said frowning. "I was amazed at how many comments I got about the haunted house when I started this project. I eventually had to ask the workers to stop discussing it."

Noel nodded and jotted down notes. "Who was the next owner?"

"No, wait. Look, a picture," Claire interrupted. They all three bent over the book and Claire felt a slight lightheaded feeling wash over her. The picture was an exact replica of the portrait from Cole's room, or at least part of it. The copy filled the page with a close up of the man's face that made the resemblance to Cole more eerie.

"Another twin?" Noel asked, looking toward Cole's serious face.

"Look at the date. 1860. He really does look like you. Older maybe, but the resemblance is uncanny," Claire responded, looking from the picture to Cole.

"I've seen this before. It's been a few years since we found the book, but when Dad and I found the portrait, we immediately took it out and had it cleaned. It was in bad shape from water damage after being stored in one of the attic rooms. We found the portrait of a woman we think was his wife up there as well, but didn't come across it until a later date. We decided to hang them together since it seemed they belonged that way. The attic is full of paintings like those, I just haven't taken the time to investigate them."

"Like the one in my room?" Claire interrupted. "Who is that?"

"One of the ancestors, but I don't know who. That painting was already there when we started renovating the room. We just rehung it after we were finished. It's approximately the same age as this one, probably one of the inhabitants who stayed in that room pretty early on."

Claire found herself imagining the image on the painting. She had always assumed it was the original owner's wife. But now that she thought about it, it seemed more logical the portrait hanging in Cole's room, the pair to the one that matched the portrait in the book, was really his wife. If that were true, the woman in her portrait must have also stayed in her room. It appears the painting was meant to hang there, and even when she had attempted to take it down, it had been rehung. Now she wondered if her mysterious maid was responsible for it, or if the lady in the portrait had put in her own spiritual hand. And perhaps she had accomplished the message in the mirror as well.

"I wonder how we can find out who she was. The lady in my room, I mean."

"I'm not sure, but we'll check in the library when we get back. And we can look at the painting itself. The portrait may have some information on the canvas or frame. I haven't looked closely at it in a long time." Cole paused and took a long swallow from his drink.

"Okay, to get back to the book. Who was the next owner after the first family was run off?" Noel asked, pen in hand.

"The son, Nathaniel Edwards," Claire volunteered, looking up from the book. "Mary's aunt stayed on at the house for a while, the poor relative of the family. Then, when Nathaniel came of age, he moved in with her. Anyway, as far as the book goes, he never married, never had a family except for his aunt, and pretty much lived alone after her death."

"And he died of old age," Noel finished, looking over Claire's shoulder.

"Well, that was never determined," Cole explained. "The old man was just found dead in the parlor. Rumors were he had died of heart failure, with the cause unknown, but some of the more superstitious in town said he was scared to death. They say his expression was," he paused frowning, "unbelievable."

"Oh, that does sound like a bad ghost story," Noel responded.

Claire looked grim. "In that parlor, I can believe you could be scared to death."

"All of this implies the ghost was already there when your family moved in," Noel observed, looking at Cole's strained face.

"Yeah, it does." He actually looked slightly relieved at the thought.

"So, who was next?" Noel asked, looking over Claire's shoulder again to the open book.

"In the 1920s a distant relative, nephew or great nephew, takes his family there. Money wasn't good and the place was in bad shape, but he wasn't financially at his best..." Claire ran her finger down the page. "But it looks like he only stayed a year or two before he left. It mentions he had an interest in livestock and had plans to turn the place into something of a breeding farm."

"Horses, or thoroughbreds?"

Claire shook her head. "It doesn't say."

"He's the dog man," Cole exclaimed. Both girls looked at him, puzzled. He laughed aloud and for a moment looked like a much younger man. "Dad told me that one. He loved the story. I sometimes wonder..." His face grew solemn and distracted. Then he recovered, answering the questions that was on Noel's face. "It was my dad's idea that we renovate Talitha. I was telling Claire earlier about how much he liked the house. He used to bring me out to see the place often when I was younger. Dad would tell all the stories about the house to my friends for a joke. He was the one who found that book in the library. But now that I think of it, he was particular about the house as well. He used to prefer certain rooms, certain parts of the house. The greenhouse, the ballroom. He avoided the library or the parlor, always said they were too dim." He sighed and leaned back. "I guess it may have been just that..."

"Or maybe he had seen or heard something." Noel's eyes took on a new excitement. "You know, maybe he was sensitive about the place. He didn't want to let on since you were so young, but he knew something didn't feel right."

"He may be like me. Affected by certain places or things," Claire said slowly.

Noel looked reenergized. "It would explain some of his interest in the house. Why he liked some areas more than others."

"And why he's back," Cole said gravely.

They sat in silence for a moment. Noel did not dare to ask the question showing so transparently on her face. She understood that Cole's father had died at a young age but little else.

Slowly Claire looked back down to the book. "You said your father liked the story?" she prompted.

Cole's face cleared, and he relaxed against the back of the chair. "Well, the story says that the owners were a small family with a large group of animals. They brought dogs, cats, some horses, and even a few chickens. Dad said the chickens went first, but there was no proof some local poachers didn't eat them. But then the cats started going, and the wife said she actually saw two of the dogs running away from the house, tails tucked and yelping like mad. When the horses disappeared one night and were found two weeks later, half-starved on the other side of Shelbyville, the people decided to start looking for a new house."

"Animals always know," Noel said nodding, and Claire smiled back. Her obvious enjoyment of her new" Nancy Drew" role made Claire feel better. Following Noel's lead, she opened the book to the next chapter but was disappointed in the lack of information. "It just says the next owner took possession in the 1930s and stayed for an undetermined amount of time. Appears he didn't entertain or do much else. The following one inherited the house in the late 1930s. It was a cousin, William Pratt, who lived there for quite a while. Let's see, up until 1948. That's when he died and apparently his line with him. The book ends there." She closed the book and handed it to Noel.

Claire looked at her friend more closely. The late night was beginning to wear on her. Her bright hair stood in careless spikes on her head and dark rings of mascara circled her sleepy eyes. The rest of her face was unusually pale, her mind running on sugar and adrenaline.

"But they never said anything about the name. I was wondering where they got the name for the house."

Cole sat forward and took the book from Claire's hand. "Well, I don't know much about the name, but I have heard a little more than what you found in that book. The ending I heard was much more dramatic than that. This is the biggest rumor of all, so I don't know the validity of it but..." he paused like a true storyteller and smiled. "Old Willy didn't believe in ghosts and lived in the house for many years with no complaints. He said he had never seen a spirit and if one showed up he'd send them packing. He grew old and stubborn with the house deteriorating around him. He could afford only one caretaker, a man named Samuel Lead who patched the roof and cleaned out the gutters, did menial jobs around the house but no cleaning or painting. In the evenings, Samuel would come in and have a drink with old Willy, but he always left before nightfall. One evening when Samuel left, Willy was complaining about what a coward he was, insisting on leaving early. The next morning, Samuel found Willy hanging in the foyer, stung up by old sheets and curtains." Cole paused and took another drink, looking between the two girls. "Samuel had him taken down and buried somewhere on the grounds, but swore it wasn't a suicide. He said Willy was just too obnoxious to kill himself and there had to be another cause for his death. It was never investigated further. Well, Samuel continued to go to the house up until the 1960s when he just got too old. The place was abandoned completely, boarded up. No one was brave enough to rob the place, not with so many ghost sightings reported. Besides, by that time, most of the small valuables had been sold off."

"You said you visited?" Claire asked.

"Dad found out the place was ours when a distant uncle died somewhere in Canada. I was just a kid, and it was an hour's drive, so we never went out to see it much. He just held on to it, for an investment I guess. He hired Eddie Canon to look after the grounds; make sure no one broke in or set fire to the place. Later Dad took me and mom out to see it to decide if he should just tear down the house and sell the land. But I could tell he thought it was wonderful, wanted to go back and visit all the time. He decided to leave it for the time being and wait for some time to decide what to do with it. We didn't hear any of the history about it until we talked to my grandmother."

Claire glanced over at Noel, surprised to find her curled up asleep on the bed.

"I guess my story wasn't very riveting after all"

"It was pretty good, but loses something when you've seen the real thing," Claire said lightly. Her eyes were grainy, lids heavy with fatigue. But she hated to end the evening. Cole had become so human, so accessible she didn't want him to retreat into his protective mask of indifference.

He rose gracefully, but his limp returned as he moved to the door. She followed him, checking once to see that Noel was still sleeping.

"Do you need a ride to class in the morning?" he asked, turning at the doorway.

"Yes, I suppose. Class starts at 8:00."

"Then I'll come by at 7:30. Will that give you enough time?"

She nodded sleepily.

"We'll talk tomorrow about what else we're going to do. We may just have to keep these rooms for some time." He smiled, but his eyes looked dark and serious.

"We'll see," she responded.

He put a light hand against her cheek, and gently brushed a finger down to her chin. "Sleep well."

CHAPTER FOURTEEN

The cell phone buzzed unpleasantly, jolting Claire out of a deep sleep. She grudgingly opened her eyes and looked around the unfamiliar room. The clock's numbers were blurry to her tired eyes, and she had to strenuously resist the temptation to lie back down.

She reached out and grabbed the phone, pressing the stop icon out of habit and without looking at the screen. The phone stopped sounding, wake up completed. Claire swung her legs off the bed and hit the bedside light with her hand, making it rock just slightly. The room was as they had left it the night before, candy wrappers scattered on the table and empty soft drink cans filling the trash can. After three of the sugar filled drinks the night before, her stomach was decidedly unsettled this morning.

She glanced again at the clock and got up to take a shower. The smell of hotel antiseptic was a welcome change to the paint and plaster smell she had grown used to at the house. She hadn't realized how much she needed to get away from there until now. She quickly showered and dressed, putting on a bare minimum of makeup. She put her hair in a neat braid down her back and began repacking her things. She regretfully closed the bag to take back home; she hated to think the house was now home. It was almost too tempting to take Cole's offer to stay at the hotel until they could make other arrangements. But she knew she would feel guilty for the money he was spending on them, and the fact she was leaving him alone in that God forsaken place.

A light knock on her door had her opening it quickly. Cole stood, arms full again with food. She let him in with a brief smile; relieved to see he carried two large cups of coffee and some plain bagels.

"Did you sleep well?"

She nodded and smiled. "I slept like a baby. It was a good idea to get away for the night."

He looked serious again. "Are you sure you want to go back?"

She nodded again but made no comment and avoided his eyes by busying herself adding sugar and cream to the coffee.

"I think I'm going to stop work on the house. It's ridiculous to keep pouring money into the thing if it will never be usable. I can't have some guest expiring on the doorstep from a heart attack because my ancestors decided they didn't want any visitors that day."

Claire had to agree. The presence in the house was very powerful and she could see no way of getting rid of it. She knew there was a reason for the ghosts, a purpose behind their presence. But until they discovered that, she felt the house was a possible hazard to any unsuspecting worker or guest.

They finished breakfast in silence, and Claire dropped in Noel's room to explain that Cole would be back by later.

In the cold light of morning she had to admire her companion. His hair was smooth and glossy, falling in a clean line to his shoulder and reflecting the sun in golds and deep browns. He wore dress slacks and an open necked shirt, both immaculately pressed.

His freshly shaven cheeks were lean, but his hard body had put on a few much-needed pounds, giving the impression of increased vigor. He walked easily this morning, his limp gone.

She felt rumpled by comparison, in her jeans and yellow knit shirt. Her hair was beginning to pull loose and fell in soft wisps around her face. Her books were in a backpack and weighed heavily on her arms and shoulders. Cole, watching her struggle, wordlessly took them from her, and carried them with comparative ease.

His car stood in the front of the lot, tastefully expensive and immaculately cared for. He opened the door for Claire first and went over to the driver's side.

"What time do you need me to pick you up this afternoon?" He asked as they neared the campus.

"Oh, you don't have to. I can catch a ride."

"With who?" He grinned at her, his eyes light with humor. "I think we've gotten beyond the polite game. I'll come and get you whenever you're ready. I have some work in town I need to finish anyway, so I'll be in the area."

"Isn't it hard to keep up your business while you're away?"

"It's getting harder. I really should fly out to New York soon to tie up some loose ends. I'm going to Denver over Thanksgiving." He turned his attention back to the road as he skillfully dodged through traffic and pulled onto the main campus thoroughfare.

"Are you visiting family?"

"No, I don't have any close family left. My mother passed on a few years ago, and my Grandmother is going to Florida for Thanksgiving."

She had a hard time picturing him with a grandmother; a sweet gray-haired lady baking cookies and toting her tow-headed grandson to movies and baseball games.

"What are you smiling about?" Cole asked, interrupting her thoughts.

"Nothing, nothing at all." She watched as they passed the

several of the University buildings and pointed to a lot outside the education building. "You can just pull over here."

He stopped the car in the space and switched off the engine, then turned to look her in the face. "You want me to pick you up here?" He asked, gesturing to the building. When she nodded, he asked what time.

She watched, amused, as a couple of her classmates passed, waving tentatively as they peered through the window.

"I'll be done at noon. I can be back here at quarter after. Will that be alright?"

"Twelve fifteen it is."

It was close to impossible to pay attention to class with so many concerns invading her mind. She took notes as best she could, finding herself sketching stained glass windows and wickedly pointed turrets on the margins of her paper, like a high school girl in Algebra class. When her last session was over, she walked quickly back to the lot. Several classmates accompanied her, showing unusual interest as they questioned her about the expensive car she had arrived in. She almost laughed to herself. It was strange how graduate students could suddenly behave like freshman coeds when a new man was in the picture.

To her surprise, Cole had already parked and was standing outside of the car, resting carelessly against the bumper.

Claire paused to admire him again. He looked polished, at ease and totally sure of himself. She was amazed at his composure considering the havoc the house had wrecked in his life and his business.

"Who is he?"

"Gorgeous!"

"He's my ride," Claire said, waving at him as he glanced her way. He moved toward them, his long strides eating up the pavement more quickly than their shorter ones. He reached for her bag automatically and responded politely to the introductions.

"Are you ready?"

She nodded and let him open the door for her. She waved as she passed the other girls, smiling to herself at their envious expressions. She was almost embarrassed at her response. Obviously, she wasn't much more mature than they, but she was enjoying it and decided she would relish being petty for just a few more minutes.

"How was class?" he asked, turning towards her as they sat at a light, waiting for the traffic to move.

"Fine. Boring but fine. I guess I've lost interest in some of the classroom techniques used these days. I can't picture dealing with some of the behavior problems they're listing, much less disciplining the children."

"You don't sound too enthusiastic about teaching."

"It's what my mom did, and I guess I just fell into the groove. I don't plan on it being my life long career. Just a jumping point, I suppose."

"And what do you want to be when you grow up?"

She felt her cheeks heat and looked at him pointedly, unsure if she should be insulted by the lightly stated words.

"I don't know. I hesitate to even admit this, but I'd like to be an author. Maybe write children's books."

"That sounds much more fitting for you, I think."

"Why do you say that?"

"I just don't picture you standing in front of a chalk board calling out names and spelling words. You seem much more introspective than that."

She frowned, her mind racing. Was that how she looked from the outside? Thoughtful, serious? This last year had taken its toll on her. She felt like she had aged. She had finally concluded she wasn't unstable. It hadn't been her imagination. And now she was just trying to handle her new knowledge.

"I think I'm learning as I go along, figuring out what I want to do. I had always felt like it was just a given I would follow in my mother's footsteps. It seemed natural. Now I'm just trying to look at it day at a time. It's all I can do."

He nodded his agreement and turned his attention back to the road.

By the time they pulled up in front of the house, Claire was starving. The workers were crowded into the bedrooms on the third floor, their efforts ringing loudly down the staircase. Cole explained they would finish out the week and not return until after the Christmas holidays. Hopefully something would be resolved by then.

Claire found Noel in the kitchen and as soon as Cole had them settled, he disappeared into the library.

"He's changed since he's been here. He's gotten so, I don't know, normal," Noel said in a stage whisper after Cole had left the room.

Claire grinned back. Noel had regained a great deal of her composure since last night. Her hair was slicked back in a shiny cap of bright red and her newly applied lipstick matched exactly. Her jeans were a well-worn purple with a white long sleeve shirt. Her shoes had enormous rubber heels, which increased her already respectable height.

"I think he's looking better since he added a few pounds. His clothes definitely fit better. He's got that businessman look on today."

"I can't complain," Claire agreed, her voice a little wistful.

"Did he ever tell you about what happened? If he was sick or in an accident? I mean, the limp is better, but you can still tell some-thing bad happened to him."

Claire shook her head. "Are you kidding? This is the most

conversation I've gotten out of him since we met. H's never said what he was doing before coming to the house. But I just have this feeling..."

"What do you mean?"

"I think something happened to make him want to come back here. Maybe even to start the project. He's blown a lot of money on this place and hasn't gotten a very big positive response."

"Well, I don't know what his purpose is, but after last night I've definitely gained a lot of respect for him," Noel responded, starting to put dirty plates and silverware in the dishwasher.

"Last night? What do you mean?"

"He could have buried the whole thing. With his kind of money, he could have covered up the incident and gotten rid of us, or just shut the thing down and scrapped the project. Instead, he's listening to us and seems to be truly concerned."

Claire nodded thoughtfully. She was having a little difficulty being objective since she had realized her feelings for him. She certainly wasn't going to call it love, but she did care for him, more than she was comfortable with.

"You really like him, don't you?" Noel said, noticing her expression.

"Who wouldn't? He's a nice guy," Claire said lightly.

"It's something more than that," Noel scolded. "I've known you long enough to tell when you're getting serious."

"I can't be serious. Not right now with all this going on and not with him. He is so far out of my league."

Noel frowned at her. "Don't put yourself down. I think maybe you'd better let Cole decide if you're his type. And from what little I've seen, I think it would be safe to say he's considering it."

Claire shook her head and stood up, visually shaking herself out of her mood.

"So, what are we doing today?" she asked, purposefully changing the subject.

"Well, we have a key, we have a ghost giving us a message; I say we chase it down."

Claire agreed and went upstairs to her room to retrieve the key. Her jeans, forgotten since the day before, were now laid out neatly on the bed, the key taken from the pocket and placed on her pillow. Her church dress was again laid out with matching shoes and even undergarments. The soft floral smell of her perfume filtered through the air.

She took the key, and bidding her new caretaker a silent thanks, went back downstairs. Noel met her on the stairs, a pad of paper in hand.

"We'll have to start on one floor and do each door separately. I'm guessing each lock was keyed separately, but maybe not. This house was constructed with such unusual style, I can never figure out if they stuck with tradition or decided to go their own way."

"Let's start on the top floor," Claire responded firmly.

"In the attic?"

"No, the fourth floor. Those rooms are the least disturbed, and I just have a feeling the maid would have had her room up there."

"Of course," Noel responded enthusiastically. "I had just assumed the key was for someone else, but the maid would have had a key for her own room."

The fourth floor had minimal lighting, cast by bare bulbs hastily screwed in by workmen. The doors were mostly closed, the scuffed wooden floors still heavily soiled and thick cobwebs hanging in tattered loops from carved crown molding. The wallpaper appeared to have been replaced more than once, and the existing paper was a sickly green with reptilian vines snaking up from the floorboards and curling at the crown molding.

They started at the far end, opening doors and trying the key in the locks. After a few minutes, they discovered the key was not only too large for the locks, all the doors were unlocked anyway.

"Well, now what?" Claire asked, pushing a strand of hair out of her eyes with dirty hands.

"It has to be to some door around here. Let's make sure we haven't skipped anything." Noel led the way back down the hall to the elaborate door that lead to the turret room. Although the rooms on the fourth floor were all smaller than the ones downstairs, and mostly empty with the exception of a few tipsy pieces of furniture that hadn't withstood the passage of time gracefully, the turret rooms were both fully furnished. The door was unlocked and opened into a room like a fairytale chamber. The floor was cleaned and covered with a large area rug, and the walls were newly painted. The windows had been scrubbed, and a shade had been hung at one to shut out the strongest of the morning sun. The furniture was spartan with a single chair and table centered by the far window, a few books and papers scattered on the surface of the scarred tabletop. Claire spied a door at the far end of the room.

"What is this, a closet?" she asked.

Noel quickly pulled the door open, revealing an even smaller room. "No, just some extra space." She stood thoughtfully. "Let's see if there is another one of these in the other turret."

Their search revealed the second one in the other turret, a small, oddly shaped room apparently a result of the angle of the turret walls. This one was remarkable because it had the only locked door. The key fit the lock, the catch turning grudgingly.

Noel could barely contain her excitement. The adventure seemed to be bringing out the sleuth in her because she went through the contents of both rooms with special care. At her insistence, they returned to the first room and found it contained little else but an old sewing machine and piles of dry rotted fabric, which shredded at a touch.

The second was more promising with two trunks pushed against the far wall. Both were locked, and Claire ran to the hall below to search for a hammer. It took several strikes to knock the locks off, but the trunks themselves were no worse for it.

Noel lifted the lid on the first one and momentarily paused, fascinated by the mess. Fabrics of dirty yellow and brown made up the first layer, a blanket of some kind. Beneath were books, hard covers with brittle pages that stuck together in places. At the bottom was a small wooden box, painted black. When opened it revealed a stack of letters, some tied together with ribbon.

The handwriting was elegant with strong loops and slants. A man's hand, Claire had no doubt.

The second trunk was almost empty with a wooden tray at the bottom. Packed in coarse linen were bottles of all shapes and sizes, their labels little more than symbols painted onto the corks of the bottles.

"What do you suppose these were?" Noel asked, holding one up to the weak light shed by the bare bulb.

"Don't know. Spices, medicine maybe. I don't think I'd open it until we know what's inside. Could be an ancient poison."

"Or love potion," Noel added, grinning.

"Um, yeah. Maybe I need that," Claire said, catching the bottle between blackened fingers.

"Let's take a few down and the letters too. Look for any notes or anything in the books. We can take this stuff to the music room."

"Far away from your friendly ghosts," Claire agreed.

Noel stopped, her expression growing serious. "What about Cole? All of this is his. Maybe we should let him read the letters."

"I'll tell him what we found. We'll let him decide if he wants to do this himself. We may want to get cleaned up before we settle down."

Noel agreed and they carried out armloads of material, closing the trunks again before heading down the stairs. At the foot of the staircase, they dropped the things in the hallway on loose newspapers. Parting, Noel went back upstairs to her room, and Claire crossed to the door leading into the library. Cautiously she knocked, noting how filthy her hands looked.

"Come in."

She eased the door open, watching him for a moment as he typed quickly on the computer. His desk was covered with documents, stacks of papers piled neatly.

"I need a secretary," he said grimly, turning around. His eyes widened in amazement as he looked at her. "Good Lord, what happened to you?"

"We've been looking around and, well, we found where the key fit. And we found some other things, a couple of trunks with some old letters."

He got up, slowly approaching her, his smile widening until his amusement touched his eyes. He lifted one hand and pulled a long twist of web from her dusty hair. "What's this on your face?" His fingers carefully slid down her hot cheek.

"Dirt. Dust I suppose. We just wanted to make sure you were alright with us going through your things."

"Whatever you want. Take the place apart if you think it well help. But take care of yourselves and stay out of the dangerous rooms. If you find something good, let me know."

"We thought we'd use the music room."

"That's fine," he paused, his eyes darkened as his thoughts turned to more serious issues. "Are you staying here tonight, or do you want to go back to the hotel?"

"I'm fine here. Really. I'll let you know if anything else happens." She backed out of the room, feeling as though her face was afire. Here she was, being threatened by spirits, her life turned upside down and all she could think about was his concern for her. And his touch.

After a quick shower, she took extra care with her makeup, twisting her wet hair into an intricate knot at the nap of her neck. She pulled on jeans and a top and hurried to meet Noel. She was acutely aware of the time, knowing she would be going home for the Thanksgiving holiday in several days. Would she even want to return after that? Exams would be fast approaching and after that, Christmas break.

Noel looked up from the mess on the floor as Claire entered. The papers had been spread out on the floor and Noel was sorting them.

"Letters," Noel said, gesturing to a stack, "bills, ads and some legal stuff."

Claire looked puzzled. "Why would a maid have stuff like this?"

"This wasn't the maid's. I'm willing to bet money these belonged to the first mistress of this house. The letters are all addressed to Beatrice and look at the date, 1854. That's when this was first built. And from the sound of the letters, it seemed our lady had a boyfriend."

"A boyfriend?"

"Definitely a lover, and he wasn't her husband. Listen to this, 'I worry that one day he will discover us and in his rage, I am uncertain what he may do'."

"So, she was having an affair," Claire said, leaning over Noel's shoulder to look at the stained paper.

"And how. This stack is full of letters from him, and he even mentions the maid. Listen. 'Have Etta place your next correspondence at the Inn, for I fear our current place is becoming too dangerous.'"

Claire sat still, picturing the lady's maid as she carried the letters back and forth between the lovers. Had she hidden them then, after her mistress had left? It made sense. Claire said as much to Noel.

"Covering for her. Yeah, it follows. They had a steamy affair, and when they finally left, Etta took the letters and hid them in her room."

"Do you think the turret room was Etta's? I was wondering if maybe it was the lovers' meeting place. It's too nice a room to give a servant, but if her mistress was using it as sitting room, or a romantic hideaway..." Claire paused and looked appreciatively out the window to admire the panoramic view outside. It would be that much more impressive from above.

"Then Etta could just keep the key after they left and hide their things in the closet room."

Claire abruptly shook her head. "Stupid! We've forgotten the timeline! The turret rooms didn't even exist when Beatrice and her husband, what was his name, that's right, Henry. It wouldn't have existed when they were here. They were built after the house had been abandoned the first time. This couldn't have been Etta's rooms. Or Beatrice's."

"But the turret is involved, even if it wasn't Beatrice's doing. And the rest?" Noel looked around slowly.

"The rest makes sense. But if the lovers got away free, and Etta hid their things, then who's doing the haunting?"

"Good question."

"And I remembered one other thing. Remember after we first moved here when I asked you who had lit the lamp in the turret? I thought it was John, but you said he was out for the evening. Whoever it was had to have a reason for being here, and I think we just found it."

"So, we're back to the first question. Who lit the lamp, and who is doing the haunting?"

Claire sat silently for a minute, looking intently at the letters. "It would be the one person who was unhappy with the situation."

"It's her husband. He got angry after she left and closed up the place and died here, an unhappy hermit. Now he's staying here because he knows this is where they did it. This is where they betrayed him."

Claire eased up onto her knees. "But that doesn't follow exactly. He wouldn't be in the turret either. It wasn't here while he was alive. And if it were just him, why the two ghosts holding on to each other?" She stopped and turned to look out the window at the beautiful view. The trees were a riotous mass of color; red, flaming orange, bright yellow, and green fought for dominance in the dusky landscape. But Claire barely saw it, her eyes turned inwardly. "I don't think she ever left here."

Noel's eye widened but she caught Claire's implication quickly.

"He killed her. Beatrice." She said in a breathless voice. "He found out, and he killed her. Then he got rid of her body, claimed she left, and pretended to be upset because of her unfaithfulness."

"But did Etta know the truth?" Claire asked, mostly to herself.

"Probably. I don't know. Why protect the letters if he found out about the affair?"

Claire paused. "Only Etta knows that."

CHAPTER FIFTEEN

Claire stopped the car and looked up at the lighted windows of the house. Her mixed emotions showed vividly on her face as she pulled out her small suitcase. Being home with her family had been wonderful, rejuvenating.

Her brothers had teased her unmercifully, her mother had cooked rich seasonal fare until she felt she was as stuffed as the Thanksgiving turkey, and her father had declared how proud he was of her. She was the first in a long line of Martins to finish her master's degree.

She had smiled, laughed at the good-natured ribbing, but died a little inside. She had so desperately wanted to lie with her head in her mother's lap and cry. She hated that she had created such a barrier between her parents and herself, even though she knew the beginnings of the rift had been formed long ago. She had taken that incident at the abandoned house and locked it tightly in her mind, bound by embarrassment and fear. And at the same time, she had subconsciously decided there was something about herself she needed to hide. It had taken Talitha to make her see what a mistake it had all been. But it still didn't diminish her desire to be protected. She wanted to spill out all her fears and lean against their solid warmth.

In the end, she had said nothing and driven back with a firm determination to see it through. She had decided at the last minute to take a detour into town with a very specific list of errands to run. She had stopped only twice, once at the church supply store where she picked out a lovely brass crucifix to hang on the wall in her room and an ornate silver cross pendant on a chain for Noel. On impulse, she had bought a plain silver one for Cole as well. Her second stop had been at St. Francis Catholic Church on her way out of town, and she took with her the small bag.

Thundering organ music signaled the end of 12:30 mass, and Claire walked in as the other parishioners filed out. Father Walters stood at the door, shaking hands and exchanging remarks about the weather and the upcoming parish building project. Claire waited until the church had cleared before approaching him.

"Father Walters, hello," Claire said as she approached him.

"Claire, I heard you were coming into town. Did you attend an earlier Mass?"

Claire took his outstretched hand, smiling at his firm handshake. He had been at St. Frances for 10 years, retiring there and content to stay in the familiar setting, to say a few masses between fishing trips and hospital visits. His white hair and lined face hinted at his age, but his handshake was firm and his eyes clear.

"We went to 9:00. Mom and Dad still like to get us up as early as they can."

"Your brothers still in town?"

"No, they left yesterday and I'm on my way out."

He looked at her closely, his expression concerned. "Are you feeling alright? You look a little different, tired or worried."

"I'm fine, just dreading finals. I'll be home again at Christmas, but I wanted to ask you a favor."

"What can I do for you?" he asked, waving her towards the front of church.

Her eyes went to the illuminated windows, the plaster saints, their eyes raised to heaven in silent supplication. This place was special, as full of life and spirit as the Talitha house. But here the air fairly hummed with serenity, the silent song of angels. She had always felt a special comfort in this place. And never, even in her childhood, had she seen one of the shadowy specters.

Her mind suddenly snapped, like a picture being brought into focus from a blurry lens. But perhaps that wasn't exactly true. When she was just over six years old an elderly man had suffered heart failure during mass. She could see the memory now with crystal clarity. The service had stopped, and one of the parishioners, a nurse, had administered CPR as they waited for the ambulance in silence. Claire had stepped out into the aisle while everyone in the church had frozen, kneeling in prayer, as the priest stood at the altar giving a ritual blessing as old as the faith. She could picture it now. Her shoes had been shiny white patent, and she had slid a little on the marble floor. She had tiptoed to see, only knowing the flurry of activity in the front had continued, the woman in the pretty blue dress leaning over the old man and pressing on his chest. The priest had been muttering softly, and over his voice, the sobbing of a woman echoed grief into the still air. And then it happened. In that short time, Claire had seen him, like steam rising from his cooling body. The man had stood and walked a few short steps to the altar. His face was ablaze with a strange light, and he was smiling. Claire had heard another sob and tried to call out, to tell them he was going, but her voice had remained silent as though frozen in her throat. The spirit had stopped and, turning for one last look at his grieving family, had again melted into an indistinct shape that floated, no flew, upwards into the hot white light streaming through the open window.

Claire had cried then, for the pure joy of it in her childish heart.

It was easy for her to see the purity and the ecstasy, even if her young mind had no words for what she was seeing. And she finally discovered where they were meant to be; those poor lost souls that had become her companions. But she had never told anyone about that incident, although the church became a place of solace.

They stopped at the altar, and Claire realized the priest had been speaking to her.

"What? I'm sorry?"

"I said, are those gifts for me, or are you here to show me something?"

She smiled back. "Actually, I'd like them blessed if you don't mind."

"No, of course not. Haven't blessed anything for you since first communion rosaries."

She took out the objects and handed them to him, one at a time.

"Wait here for a minute while I get my things," he instructed and disappeared to the side of the altar. When he returned, she had spread out her purchases and prayed with him while he read from his prayer book.

After he was finished with the blessings, they had made small talk, but the question was in his eyes. She knew he blessed things all the time, jewelry and rosaries, and even more elaborate things. But she hadn't asked the favor for a long time. When she left, he took her hand again in a tight clasp.

"If there is anything I can ever do for you. Anything at all, you know where I'll be. God bless you, Claire."

Tears had blurred her vision as she walked quickly away, listening as the church bell tolled the quarter hour.

Now, approaching the house, she held the paper bag in front of her like a shield. Ben's car was nowhere in sight, and Claire wondered if he had brought Noel back yet. They had together gone to Noel's mother's house for the holiday and were planning to stop in at his parents' before returning to Talitha. Claire found it touching that they had progressed so far in their relationship, enough to want to share it with their families. Noel had changed as well. Gone was here careless disregard for the future. She had acquired the glow of love in bloom that came with an anticipation of things yet to come.

Claire hesitated and looked back to her car. If the house was empty she wouldn't go in, she thought desperately. She couldn't, not by herself.

The front door opened and a figure stood, framed in the doorway. Soft light illuminated features, fine sculpted and familiar. His hair was pulled back off his face, raked back with impatient hands. The dim light seemed to emphasize his eyes, large and luminous in his shadowed face.

"Are you coming in or running out?"

She walked up to the foot of the stairs where he met her, his warm hand brushed hers as he bent to take her suitcase. She could smell his scent, warm and intoxicating.

"I didn't know if anyone was home. Ben is bringing Noel, and I didn't see the car..."

"They're not here yet. I've been back for most of the day. I didn't want you to come back to an empty house."

"I wouldn't have stayed. I'm not that brave." She dropped her eyes from him and looked at the rough stone of the porch. The open door yawned before them, and Claire felt herself holding back. She hated the foyer, hated it with a passion that was uncontrollable and frightening.

"Are you okay?" His hand went to her arm, turning her away from the door. "Claire, are you alright? What do you see?"

She shook her head and looked up into his concerned eyes. She could almost melt in the depths of them. "Nothing. Nothing at all. I'm fine." She walked determinedly in, noting that he trailed her closely as she went up the stairs and into her bedroom.

It had remained untouched except for the dress that continued to rest on the bed. She took the suitcase from him and placed it on the bed, holding the bag in front of her. She didn't know what religion he was but suspected since the funeral that he was Catholic. She felt strangely vulnerable, bringing to him a symbol of something so intimate, so special to her. But she dug into the bag with greater resolve and pulled out the necklace.

"I don't know if this will help, I mean, it's just a symbol to some people, but I got you this." She held it out, the silver catching the light.

He lifted his hand, taking it gingerly. "I used to have something like this. My grandfather's family was Catholic." He smiled, putting the chain around his neck. "Not a bad time to go back to the Church." He unbuttoned the first button of the shirt, slipping the cross inside, next to his heart. "Thank you. I appreciate your concern for me. It's been awhile since someone has cared." He stopped awkwardly.

"Perhaps it's time for that to change," she said impetuously, feeling a well of sympathy for him, for the bleak expression on his face as he gazed slightly beyond her.

The door below slammed and Noel's voice carried, loud and sharp, up the stairway. "Claire, where are you?"

The rest of the evening was spent settling back in. Noel had brought leftovers from her turkey dinner which they reheated for a late supper. Ben had followed her in and stayed to make sure they were comfortable. Claire felt sure Noel had told him about the recent events at the house.

Cole especially seemed to enjoy the meal, and Claire was surprised again at the sharp prick of empathy she felt. While she was basking in the glow of familiar warmth at her home, he had taken a business trip to Denver. When she asked about his Thanksgiving, he brushed the question aside, choosing instead to distract the flow of conversation to her vacation away from the house.

Ben left slightly before 10:00 and Claire took Noel upstairs to give her the cross necklace.

"It's beautiful. You said you had it blessed? That's so cool." She hung it around her neck. "Now I'm ready for anything, vampires, werewolves, the boogieman."

Claire shook her head smiling. "I think you need a silver bullet for werewolves, but we haven't spotted any of those yet."

"Yet is the word," Noel said, rolling her eyes. "Around this place you can never be too sure. But seriously, thank you. I know how much your religion means to you, and right now I think we all have a good reason to look to a Higher Power for some help."

Monday morning was spent in classes, and Claire had never felt so eager to get back to Talitha. She felt a strange suspended sensation, as though her life and the lives of all around her had been placed on hold until the situation at the house was resolved. Cole had declared no cleaning was to be done until the following day, and then only light housework would be necessary. With the laborers gone, their services had been reduced to cleaning the renovated areas of the house and cooking meals. No promises had been made about the job following Christmas, but Claire wasn't prepared to think so far ahead anyway. When she drove through campus to pick up Noel, she was pleased to note that the car was working well. With cold weather setting in, she didn't want to become stranded anywhere.

Once home, Noel decided some additional exploring was called for.

"Come on, what else do you have to do this afternoon? Don't tell me you think you can concentrate on your schoolwork. I can barely pay attention while the class is in session."

"I agree. But don't you think we should check with Cole before we go exploring any further?"

"He won't care, and you know that as well as I do. I think we might just find some good stuff in the attic. We may even find some things that will give a clue to our ghosts."

"I think that's what I'm afraid of."

"Well, I prefer to be an informed victim."

"I know, I know." Claire reluctantly acquiesced and followed Noel up the steep side stairs to the third floor. Noel grinned as she dragged a reluctant Claire up the final set of stairs into the attic. The silence in the house was complete except for their footsteps as they climbed the stairs. They started at the far end of the attic, opening the door into utter blackness. It was no surprise the place was sound, no crack of light invaded the place. The leaks that had previously plagued the roof had been repaired months ago, and the house felt as tightly sealed as a tomb.

A series of bare bulbs provided light, the wire so new that no dust had settled. It was apparent they had been recently installed with the renovation of the upper floors. The attic was cut up into many rooms of various sizes, some shut behind thick wooden doors and others open without so much as a doorframe.

The dust was thick and choking, even when the girls walked gingerly along the path left by the workmen as the lights were installed. The attics were full, packed with decades of furniture, representations of each phase of decor.

The oldest was in the main part of the attic, just above the original rooms. Here were large, lumbering pieces of furniture; the fabric thick and dark with little pattern, ripping a little at the hand sewn seams. Over all, it was well made but unattractive.

Many of the corresponding decorations were piled atop the furniture, graceless lamps and dark tapestries depicting hunting scenes; many shrouded in sheets for protection. Stacked neatly against the wall were paintings, their frames chipped from careless handling. It was apparent the new owners had wasted no time in moving all the old things up into the attic since none of them resembled the more elaborate pieces still in place on the lower floors.

"Bingo!" Noel exclaimed, laying out several portraits face up.

"Oh lovely. The Addams family revisited," Claire said dryly, moving them closer to the light.

The portraits were poorly rendered, heavy handed with stiff expressions and dull eyes. The first was a man, dark haired with coarse features, his eyes hooded by thick brows that met in the center of a lined forehead. His nose was slightly bulbous, his lips a dark slash above a square chin. His skin looked browned by the sun, but the colors were difficult to determine because of the dust and grime accumulated after years of storage.

The second was a woman, as light as the man was dark. Blond hair was gathered atop her head and girlish ribbons twined in the curls and fell to bare shoulders. The overall impression was of youth and beauty, a stark contrast to the man.

"Could this be Mr. and Mrs.?" Claire asked softly.

"I was thinking Beauty and the Beast," Noel responded grinning.

"Let's look at the others. Maybe they were just some other relatives."

Noel looked skeptical but pulled out the rest of the pictures. Hunt scenes, poorly painted landscapes, and a still life. All were different, by various artists according to the flourish of a signature, but none were impressive in quality. They hadn't pressed for much decoration or some of the pictures were gone, because there were too few for such a large house. But no other portraits of the inhabitants were found in the area, and the two girls carried their find downstairs.

The library was conspicuously empty; Cole was busy with meetings in the city. They laid out the portraits and, taking only a dry cloth for fear of damaging the paint, dusted as best they could.

The cleaning did little to improve the quality and the subjects stared flatly out at them from the warped canvas. But at the bottom of the frame they struck pay dirt. A small plaque, blackened with age, had been engraved with their names; Beatrice Ann Hagen and Henry Maximillian Hagen.

"Do you think?" Noel asked.

"I'm pretty sure. This has got to be them. He built this place for his wife. And she's definitely attractive enough to acquire a lover."

"What was his name, the lover, I wonder?"

"I don't know. The letters were signed Gemini, but that could be anything, his birthday or just a nickname."

"Not a huge surprise he wouldn't want to put his own name on something. If her husband did get his hands on him, at least the pen name gave him some anonymity."

"Didn't seem to help them, though. If we're right and she is the victim, I guess her husband knew what had happened. Doesn't bode well for the lover, does it?"

Noel sighed and propped up the portraits. "Okay, so we know who we are dealing with, but how do we prove it?"

"We have to find her."

"Gross," Noel said, drawing back. "You mean her body?"

"Yes, or whatever we can find. Everyone thinks she ran away. We've got to prove she didn't. I bet a hundred bucks she never left this house."

"You mean he buried her here. I bet in the basement." Noel's eyes widened and she grinned wickedly. "This is just like a movie. We'll find her molding bones in a shallow grave in the cellar..."

"No. Cole told John they had done some major excavating down there because of water leaks. If she was there, I think they would have found her."

"What's the other choices? The garden. The yards. There are acres around here. There's no way we could ever find her."

Claire felt an odd prickle along her arms and her head felt

almost light, the sensation familiar and unsettling. But no figures appeared, no shadows formed in the harsh afternoon light.

"She's here. In this house and close by. That's why he's holding her. She wanted to leave, so he killed her and kept her close, even in death."

Noel looked at her curiously, then with alarm. "Let's get outside. Now."

Pulling Claire by the hand she led her out the front door. The afternoon sun was slipping behind the trees, casting foreshortened shadows against the shorn grass. The handyman, Eddie, was still at work, the sound of his mower leaving a droning buzz in his wake. The air smelled of fresh grass and fallen leaves. A hint of burning was in the air, stale since the bonfire had been extinguished.

Claire sat on the lowest step, her long legs stretched out in front of her. Her breathing seemed odd, like she couldn't get enough oxygen, but she didn't feel afraid. She found herself frowning as she examined her stained fingertips, her mind strangely empty. She felt a little light headed then. Her eyes scanned the scene around her. The porch had leaves gathered in the corners, rustling against the steps and stirring lazily in the breeze. Orange, red, yellow-green; the early foreshadowing of the chill yet to come. The leaves were lovely in their rustic way. The colors, the colors were…

Clair was surprised at Noel's tone of voice when she spoke, "Claire!"

She jolted a little. "What?"

"That was friggin' scary. Are you all right?"

"What do you mean?" Claire asked, distracted, her mind still grasping at what seemed to be a shadow of a dream.

"That trance, or whatever you were doing. Didn't you hear yourself? Like something from a séance."

Claire rubbed fingers over her eyes. She had a vague feeling of vertigo still. "What do you mean, what I said?"

"You were saying something. Like 'find me, find me'".

Claire felt a little shock. "Oh, my God," she said softly. "We've got to finish this and soon. I don't want to lose what little mind I have left." She turned to her friend and looked into Noel's imploring visage. "You don't think I'm going crazy, do you? I know I should leave now, get out of this place, but I really feel the need to see this through."

"This can't be good." Noel looked a little sick.

"I know. I know this has gone far beyond normal. But it's not going away either." At Noel's silence, she stood slowly and dusted off her jeans. "I think we should go back in. I need to find her. To know what happened to her."

Noel shook her head. "I'm not so sure. What if they come back, the spirits? Claire, I'm scared for you. For you and for me."

"Noel, I have to know. I just have to."

CHAPTER SIXTEEN

Two frustrating hours later, they were almost ready to give up. The walls were sound, no hidden doors or tunnels, no passages in the library or hollow panels behind the bed. Even the fireplaces were sound.

"Let's go back to the master bedroom." Claire suggested as they left the parlor. "It was John's room so..." she left the rest unsaid.

Noel looked at her with curious expression. "Is this a hunch or some vibe you're getting from the house?" she asked sharply.

"I'm not even sure. I just feel like we've missed something. I know it sounds strange. I'm not hearing voices or anything, I just feel something, you know?"

Noel nodded slowly. "Okay, we'll go up but let's get Cole. It's his house and his ghost. If we find something I think he should be there."

Claire nodded her agreement, but worry lined her face. Her hands were icy cold and damp and a headache was beginning to edge into her temples. She remained on the steps, head in her hands as Noel went to get Cole. She felt alone and vulnerable in her knowledge. It was as though the inhabitants of the house spoke to her in different voices, and she couldn't find the right response. She could almost be certain the urge that made her realize the body was close by had nothing to do with the presence in the foyer or the parlor. Spirits, like the people they once were, all seemed to have their own agenda, each working toward their own purpose. The maid, the woman in the portrait, the twisted spirits, they all seemed to have their own message.

Her eyes skimmed up the heavy front doors to the plaster walls, now stripped of wallpaper. She turned to look up the staircase, her eyes lingering on the carved railing, vines creeping like carved snakes twisting around the posts. The place was a mixture of fine workmanship fronting a darker, more macabre heart.

She heard footsteps and watched as Noel approached, Cole following behind. He looked skeptical, his eyes dark with concern, but said nothing and silently went up the steps behind them and into the old master bedroom, the room John had so recently inhabited.

The late afternoon light was weaker here, the sun moving to radiate its brilliance on the rear of the house. The windows were curtained partially, and Noel swept them back briskly.

"Lousy lighting. Well, what are we looking for?" she asked, moving to the fireplace.

Claire looked over the room again. The room had been stripped of all personality; John's belongings had been carefully packed up by Charles to be sent to his family. The computer and its accessories had been sent back to some corporate warehouse to be divvied out to other workers while the desks, tables and bookcases had been moved into other bedrooms. The two pieces of furniture left since the move were the bed, bare of a mattress or any linens, and the wardrobe, its doors already open. The walls were devoid of any pictures or decoration, the fireplace swept clean of any offending ash. It was lonely and empty and so very wrong. They stood in the doorway in silence, missing John's laughter and life.

"I haven't been in here since he left," Noel said softly.

"Me neither. Charles did all the packing. I guess he cleaned it out too." Claire felt a strong surge of sorrow. "I should have been here to help."

"He didn't want any help," Cole said from behind them, and shifted to slip between them and into the room. "Charles wanted to do this. He felt like it was something he could do for the family." He sighed and looked out the window, out into the sprawling yard and woods beyond.

Noel blew her nose noisily, wiping her eyes in quick angry strokes. "Ok, so we need to do this. What are we looking for?" she asked Claire, her voice resolute.

"We left this room out earlier, so I guess we'll first just search as we did before." In their explorations of the other rooms, they had checked out the wardrobes, tapped walls, tugged on carvings, and checked for loose floorboards. Again, after their search of John's room they found all were solid with no hidden panels or passages.

"If you were going to stow a body, where would it be?" Claire asked idly. Her eyes were dark with her thoughts turned inward, trying to follow the pattern of an unfamiliar mind.

"I'd put it outside," Cole responded with dry humor, his brows creased over tired eyes.

"No, you don't understand. You want to know that nothing gets to it, ever. You want to be sure it's never moved; keep it close to you. You want to be sure..." Claire's revere was broken when her eyes landed on the bed again. "Maybe you want to sleep with it."

Cole looked at the bed, then back to her with an expression of distaste. "Keep a body in your bedroom. Or are you saying he kept her in the bed..."

"Or under it," Noel breathed.

Cole slowly looked to the bed, its height increased by the huge platform. Noel walked slowly; her eyes riveted on the wooden boards beneath the empty bed frame.

"It's the right size for a body," she said, kneeling to peer under the frame.

"You don't think he murdered his wife and put her down there! Good Lord, you can't be serious. Think of the stench."

"Maybe he moved out for a while. He became a hermit afterwards, no one even saw him. He could have been sleeping in the attic for all anyone knew." Noel seemed to warm to the subject. "If you're crazy enough to kill someone, maybe you don't have any qualms about sleeping with the body. I've heard of it before. Keeping a loved one's body after they die..."

"That's grotesque."

"That's real. People have periods of grief that are so severe they can't let go. Maybe he killed her and in a fit of remorse, put her there."

Claire turned, watching as they debated the subject, each looking at the bed as though unable to look away. "There's no resolving this unless we look," she said flatly.

Both turned to her, surprised.

Cole sighed. "You're right. I think it is a bizarre idea, but if this settles something, it will be worth it. Wait a minute while I get some help."

He disappeared, leaving the girls in silence.

"Claire, what if we find something? It's easy to discuss in theory, but to find something or someone, that's another matter entirely."

"But maybe it will solve some of the mystery of the place. If she really is here, maybe a proper burial is what she wants."

They waited in silence until Cole returned, a man following slowly behind with reluctance evident in his hesitant steps. Both carried tools, and they had matching grim expressions.

Claire wondered how much Cole had told his companion. It took her a few minutes to recognize him as Eddie, the gardener. Time and the exposure to the wind and sun lined his weathered face.

His eyes were blue slits under bristly gray brows, permanently squinted from working in the harsh sun. Claire knew the man had worked here for a very long time, had known Cole and his father before him. But he had never spoken to Claire, content to work in silence in the great lawns and tangled gardens.

"Let's get this bed frame out of the way and start. I don't want this to last past nightfall. The lighting is bad enough already." Cole rolled up his pristine shirtsleeves. His long-fingered hands, graceful and quick, looked more at home at a piano than completing manual labor. But he bent to the task willingly, using the tools with familiarity bred from experience.

The gardener stood at the front of the platform, rubbing his neck in an agitated manner as Cole took apart and removed the pieces of the bed frame. As he carried them across the room and out of the way, the gardener began to dig at the nails on the platform with the slender claws of a hammer. The hard wood came up with a protesting creak. Despite the care he was taking to leave the boards undamaged, scuffs and gouges marred the surface. He pried the wood up, one piece at a time, revealing the dark floor beneath. After the first five boards were removed, he stopped with a muffled exclamation.

Noel surged forward, but Claire hung back, knowing she had been right.

"Hot damn. You were right. There's somebody down here," he said softly, something like fear clouding his eyes.

Claire approached slowly, breathing in the dry scent of decay. Lying on the floor, looking much like a figure in a casket, the body was stiffly positioned. Sparse hair clung to the skull; the clothes were rotting but intact. Empty eye sockets glared up from a mummified face, the skin stretched like old leather over heavy bone. A tattered shirt of indiscriminate color was overlaid with a dark blue box coat with notched lapels trimmed with braid. Matching pants and a crumpled bowler placed conspicuously close to the fisted hand completed the clothing. No boots or shoes covered the skeletal feet.

"That is no woman," Noel breathed, stepping back to catch Claire's arm.

"It's him," Claire said tightly, turning anguished eyes on Cole. "It's Henry, the man who built this place."

The silence was unbroken until Cole moved with swift efficiency to force them all out of the suddenly suffocating room.

"Go downstairs, wait for me in the music room. I have some calls to make, and for God's sake, get a drink or something. Lord knows I will."

It was hours later before they left, the investigators and the coroner, a black bag encasing the fragile flesh and bones. Nothing remained in the cavern beneath the bed, and Cole left it open, unconcerned now that it was empty.

Claire and Noel ate a late dinner in the kitchen, the bright lights illuminating the smooth surfaces and gleaming floors. The smell of roasted chicken and fresh oranges warmed the room, making it seem fresh and inviting. The stark contrast between the slick efficiency of this room, and the almost brutal abandonment of the upper floors struck Claire anew as she lingered over her coffee, well spiked with amaretto liquor.

"Do you think it's over now?"

Claire shook her head absently. "I don't know, but I doubt it. This changes everything. I mean, I can see why he would be haunting the place, he was murdered here..."

"I guess that's for sure. You don't just conceal the body of a person who died naturally beneath the bed."

Claire nodded. "But what happened to her? Was she the one who killed him, or maybe her lover did it for her."

Noel looked indignant. "Wait a minute. Who says she didn't do it herself? She could have easily offed him and put him there."

"Yeah, but do you picture her nailing those boards down? That's a pretty radical change to go from embroidery to burying a guy in your bedroom."

"Entombing him, you mean," Noel said gravely. She took out her necklace from beneath her tee shirt and unconsciously caressed the cross. "How could you do that? Kill someone and then shove him under your bed. And this wasn't just a stranger, this was her husband."

"I wonder how he died," Claire said slowly. No outward damage had been seen on the body, no bloody stains on the clothing or the floor, but the state of decay would make it difficult to determine much without a formal investigation. Since the crime was so old and the perpetrators long gone, the coroner expected a swift identification, if possible, and immediate burial.

"Well, where do we go from here? We can't just leave it this way. What happened to the widow? Why did they do what they did, assuming some stranger didn't come along after they were long gone and do this. I can't stand not knowing more."

Claire looked up from her own grim thoughts. "Let's get out the letters. See if we can find any more clues to their plans. And maybe we can visit the library tomorrow. See if any mention of them was made in the press. Maybe they attended formal functions or something."

Noel visibly brightened. "Sure, we can see if they have any more pictures. Maybe we can find some information about their friends. I wonder if there's anyone alive that would know more of the story."

Claire shrugged and ran her fingers through her hair. "I think I'm ready to turn in. I have some homework I need to get done before tomorrow afternoon, and if we're going to the library, I need to be up extra early."

Noel nodded. "I'll be up in a little while."

After Claire completed her shower she sat on her bed, attempting to read a novel to get her mind off the events during the day. It was tempting to just leave. Their suspicions, although off in accuracy, had revealed some truth. There was a violent death, and Henry was probably trying to keep his cheating wife from escaping. The feeling of revenge was almost palpable, and Claire shuddered, thinking of how close the body had lain.

To sooth herself, she got out her sketchpad and a couple of sharpened charcoals. Her drawing quickly developed, a harsh and angry face, Henry's face, contorted in anger. It was better than her usual cartoons, but still looked stiff and childish. Frowning, she ripped the page out and crumpled it into a tight ball.

She went and stood at the French doors, finally pulling the curtains open and flipping the latch to let the door swing in. She didn't see the dove outside, but that didn't mean she wouldn't come. She had been leaving an occasional heap of seed out on the balcony to feed both Leta and some of the other birds in the neighborhood. It made her feel better that something alive was visiting her room.

She had seen the little dove a few times in the evenings before full dark and was reassured by her solidity. She didn't know when the bird was leaving on the nights when she stayed in Claire's room, and she certainly didn't know who was closing the door after her, but now with Etta's visits, she thought perhaps she had an idea. It amused her that Etta would help her care for her little feathered friend. Perhaps Etta was an animal lover?

Her hallway door swung open, causing her to start. She quickly closed the pad, dropping it next to her on the bed.

"Noel, you scared the crap out of me! I'm thinking I'm living with ghosts, and you come tearing in."

"Sorry, sorry. But you've got to hear this. It seems our lovers did have some escape plans but I just didn't notice it at first. These letters are so hard to read, but here he talks about a ship, a steamer.

Sounds like they were headed to the Ohio River to catch one of the passenger paddle boats. He even makes a reference to going to the coast sometime in the spring of the next year. I guess she had decided to leave her husband."

"Then why kill him?"

"Don't know. Maybe he found out. Maybe there was a fight. He doesn't look like the most forgiving man. Maybe he threatened her."

"So, in a fit of passion, she killed him."

"And her boyfriend comes over, helps her do away with the body, and gets the caretaker to check on the house."

"What about Etta? She must have stayed behind."

"I doubt she stayed for long. Someone must have gotten her out of there, paid her off. Or worse."

Claire looked skeptical. It was just too neat. If Etta had known what happened, what had she done? Had she become another casualty in the game? Or was it possible she had remained after the murder? What kind of power could she have wielded in her position? No one would believe a maid over a wealthy member of the upper-class society.

"If they just left, maybe we can trace them. Find out their ship passage, something."

Noel sighed. "I'm not sure about that, but at least we can look her up. Beatrice, I mean. Maybe she had some family who would know where she went."

Claire agreed and leaned back, suddenly exhausted."I'm going to bed too. Do you need me to stay in here?" When Claire shook her head, Noel backed out the door and closed it softly after her.

Claire got up and put her books and sketchpad away. She dimmed the lights and returned to her bed. She wouldn't sleep in darkness, not tonight. She lay down, pulling her blankets tight around her. She thought about Cole, looking so tired and grim as they took out the body. The possibility of a successful business was becoming slimmer, and she doubted people would want to sleep in a room where a body had been found. She had little doubt the fact would hit the news at some point. Even people with great wealth were not immune to the probing eye of the press.

She knew Cole would still be awake. Working or reading, she wasn't sure, but she felt more secure knowing he was in the house.

As thought sensing her unease, she heard the tick tick of something sharp striking the glass of the window and watched as the bird slipped though the opening in the French doors.

"Leta," Claire said with pleasure. In all her research, she had finally looked up the name she had unwittingly given the bird. The origins of Leta was a shortened version of Aleta, a Spanish word for winged. It seemed to fit, even though Claire had no idea where she had gotten the title.

Funny, but she hadn't mentioned the bird to either Cole or Noel either. It seemed like she had chosen to keep the dove as her little secret. She held out her hand and the bird swooped from the doorway to perch on her finger. She was amazed at the dexterity of the wild bird. And why had it decided to trust her? Why befriend her? She certainly hadn't trained it, but the way it behaved made her think it was somehow knowledgeable of humans.

"You're just my little companion," she said softly, looking into the bright eyes of the bird. The bird let out a gentle sound and then fluttered to Claire's shoulder where it gently began to preen her hair as though caring for a child.

The bird was still sitting comfortably in the crook of her neck when Claire fell deeply asleep.

She dreamed she was painting. She was standing in that dark cellar room, the harsh light of the lantern casting dancing shadows across the uneven walls. Dabs and smears of paint covered her nightshirt, where in her passion, she had wiped stained hands on the cloth. And she painted. The subject was the same, the woman, the window, the breeze, and the night. But now she was angry, betrayed and hurt. The colors were a blur. She felt the salty tears on her face, tasted them, and felt the bitterness of years.

CHAPTER SEVENTEEN

W hen she woke, she thought she was bleeding. Smears of red and brown streaked over her hands. She sat upright in bed in a panic, choking back a cry. But it wasn't, it wasn't, because there was blue, and there green. In dots and splotches, paint crawled over her hands, her arms, the long white tee shirt with the giant poodle picture. It stiffened the cloth, and shadows of color had transferred to the sheets.

"I dreamed I was painting," she said in a whisper.

She hadn't thought of the painting in the basement. With all the scary activity of the last weeks, she hadn't even recalled the odd piece of art tucked out of sight. But now it seemed of greatest importance.

"What have I done?" she asked herself. In the dream, she had painted. And obviously, she had painted in reality as well. Sleep walking, sleep painting, what else could her crazy mind be doing?

With shaking hands, she gathered clothes for the day and crept out the door, closing it softly. She couldn't face anyone now.

Couldn't answer questions, couldn't explain. For now, she would wash away what she could and hide the rest.

The water was hot, but because she made it that way. The latex paint washed with a good scrubbing, leaving small stains of hue on her skin here and there. She washed and breathed and concentrated on the day. She would go back to see the painting, but she would go alone. She had to see what she had done. Had she ruined the painting? Had she carelessly destroyed it in her sleep? She was no artist, and the person who had originally designed the painting had obviously had more talent than her. She felt a surge of regret. The painting had been good, and now?

She turned off the water and quickly toweled dry. She was able to dress and hurry back to her room without meeting anyone else. But there were few people there now. Just Claire and Noel. And Cole.

She deliberately put on makeup and dried her hair, brushing it until it gleamed. She pulled it away from her face with a clip but let it fall down her back in a silken wave. Taking one last look in the mirror, she forced a smile. Good. She didn't look crazy.

Claire was alone in the kitchen when Cole came in. She felt the immediate surge of emotion at seeing him and paused to just gaze at him, her eyes eagerly tracing his now familiar features. When he stopped to study her, she dropped her eyes to hide her expression, and glanced into her coffee cup, empty except for a few dirty brown grounds.

"Good morning. I'm not going to ask if you slept well. I doubt anyone did." He moved to the coffeepot and poured himself a cup before sitting down across from her at the table.

"I slept alright. I'm feeling fine today. Better actually." And it was true. Considering her apparent actions the night before, she felt rested. "I feel like something has been resolved, part of the story. Don't you?"

"I hope you're right. I'm just not sure." He looked over in frustration, raking his hand through his hair in an impatient gesture.

"Well, you don't have to worry about us." She tried to look sure of herself. "Really."

He looked at her cautiously, picking up his coffee cup as he climbed slowly to his feet. He busied himself at the sink, rinsing the cup even though he had drunk very little. He turned back to her and forced a weak smile, an expression that curved his lips but didn't reach his eyes.

"I'm going out for a little while. I've got some business to attend to, but I'll try to be back later today. What are you planning on for today?"

"Noel wanted to check the library. See if we can find any more information about Beatrice Hagen. What may have happened to her."

"You think she was the one who killed him?"

"Yes, don't you?" Claire responded, surprised.

He looked somber suddenly. "I just can't picture it. She didn't look the type."

"You're looking at the portrait and assuming she was as she looked. I bet she was a much more complex character than that painter ever saw."

"I'm sure you're right. I just can't imagine murdering your spouse."

Claire nodded. "But the world was different then. She was probably forced into marriage, and he didn't look to be her type precisely. He was older, rough, he may have been a real bastard. Maybe her lover was young and handsome..."

"So that's what women fall for? A pretty face?" he prodded, chuckling.

Claire felt herself color, looking into his amused eyes.

"Just those of us with taste," Noel snapped, stomping in. "Oh, I have the worst headache."

"Have you taken anything for it?" Claire asked.

"Yes, but it may take a little while. In the meantime, is there any of that coffee left?"

Cole expertly poured her some of the now strong brew and sat the steaming cup before her.

"Do you want anything in it?"

"No, thanks. I drink mine black on days like this."

Cole took one last prolonged look at the two girls seated at the table and pulled his keys from his pants pocket.

"I need to get going if I'm going to make it back by nightfall. Are you sure you're going to be alright?"

"Yes, Dad," Noel said, grinning playfully, then dropped her head with a grunt of pain, her hand reaching for the pain pills.

Cole left reluctantly, and Claire felt foolishly happy. Whatever evil had been stirred up by the location of Henry's body seemed to have been dispelled, and she had high hopes of some sort of resolution soon. Except for the incident with the painting. Damn, she wished she could forget the painting.

Noel set her coffee down with an uncharacteristic scowl. "The weather always gives me such a major headache. Oh, just shoot me and get it over with."

"Are you sure you want to do the library today? We can always wait for a few days."

"No, no. We only have a few weeks before Christmas break. I'm just worried. If this isn't resolved, Cole is going to close this place down. We'll be back to being homeless, jobless. And Lord only knows about this place. It's already affected you. Who can say it won't still?"

"Noel, I'm going to be fine, okay? I feel like now we're working on this, they're going to leave me alone."

Noel looked skeptical and slowly stirred her coffee, inhaling the rich fragrance with relish. "Claire, we've been friends for a long time. I only want what's best for you, you know? But you've changed since we've been here. Aged. I just am afraid..."

"That I'll be haunted where ever I go."

Noel took out her spoon, taking her time sipping the hot brew.

"You haven't had these experiences for a long time, years. And we get this job and you're seeing them, and not just here. In the apartment, on the bridge, they seem to be getting more and more common. This place has opened a channel or something."

Claire nodded, her eyes clouded. "Maybe it has, and if that's true, I'll just have to handle it. I'm not a child anymore. I think I'll be more able to cope. Maybe to help them."

They left by early afternoon, intending to get some research done before Claire had to be in class. The drive between Shelbyville and the University campus was a pleasant one with only a spattering of rain accosting the windshield. Parking on campus was difficult as usual, and Noel put her tag prominently in the window to avoid a ticket. They walked between the hovering buildings, walls of brick rising on either side, until they came to the entrance of the library. The building was an unattractive mixture of architecture; the glass and concrete entrance boasted tiled floors and pale paint. The open atrium lead into a tighter space furnished with the "stacks" as they were commonly called, shelves upon shelves of loosely organized books.

The girls went first to the computer terminals to do a search online. They split up, both picking an area to search. Claire was interested in finding some information about Beatrice's possible flight on the steamer down the Ohio River, while Noel held out for the actual family tree.

By the time she had to leave for class, Claire was frustrated and in a less than studious state of mind. Names and dates swirled in her mind, but none had been right. She had looked at sheaves of old newspaper, their brittle pages protected by plastic, and she had squinted over projectors with films of microfiche flashing before her. But nothing had helped. Nothing of use.

Defeated, she walked slowly to Noel to tell her goodbye, and they agreed to meet in the same area in a few hours when Claire's classes were done.

Noel was in deep conversation with another student when Claire returned. Her companion sat with his legs carelessly propped on the desk, his mismatched hooped earrings swaying when he spoke fervently, which was often. Claire watched in fascination from a distance, smiling unwillingly as the guy gestured wildly as he talked, his face animated. He was obviously giving Noel an earful.

Noel grinned when she caught sight of Claire and waved her closer.

"Claire, this is Tonic. Tonic, my roommate Claire." She looked at Claire's blank expression and her grin widened. "Tonic works here at the library part time. He's a whiz."

Tonic turned sharp green eyes on Claire and smiled. "I needed some extra cash, and this is a great place for reading. So, are you the one looking up the long-lost ancestor?"

Noel stepped in, covering Claire's silence. "Yeah, good old Great Aunt Beatrice. You'd be amazed what info Tonic dug up for us. He's just," she paused for dramatic effect, "beyond groovy."

Claire kept a straight face at Noel's antics, but Tonic was preening, pushing the long lank hair out of his face with one tattooed hand.

"It was a cinch," he said, gloating. His face became suddenly sober, and he swung his feet down with haste, the high tops making a flat thud as they hit the floor. "Shit, here comes the boss. Gotta go. Been great though. Want my number?"

"Not now, but we'll see ya around," Noel said, gathering a stack of photocopies. She turned her brightest smile on him and blew him a kiss as she pulled Claire along.

"Oh, Ben would love that. He looked like he could really be your CLOSE friend," Claire joked as they pushed the tinted double doors open, letting in the dusky light.

Noel grinned. "All for research, you know."

The car shuddered across the bridge, and Claire found herself looking intensely on both sides of the railing. She hadn't seen any apparitions recently, but in the overcast and misty atmosphere, she found herself anticipating the worst. The very idea of seeing this specter fascinated and frightened her, now she had a name to go with the face. The place was still, but powerful, causing the fine hair on her arms to prickle as they rumbled across the bridge. The vines on the far side seemed to reach out their spindly limbs to hold the crumbling concrete. Claire turned back and watched it recede, wondering if the figure in the center of the bridge had been real, or just her imagination.

Noel sat in the passenger seat and held her photocopies close to her chest, gesturing energetically with one hand as she described her meeting with Tonic and subsequent search in the library. According to her, Tonic was a genius and had easily accessed old newspaper articles and even a picture from the society page.

They pulled into the drive, surprised to see Cole's expensive car not in its usual spot. Claire frowned at the empty space, feeling uneasy. Although their relationship was still in an awkward phase, a sort of limbo, his presence in the house was always a comfort.

The front door was locked, but the foyer light was on, illuminating the cracked tiles and scuffed stairway. An odor of dust and decay always seemed to pervade the space. Claire had a flash of John, falling and flipping, landing spread eagle on the hard tile, his blood pooling beneath his shattered body. She shivered and found herself holding her books firmly against her chest like a shield. What had he seen to make him jerk away, to move so violently to cause him to turn around and land, face first, without even the protective gesture of shielding himself?

Claire shook her head quickly and followed Noel through the doorway into the library. Cole's presence was most marked here with his closed computer resting on the desk and the stacks of paperwork scattered about.

Claire stopped for a moment when she saw a familiar plan laid out on the desk. John's handiwork, she was sure, because the precise depiction of the house was obviously an architectural plan. The first showed the facade of the building, the clean lines unmarred by the wearing of time and the elements as the house must have appeared when it was built.

The page beneath was the actual floor plan of the first level; the stairway, foyer, library, and parlor depicted in blue while the rooms in the new wings were drawn in red.

Stuck to the page using clear adhesive was a sketch where John's body had fallen. Claire felt a shock, even with the flat depiction.

Turning to the next page, she saw a similar layout of the second floor. In the master bedroom was another taped figure. It was on the tip of her tongue to call in Noel, but given a moment of critical consideration, she decided against it. If Cole chose to hold on to his own theory, Claire didn't want to appear like she was trying to snoop in his business.

But it made her shiver to see John's death connected with the body upstairs. The link was something she had avoided, lending reality to the ghosts. Did they indeed have the power to kill? And if they did, why choose John, who had had nothing to do with the things they had experienced?

She stood for a moment, laying a light finger against the drawing, her fingernail tracing a line from the top of the staircase to the place where John had fallen. Hadn't Cole told them about the last owner hanging himself in the same room? Had old Willie chosen to dangle himself over the foyer floor, or had he too had some help?

She shook her head slowly to clear it and went into the music room where Noel was laying out her copies.

"Here's the picture I told you about. Couple of the year." Noel tossed the copy across the table to Claire.

The picture was blurry, from time and the poor quality of the copy machine. The figures were stiff; their clothing formal for an evening out.

Beatrice looked as youthful as she had in the portrait, her pale hair piled atop her head in glossy curls. Her smile was bright, and the hand she looped through her husband's arm was deliberately loose. Her dress was an elaborate hooped concoction that nipped in close to her narrow waist and flared out in a graceful bell to the floor. The trimming was lace, the details indistinct in the gray and white palette.

Henry was scowling, grim lines around his mouth and a stray lock of hair falling over his broad forehead. His stance was rigid, one hand with a heavy ring holding his coat at the lapel. A bowler much like the one they had found next to his body was clamped in his free hand.

Claire felt a flash of recognition, which quickly faded as she looked more closely at the picture. Something was similar to a picture she had seen before. Not the hat, not the jacket. Could it be the ring? Where had she seen that before? It certainly hadn't been on Henry's body when they had found it. Only his wedding band had adorned his skeletal fingers. As distasteful as it had been, they had studied the body before it was removed, looking at any details they could see without actually touching the desiccated corpse.

She turned her attention to their faces. They may not have been the typical romantic couple, but they also didn't look like a murderess and her victim. What had taken them from this to the horrible ending that followed?

"Here's one," Noel said, interrupting her thoughts. "Mr. and Mrs. Henry Hagen reported they are completing the building of their home, Talitha, and are due to move in during the summer."

Claire looked up from the picture. "A mention in the newspaper; he was a little proud of his place, wasn't he."

"Yeah, it goes on to mention sculptors, masons, carpenters, and some pretty impressive designs. I wonder why, with all the money he was pouring in, he didn't choose better paintings or decorations."

Claire shrugged. "Maybe he had really bad taste."

Noel grinned, "Okay, are you ready for the real dirt?"

Claire nodded, knowing from the eager gleam in her eye Noel had a good story.

"We found a relative of Beatrice's."

"No, are you serious?"

"Absolutely. We looked up some information about the Hagen line. It seems there were quite a few of them, but someone had luckily constructed a family tree somewhere along the way. Beatrice and Henry were mentioned as only distant cousins, but it did tell what her maiden name was. We tried to find any close relatives with either her name or his, but it seems his line sort of died out. The folks still around are distant cousins, twenty times removed. But when we looked up her name, Namous, we struck gold. The name is not all that popular and we got a listing in this area. Turns out we actually found one just a couple hours away in southern Indiana."

"How did you know it was the right group, the right branch of the family?"

"Well, I sort of called about 18 of them on the list. I just lucked out. There was a bunch more I never got to."

"So, her family lives around here?"

"No, actually most of the family is out west, but the guy I talked to said Beatrice was his great, great aunt once removed, or something."

"It's amazing he even knew of her."

Noel grinned. "Not really, she's something of a family legend."

Claire raised her eyebrows, looking at her friend, her eyes alight with barely controlled curiosity.

"Apparently a lot of her story was known by her own family, and they did not approve. She was reputed to have left her husband for another man and was booked on a ship to head back home to meet with her estranged family. She told them her husband and she were separating and a 'friend of the family' was taking her out of Shelbyville to find a lawyer in a bigger city. But, get this, the tickets were never used, and the family never saw her again."

"What?"

"Well, she wrote to them, telling them she was coming in a few days but she never showed up."

"Surely someone went looking for her? Contacted someone at the house?"

"No, the family had already decided to disown her because she left her husband against counsel. When she didn't come around, they decided she finally understood they didn't want her in their lives and had given up contact. No one even bothered to check on her until years later, and by then the house had been abandoned, and the rumors she had left willingly were firmly implanted in the minds of the locals."

"So that's the end."

Noel nodded. "Unless we can find out who her lover was, it seems like they got away clean."

Claire sighed. "A dead end."

"In more ways than one," Noel said grinning.

Claire paged through the rest of the papers, finding a few mentions of the husband and wife at local parties and teas. Beatrice was more outspoken than her husband, quoted on occasion but with no great revelations. Claire sighed with pent up frustration. She could feel a breakthrough coming on, but kept butting up against one obstacle after another. It appeared the couple, to cover their horrendous act, had disappeared from society and family ties as well. Perhaps the maid, Etta, knew their fates, but she had remained silent since the first clue.

———————

The door closing reminded them of the other occupant of the house, and Claire listened as his footsteps grew closer, pausing at the library. He continued, the sound louder as he climbed the stairs. Moments later they heard him descend and he came in, the portrait from Claire's room, in his hand.

Noel rose, her bright hair catching the light in an array of red and golds, and moved to the door, closing it behind him.

Cole gave them one of his rare smiles and set his burden on the floor.

"I figured you would be in here. I'm afraid the work in town took longer than I expected." He walked up behind them to look at the stack of papers. "I saw the car outside but no lights were on."

Noel frowned. "We left the lights on in the foyer unless it blew." She rolled her eyes. "The lights aren't that reliable here."

"Sorry," he replied dryly. "Either my electrician isn't very competent, or my relatives aren't very nice."

Noel shook her head vehemently, "No, not your relatives. It had to be Henry, we're pretty sure."

He nodded and pulled a folded envelope from inside his jacket pocket. The envelope was thin with only a few sheets of paper, which he removed and tossed onto the table.

"I'm afraid I have to agree. I went to see the medical examiner this afternoon. He wasn't very anxious to give me information, but a few dollars loosened him up."

He pulled up a chair and sat down slowly, spreading out his notes before him. "It was a male, approximately 5'10" or 5'11", large boned, wide shoulders. No broken bones, fractures, or other signs of violent injury. It's hard to say at this late date about what killed him, and they were hesitant to run any tests on him." He paused and moved to another page. "We can tell he had dark hair, was relatively young when he died, thirties or forties. His clothing was worse for wear but there was a ring, a plain gold wedding band encrypted with initials, HMH."

Claire stood, stretching slowly, her hair falling sleek and soft in the dull light. Cole watched her for a moment, his mind momentarily distracted.

"No other jewelry, no other rings?" she asked, thinking of the heavy ring they had seen in the picture.

"No, one was all."

Claire nodded, her expression distant. Something was still bothering her. She glanced up, surprised, when Cole spoke again. He looked vaguely uncomfortable with a slight reddening beneath his cheekbones.

"I think now I could use a drink. We can look at your portrait later."

Cole walked slowly to the kitchen, leaving the girls exchanging silent looks.

"I think he's relieved it's not his family," Claire said softly, looking at the pages of notes.

"I would be too. But now what. We have the victim, but not the murderer for sure. Do you think Henry will feel better, now that we know what happened?"

Claire looked absently at the darkened windows, seeing their reflection in the panes. "No, I think he wants what anyone would. Justice."

CHAPTER EIGHTEEN

Claire looked up from her paper, carefully examining the portrait they had re-hung on her wall. She was pleased to see the eyes watching her now, and felt good now that they had a name to go with the face. Galiena. They had found it written in miniscule print on the back of the canvas, and had later found the matching name among the family papers. Galiena had indeed been the mysterious German aunt of Margaret; the lady who had persevered and stayed in the house after her niece had run out in fear. Claire had a secret feeling, an innate knowledge that Galiena had known a lot more about the spirits in the house than any other member of the family. Perhaps she knew the true story of the Hagens, or at least part of it.

Claire looked back down at her paper, taking a few extra minutes to re-examine her work. After a stressful week, the exams were finished and she was anxious to get home, to enjoy Christmas away from the house and its ghostly inhabitants.

She had told Noel goodbye the day before, holding her hand a moment too long before releasing her to leave with Ben.

"Are you sure you don't want to go tonight?" Noel had asked. "You know you could stay in the hotel until your exams were done."

Claire shook her head firmly, pushing her long hair behind her shoulder. "No, I just have one more tomorrow and will leave on Friday, early."

Noel watched as Ben loaded her bag, then turned her concerned eyes back to her friend. Her face looked pale, contrasting with the deep auburn flame of her hair. "I don't like leaving you here."

"I won't be alone. Cole will be staying for at least another week and nothing has happened in at least three weeks. Even Etta has made herself scarce. Maybe Henry's at rest..."

"I know, I know. I just worry."

Claire smiled, her eyes misting. "We're only going to be apart for four weeks and I already feel so..."

"Are you sure you don't want me to stay. I could leave a little later and meet Ben in a couple of days. I would in a second if you need me to."

"I know. But you need to go. I'll be fine, and you'll have a great holiday. Ben's family already adores you, so it should be a lot of fun." She playfully shook her friend, "and you be sure to call me if any important questions are asked."

Noel grinned, "Trust me, if he pops THE question, you'll be the first to know."

They had left in a cloud of steaming exhaust, and Claire had returned to the house, an uneasy premonition causing her to turn and watch them as they left. But the night had been uneventful, and the following day had dawned garish and golden, a herald of good weather. Several hours later, she put down her no. 2 yellow pencil and sighed, feeling the euphoria of freedom with the completion of her exams. Her bags were packed for the next day, and she had only a few toiletries to add in the morning.

The shrill bell jolted her out of her concentration and she

handed in her paper, filing out with the rest of the students. The walk to her car was less than a block and she felt an almost tender regret as she bade the stately brick building of the education department goodbye.

The car started on the first try, and Claire felt a small twinge victory. She had become almost obsessed with the vehicle, always feeling as though it were the only thing standing between herself and possible freedom from the house. And distance from Cole.

Her smile melted as she pondered the fact. Her feelings for him had grown, but she wasn't brave enough to put a name to them. Her life had become very confusing and in the upheaval, the last thing she needed was to find herself in the middle of a relationship. But how could she control the way her heart fluttered when she heard his voice or her breath quickened at his touch?

She rubbed her hand wearily over her forehead as she watched for the road leading out of town. The sky remained a cerulean blue, the clouds a white and gray relief from the blinding color. The air was crisp, the temperature sinking to below freezing in the evenings. A few flurries had drifted to the ground the day before, and the weather was predicted to disintegrate as the week went on.

As she pulled into the drive, she paused the car, looking at the shadowed facade of the house. It looked cold, dead. But then she noted lights were showing in the foyer, glittering through the curvy glass of the windows and giving the impression of habitation. Claire was relieved and pulled her car around back so she could enter the rear door. She no longer trusted the house, even if they had lived in relative peace for the last few weeks.

When she unlocked the door, she heard noises from above and dropped her books off in her room before following the noises up to the attic. It had to be Cole, and like a thread pulling from her heart, she followed the tug of emotion.

The bare bulbs illuminated isolated patches all along the attic floor, turning motes of dust into flakes of fire. The piles of furniture and knick-knacks, boxes and trunks, created a narrow alley to the middle of the attic. Claire followed the lights, nervous and regretting now she hadn't picked up a flashlight in her rush. She stopped as the room widened; relieved to find she was not alone.

Cole was sitting at a dining room table, a desk lamp placed on the tabletop. He looked up quickly, his smile welcoming.

"How's it feel to be that much closer to graduation?"

"Great! I'm just glad for the exams to be over."

"And just one more semester left?"

She nodded in agreement and skirted the table, curious to see what he could be working on in such a dirty and cluttered space.

"Since we haven't gotten any more messages from the other side, I thought I'd take advantage of the quiet and do some investigating."

"Yes, I noticed you had been doing something like that in the library," she said, glancing down to avoid his probing gaze.

"In the library?"

"The blueprint. I didn't mean to pry but I happened to see John's drawing on your desk..."

He raised his hand to silence her and smiled wryly.

"That's fine. I wasn't trying to hide it. I was just mapping out the house, looking to see if the proximity of the bodies had anything to do with John's death."

"And did you decide anything?"

"Well, we've got the stories of the house to validate some of this. One man supposedly died in the parlor where you've experienced your sightings. And the parlor is situated almost precisely under the original master bedroom. In addition, John was killed in the foyer where we have another story of an ancestor hanging himself. There is some correlation there, however circumstantial it is."

She nodded slowly and walked behind him, leaning over to look at the thick album in front of him.

"This was in a trunk with a pile of other mementos. It looks pretty old." He flipped back a few pages. "Just look at those faces. They must have been ordered not to smile."

As he turned back in the album, the black and white photos gave way to earlier forms of photography, tin types with formal poses, stiff and lifeless as porcelain dolls.

Claire pulled up a second chair and they sat in companionable silence, both absorbed in the images in front of them.

"Some of these must be before they moved into the house. None of this looks familiar," Cole said, pointing to a family posed in front of a Victorian home.

"So, when the next family moved into the home, after the Hagens were gone, they brought their own mementoes that ended up in the attic as well."

"I suppose. Since the house hadn't been empty for too long, I guess there weren't as many repairs to do. They just brought their things and moved in." He flipped another page and made a strange sound in the back of his throat, like he was choking back an exclamation. A larger portrait dominated the next page, two men sitting stiffly in matching upholstered chairs, and set in front of a huge fireplace.

The fireplace was unchanged in the parlor, the rest of the room surprisingly warm and attractive with soft florals, but most surprising were the men. As identical as clones, they stared solemnly at the photographer. Their clothes were similar, one suit a shade darker than the other, but the hair was the same dark shade and they were both clean shaven. It was a toss-up as to which had posed for the portrait in Cole's room, not that it would have mattered. They both resembled Cole strongly; the strong boned face, dark hair, and crystal eyes.

"Twins," Claire breathed. She felt the surprise punch the air from her lungs, as though a huge revelation had emerged.

Cole gingerly pulled the picture loose, its corners held by small black tabs. On the back was a brief line scrawled in a loose, but distinctive hand.

"Matthew and Michael Edwards, Matthew's home, Talitha, 1857." Cole's voice was odd, restrained, as he read the words.

"Gemini, the twin," Claire said. "It's the same handwriting, I'm sure of it."

Cole's face seemed to tense as he realized what she was referring to. "Where are Beatrice's love letters?"

"Down in the music room. We left them there with the rest of the papers. Do you want me to go there?"

"No, let's both go. I'll bring this with us. At least the lighting should be better."

Claire ran down the stairs first, feeling as though she were being chased by darkness, by deception. Her unwilling mind spun out of control, the missing piece of the puzzle shifting into place.

Cole followed, turning off lights and shutting the door to the attic. He moved with quiet efficiency, almost automatically, taking her elbow lightly with his free hand at the base of the staircase.

She went immediately to the table in the music room and shuffled through the papers, taking out the stack of letters.

Cole went around the room, illuminating it with table lamps. His gestures were quick and steady, but she got the impression he was trying to keep himself busy, and that he was as anxious as she was.

Carefully, she smoothed out the letters, easing the brittle pages until they lay flat. Next to them she placed the picture, face down.

The writing was distinct and a match. The slants, the stroke, the uneven rounding of letters was the same.

"The bastard," Cole said softly, flatly. He stood, looking over her shoulder much as she had shadowed him in the attic above. "I should have known..."

"How could you have known? How could anyone?"

"But I knew something was wrong," he said harshly. "I just had a feeling the two families had to be linked. There had to be something stirred up by my coming back here." He wiped his face with his hand. "I still don't understand. The house wasn't his. It was Matthew's. It was Michael who was seeing Beatrice. It's his hand-writing. Why did his brother end up buying it?"

"Wait," Claire held out her hand. "So, while Beatrice was still married to Henry, she was having an affair with Michael Edwards. Your great great grand something." She paused to catch a breath. "And after she disappeared, and Henry was supposed to be living here as a hermit he was actually interred upstairs. So was the house was just left here? Maybe taken care of by just the staff? Then when Henry 'died'," she used a gesture to indicate the false death that had been reported, "Michael's twin brother swoops in and buys the house."

Cole rubbed his eyes wearily. "I always wondered how he found this place. Matthew, I mean. They lived several hours away, in Ohio I think, and pulled up roots to move here. The book stated as much. But now it seems obvious. He had family here."

"His brother," Claire said, flipping the picture to see the two handsome faces, so alike.

"Michael must have influenced him, promised him the house at a great price. It had been years since the murder and the house had reverted back to the state."

"But why? Why move your family into a house where you know a body is boxed into the floor? Never mind the fact he was involved in the murder himself."

"But that's the beauty of it. How better to insure the body is not found than to move your own family in? I'm sure he influenced how much construction was done."

"But Beatrice..."

Cole picked up the picture, holding it closer to the light. "I don't think Beatrice ever left the house either. You said you felt two spir-its, fighting. Beatrice and Henry. Together forever. I don't know how she died, suicide or murder or maybe just an accident, but I bet

Michael here was involved. If we tore this place down I bet we'd find her."

Claire shivered, wrapping her slender arms around her middle in an unconscious gesture of protection.

"You think he killed her," she said flatly, her eyes sliding from the picture in his hand to his eyes, glittering with an icy intensity.

"I don't want to believe there was another murder, and I'd rather not have monster in the family, but yes, I think he did something with her. Maybe she panicked, wanted to go to the authorities, or maybe she just had a breakdown..."

"No, you're making her out to be a victim. She wasn't. She murdered her husband and helped hide the body. I think she was a lot stronger then you give her credit for."

Cole looked puzzled. "You have a feeling about her."

"Yes. Maybe it's just women's intuition. But I'd bet a bundle she gave him a reason for wanting to be rid of her."

"You think she's one of the ghosts."

"I'm sure of it."

Cole got up, pacing across the room to the window. "Okay, enough of this. I think we need a break. Let's get some dinner. You'll be leaving tomorrow, and we'll have a nice long time to look up more facts, but this time away from the house."

"Facts about Beatrice?"

"About Michael. We know what happened to his brother, but what happened to Michael?"

"You don't think he's here too?"

"I don't know. I don't know what to think anymore."

They ate dinner in the brightly-lit kitchen, wolfing down peanut butter and jelly sandwiches and potato chips like first graders.

Cole looked mournfully at the crusts left on his plate. "God, I miss Noel."

Claire grinned and gave him a companionable shove. "Look, I told you I didn't cook. We should have ordered pizza."

Cole frowned. "No one delivers out here."

Claire laughed again. "At least we have ice cream for dessert. Noel bought some really good stuff before she left."

Weighted down with bowls full of bananas, ice cream, several toppings and whipped cream, they retired back to the music room. For those few golden minutes, they had avoided the subject of the house. They had talked of their childhoods, their favorite movies, their favorite food. It was fantastically good to think of something else besides the betrayal and sorrow that hung heavy in the atmosphere of Talitha.

Cole pushed his empty bowl away and his face sobered as he looked again at the photo. With slow deliberate movements, he pulled out the book and opened it to the page with the portrait revealed. Then he rummaged through the stacks of photocopies and pulled out the newspaper clippings.

"There's something I feel like I'm missing," he said softly, looking at the group of pictures. "Let me get the portraits together."

A moment later he returned with the stack of framed canvases and laid them out together with care. They looked at the faces, the stiff clothing, the backgrounds, searching for clues until Claire caught her breath.

"It's the ring," she said excitedly. "I knew I had seen it before. Henry was wearing it in the newspaper photo, and here it is in the portrait."

Cole leaned over to look closely. "You mean Henry and Matthew wore the same ring?"

"Look. They are exactly the same. This is the proof we've been looking for. How else would Matthew have gotten the ring unless it was taken from Henry, or Henry's wife gave it to her lover?" She made a face. "And then he passed it on to his brother?"

"Well, there are several other ways, like he might have found it in the house after he came here, but I admit it is pretty good evidence." He looked rather disappointed as he said this, and she felt a sense of regret for proving her theory.

"Just because you have one skeleton in your closet doesn't mean you're all a bad lot," Claire said, gesturing with a spoon.

"Skeletons, now that's appropriate," he responded smiling back. He cocked his head, a gentle smile easing his stern features. "You know, you're one of the bravest people I know. Not many would stay in a house after seeing what you've seen here."

Claire sighed, swallowing uncomfortably at his praise. "This isn't the first time I've seen these things. I think I've been haunted all my life; I've just been trying hard to pretend it wasn't real. There have been spirits in every house I've lived in, to tell the honest truth. Yours are just a little more," she paused, "insistent."

"Noel hinted you were more sensitive. She cornered me in the library one day and gave me quite a lecture. I think she wanted me to understand you were more susceptible. Vulnerable."

Claire nodded. "I'm sorry Noel felt she had to speak to you like that, but she has a strong protective instinct, at least where I'm concerned. Like I told her, I don't feel vulnerable, just available." She found her cheeks heating at the double meaning. "It's like I have a special spiritual cell phone, and mine is the only number they have."

She looked down to her bowl, now soupy with melted ice cream and chocolate. "It sounds odd, I know. I haven't ever said much to anyone because the subject makes most people uncomfortable. Especially my family. Everyone has hesitated to believe me, except Noel and you."

He took the bowl from her hand. "Don't worry, I've become a

firm believer. How could I not? I'm the sole owner of the MOST haunted house in the United States."

While he was taking care of the dishes, she scanned the letters again. They certainly sounded amorous, but maybe extreme. Could he have planned her death? Could it have been an elaborate scheme from the very beginning, or had he been washed away in the tide of passions leading to this grim conclusion?

Cole returned and stacked the letters and picture. "No more tonight," he said firmly. "It's getting late, so let's just do something more relaxing."

"Play for me?" she asked hopefully.

He nodded and sat down at the piano, his long fingers gracefully relaxed on the keys.

"Any requests?"

"Something cheerful," she responded, sitting back in her chair.

He played, piece after piece, his fingers deftly caressing the keys. Some songs were familiar; soft rock tunes and light jazz, interspersed with some aching love songs. She felt her eyes closing, listening to the music as it surrounded her, moved her. For a few moments she ignored the house, the history, and the spirits.

As the music silenced, Claire opened her eyes and sat up straight. She smothered a yawn behind her fist as she looked at her watch.

"It's almost 11:00," she noted, surprised.

"Time for bed," he agreed, rising from the bench and closing the lid over the piano keys. "You've got a drive tomorrow, so you need rest."

She nodded, feeling as though so much was left unsaid. Would he still be there when she returned from her break? Or would the house be abandoned, left alone to rot to the ground?

Together they walked up the stairs, choosing still to go up the side set of stairs instead of the main grand staircase. At her door, he hesitated and watched as she opened the door and slipped inside.

"Call if you need anything," he said, and smiled quickly as he turned away. Slowly she closed her bedroom door, listening to the sharp click of the latch catching, echoed by a second one down the hall.

She had hoped she would have a visitor that night. Aleta had been scarce over the last several days, and she worried the cold had sent her avian friend heading for warmer climes. The move to Talitha had brought several welcome things into her life. The bird was one of those strange blessings she would miss when she left. She had experience with other pets, other companions, but never one like this.

As though the dove could sense her there, Claire heard a fluttering flapping sound and felt the air fan her cheek as the bird soared past her and into the room, seeming to pull in a breath of crisp air and the scent of the evergreens.

"Leta!" Claire exclaimed, watching the bird in her graceful glide around the room until she came to rest on the desk. Claire turned back toward the night but froze. She couldn't close the door, so she pulled it to just a little and then hurried to get her robe.

The bird was at the desk, but instead of watching Claire, she seemed to be nibbling on some of Claire's papers. Her sharp beak was making little notches out of the sheets, and Claire hurried to see what she had been working on. Several of the books there were Cole's, and she didn't want them destroyed.

She bird made a low coo, and Claire bent to see what she had. But it was just one of the pages from the book, which with some tugging, was coming loose from the binding. Claire bit her tongue before she could scold the bird. There was nothing here at Talitha she would take for granted, not even the movements of a wild dove.

She took the book from the desktop and gently opened it to the page that now stuck out from the rest. It was another of those awful black and white photos, but this one showed a line of people in work clothes, two men with tweed suits and boots, one holding the bridle of a giant black horse, and a woman, small and pale and...

"Etta," Claire said softly. "You found Etta," she told the bird.

As though in response to the statement, the bird seemed to nod its sleek head, and then take flight, the familiar flutter of its wings sounding close as it flew by Claire and then to the door, out into the cold night.

CHAPTER NINETEEN

Morning brightened the windows, the light glaring harsh and white between the curtains. The shaft of light played over the swept floor and widened to bathe the fireplace opposite. Claire sat up and ran a slow hand through her tangled hair. She turned to look sleepily at the clock next to her bed, seconds passing before the numbers registered: 10:14.

"Oh, good Lord, I'm late," she breathed, stumbling to her feet. She stepped over the pile of dirty clothes she had shed the night before and rummaged through her drawers to find something to wear. Most of her wardrobe was packed, so the options were limited. She pulled out a pair of jeans, too tight across the seat, and an old sweatshirt, adding undergarments to the pile before heading for the door. As she crossed the room, the sun struck her with its blinking brilliance, causing her to squint. Slowly she approached the French doors, pulling the heavy drapes back with a quick jerk.

Her gasp of surprise was followed quickly by a muttered curse. The world outside was a winter fairyland; the trees heavy with piled snow. The railing on the small balcony was topped with the stuff;

blown snow gathered in a sparkling slope and pressed against the glass at the base of the window. When she leaned a little further, she could see the fountain, the horses drowning with snow reaching their straining necks.

Slowly she dropped her clothes and sat on the edge of the bed, feeling deflated. She didn't need the radio to tell her she was stranded. It had to be a freak of nature to cause snow this unexpectedly deep, deep enough to bury her alive in this tomb of a house. How quickly her plans had changed. It was as though the world had decided to conspire against her ever leaving the house.

Slowly she stood again, picking up her belongings, her mind churning over the problem. Surely not all was lost. December snows were usually short lived, unlike their January counterparts. She would be on her way by tomorrow. There was no reason to believe anything would happen to prevent that. And the house had been quiet, hadn't it?

She added a short prayer and hurried into the bathroom, taking a long hot shower before emerging in a fragrant cloud of steam. She took her time drying her hair and adding a little makeup to give her cheeks and eyes some color. She pulled her crucifix from beneath her shirt and left it hanging prominently against the soft material, as though daring any evil to invade her hard-won serenity.

Once back in her room, she reordered her belongings as though she thought she might need to pack them at a moment's notice, wishful thinking she knew, and neatened the bed. A soft shuffle and clicking sound drew her attention to the balcony doors. Out in the snow, a shade darker than the eye straining white, was the feathered shape of her dove.

"Oh, no," she breathed, and hurried to open the latch. The bird flew in with a breath of frigid air and a puff of icy snowflakes that landed on the wood floor and melted into invisible puddles. She closed the door on the weather this time and bent close to the little bird. She was fluffed up, but appeared healthy enough for her night out. Claire bent down and put out her hand, pleased when the bird perched on her fingers. Her little clawed feet were very cold against Claire's skin.

"Now what are you doing out in this weather?" she asked, "you could have stayed in here last night." But the events of last night could have easily been a dream.

Claire walked the bird over to her desk. Slowly she scanned the surface, and felt a surge of relief when she found the paper that had been pulled from the book, still with marks from Leta's sharp beak.

Taking it and the book and other papers and dropping them onto her made been, she pulled open the desk drawer where she kept the seed container. She pried off the plastic lid and smiled as the bird hopped to the desktop. With amusement, she watched the bird gobble up a few of the larger seeds, dropping the hulls carelessly on the desk top. After a moment, Claire realized the bird probably had not had any water since the weathered had gotten so frigid. She cracked the door open and seeing no one in the hallway, slipped out, closing the door behind her and hurrying to the bathroom. She grabbed up a little paper cup and filled it with water. Back at her door, she hesitated in the silent hallway. No sounds from below hinted that anyone else was stirring. She eased the door open, and seeing that the bird was still eating at the desk, she ducked into the room and closed the panel behind her.

After a moment, she laid out the last of the bird supplies. She had placed a towel on the desk with the seeds, the water cup, and a little nest of hand towels for the bird to snuggle in if she were so inclined. She didn't know what else she could do for her just now, and she was eager to see what Cole might be doing. She paused and closed the curtains securely over the harsh light from the French doors.

"I'll be back," she reassured her temporary roommate, and closed the door after her.

When she descended the stairs, she felt better, a whole day

yawning before her with nothing to do, but pleased she had been able to care for the dove. Seeing it in the light of day gave her faith she wasn't really losing her mind. She might be painting in her sleep, but she hadn't made up her night visitor.

The kitchen was warm and smelled of freshly brewed coffee. The pot sat half full, a bag of bakery goods lying out on the counter. Claire dug in with appetite although the pastries were a little stale, and read yesterday's paper as she finished her breakfast.

She cleaned up after herself, taking extra time to wipe the countertops and sweep the kitchen floor. When she was finished she went back up toward her room, walking slowly and listening for Cole as she went. The house was silent except for the low buzz of the radio from the library. She wondered if he was working or just sitting in there, enjoying the quiet.

Forcing herself to move more quickly, she climbed the last of the stairs and opened her bedroom door, peeking to see if the bird had settle down. She could see the feathered shape had indeed cuddled down in the next of towels, and she tiptoed into the room to consider her options. She had packed already, arguing with herself about what to take, with the future looming and questions unanswered. However, she was hesitant to leave anything of sentimental value. She knew Cole would let them return to pick up their things even if his project was abandoned, but she didn't like the idea of her belongings being left in an empty house.

Sighing, she looked around the room. She could live without the cheaply framed prints, the meager furnishings, and the comforter that had served her for five long years in college. She could even do without most of the clothes left hanging in the closet or stuffed into drawers. But her books were invaluable to her, and she had to restrain herself from unpacking clothing so she could fit a few books in her duffel bag.

Her eyes landed on her cell phone, and she sent a quick message to her mother, promising she would call when she knew better what her plans were.

A light knock on the door jarred her thoughts and she quickly walked to the door and swung it open. Cole stood outside, his hand still raised as though to knock again. And he looked good to Claire, with his unshaven jaw and clothes that were deliberately casual, faded jeans and a knit shirt, which was showing wear on the cuffs and at the elbows.

"I heard noises. I assumed you were awake," he shifted uncomfortably. "I didn't want to wake you early. What with the weather..." he gestured vaguely to the French doors.

She nodded, mildly amused at his discomfort. From his expression, it appeared he felt responsible for the snow.

"I guess we'll have to stay in today, but surely by tomorrow it will start to melt. I still have a week till Christmas," she said calmly.

"That's true. We'll start digging out early tomorrow morning. I've called the plows. They're due out later tomorrow afternoon. We can at least get into town..."

"Yeah, we'll make it that far. The interstates should be cleared first, so once we get out on the main roads, it should be easy going." She looked around the room, slightly embarrassed by the disarray. "I was taking the morning to neaten things up, but I got distracted." She looked rather wistfully at the beautiful carved beds, the clever fairies gazing at her with tiny smiles. "It is a gorgeous room."

He nodded and stepped further into the room, his eyes scanning the finishes. "It is that. Such a shame things couldn't have gone better." He let out a sigh. "But I am grateful to you and to Noel. You both have worked very hard. You've gone beyond what was asked of you. Frankly, I'm not sure exactly why you're still here."

She felt herself blush, pleased by his praise but more by his expression, his smile so warm, his eyes intense. The shrill of a phone sounded downstairs, breaking his gaze.

"I'd better get back to work," he explained, "but come down anytime if you want a little company, or to use the library."

Claire nodded her agreement and turned back to her room. She hadn't pointed out the bird to Cole, and she wasn't sure why. Perhaps it was her little secret, at least for now. She shook her head, deciding she could put off her tasks no longer. She shut the door and gathered her cleaning supplies, getting to work with grim determination. By noon the room was done, thoroughly cleaned with fresh linens and sparkling windows. She wiped up the bathroom and went back to the kitchen for a quick lunch.

The house was still quiet, like some dangerous beast sleeping. She knew Cole was working in the library; she could hear the faint rumble of his voice. But there was something preying on her mind, and she just couldn't let it go. The painting. She knew she had been in the lower level, and she knew she had awakened with her hands smeared with paint. Her question remained the same. Why? What had she been doing?

The bird appeared to still be dozing, so she slipped into the hallway and listened again. Cole was still talking, his voice an even rhythm. So, she would go down. She didn't want to say anything to anyone until she had a chance to see the damage. If she had destroyed the painting in her sleep, well, she would tell Charles at some point. But frankly, she didn't even know if Cole was aware of the painting's existence. And seeing it after it was ruined would do him no good.

On the other hand, if the painting was still recognizable, she would show him. He should see. Whatever was happening in the house, she was sure the painting was related to the rest. There were no coincidences. There were no construction workers that just happened to go down into the cellar and decide to paint their private masterpiece.

And that left? Who? The artist remained elusive. She refused to even entertain the thought that niggled at her mind, that she was the artist. No.

Claire found one of the powerful battery lanterns, and switched it on as she descended the stairs. The main room was still lit with the utilitarian fixtures. The little room was open, the door hanging wide. A block of light slid before her, swaying with her movements. But the lantern did a good job of lighting up the space, and she had to pause in amazement again.

The painting was finished. More layers had added dimension and depth. The woman's features had become more defined. Her light hair, curls spiraling down her back, was highlighted with gold. It was without a doubt the most finely done painting in all of Talitha. It was the painting of a beautiful woman. It was a painting of Beatrice.

And the artist? Claire realized now that she was seeing the finished work the artist had been a man in love with Beatrice. The colors and shapes, the way the light hit her and lit her with dazzling beauty, all spelled out a desperate love. But the way the woman gazed out the window made Claire feel a wave of sorrow. She hadn't loved him back.

Claire's eyes followed the line of light to the floor where she could see footprints in the dirt floor. They were tangled and over-stepped, layers of boot marks, scuffs, and distinctly, bare foot prints. Her breath caught. She knew whose footprints those were, the familiar arch of the size 8 foot made her breath hitch.

She was the painter. Sleepwalking, sleep crying, sleep painting, her mind absorbed by the ghost of a man who had loved his wife and then been betrayed in the very worst way. Henry.

Claire spent the rest of the day in library, shuffling through old books in the bookcase in hopes of finding something that would be of interest. To her amusement, she found two rather gristly books, compilations of ghost stories that depicted graphic scenes of murder and revenge. All the stories were stated to be true and all located in the general area of Kentucky, Indiana, and Tennessee.

When Cole discovered her reading material, he chuckled, picking one up from her lap.

"Dad must have bought these. It was right down his alley. He loved to read about other haunted houses." He sat opposite her, absently prodding the fire with the poker. A shower of golden sparks drifted up the chimney, lighting his face with their glow. "I guess he really did feel something. Or know something. Nothing else explains his interest. Now that I think about it, he questioned Grandma about the house a lot." He paused, his eyes drifting to the phone. "You know, maybe Grandma has some information we could use." He pulled out his cell phone and scrolled through the contacts list.

"Are you going to call her now?" Claire asked.

"Not going anywhere, are we?" he asked, smiling wryly.

While he sat to make his phone call, Claire waited, feeling slightly awkward. She didn't want to eavesdrop, but she would feel foolish stepping out.

"Hi, Grandma, it's me." He paused, sitting at his desk, his eyes focused on the blotter in front of him. "Yes, I'm still at hell hole motel." This time, the pause lasted longer and Claire let her eyes wonder to his intent face as he doodled on the calendar in front of him, his graceful hands sketching lines and curves between the squares. "Yes, I'm hoping to be in by the twenty-third, but we got several inches of snowfall last night. Eight I think."

Claire's attention wandered and she returned to the book, idly paging through the chapters. Surely if this house were contained in the book, his father would have told Cole. She found herself enthralled momentarily by a tragic story of young lovers when her attention was drawn back to Cole's conversation.

"Well, I don't know about ghosts, but we have seen some odd things. What I wondered was if you knew anything more about the first owners, or our family, the ones who moved in right after."

This time the silence lasted much longer and Claire could see him writing notes instead of doodling.

"Did you know he was a twin?" Cole interrupted. After a moment he nodded, his grandmother needing little encouragement to continue her talk.

"Have you ever heard of a maid? Maybe Etta?"

Claire sat still, thinking of the picture upstairs in her room. She would have to tell him about finding it, but how to explain her firm belief it was Etta? She shook her head briskly and listened as he spoke with his grandmother, watching his face change from curious to serious. Once or twice he looked honestly surprised at what he was being told, and Claire wished she had thought to ask him to use the speakerphone. Toward the end of the conversation his expression warmed, and they discussed more personal topics. Claire turned tactfully away but heard the affection in his farewell. When he hung up he leaned back in his chair, the notes in front of him.

"Well, we should have called her a long time ago. She knew more than any book." He got up and walked closer to the fireplace. He paused for a moment to throw another log on the fire.

"What did she say? Did she know about the twins?"

"Apparently. She said she knew the house was bought by the family after standing empty for some time. She knew there were twins, but she didn't know much about their relationship. But the most interesting thing was Etta. Seems that she was hired on at the house and was the lady's maid for Matthew's wife."

"What?"

"I don't know if it was blackmail or just ignorance, but she moved into the house with the family shortly after they bought it from the state and cared for Margaret, Matthew's wife."

"The portrait in your room. I guess that was Margaret."

"I suppose," He agreed, "it would make sense if he had a portrait done of himself, he would have one done for her as well."

"Here's the real question. Why and how did Etta end up back in the house? If she knew about the murder, it seems like she would have stayed clear, as far from the house as she could."

"I think Michael must have given her some kind of incentive."

"I'm sure," Claire agreed, "but I don't think Etta was black-mailing anyone. She knew something had happened to Beatrice, maybe she just stayed on to find out what."

"And she never did."

"No, I don't think she did. At least not in life. And now she's trying to help us."

"But you haven't seen her for some time now."

"No," Claire smiled, "I think she gave up trying to dress me properly." Again, Claire thought about the photo in her room.

The clock on the shelf slowly struck 7:00, the rich tone sounding far too loud for such a small clock.

"Okay, let's call it a day on the investigation," Cole said rising. "What else do you know how to cook? I can make a mean instant pudding."

Dinner preparation was a haphazard event, but more fun than Claire had experienced in weeks. Cole was inept with anything involving the stove, but made a fine salad and insisted on marinating and tenderizing the steaks. While the potatoes cooked, Cole went down in the wine cellar to pick a bottle of good red wine.

They spent the dinner carefully avoiding the subject of the house and instead spoke of their families and interests. Claire sipped wine, listening as he discussed his love of old films.

"So, you've watched some of them repeatedly?"

He smiled self-consciously. "I have a mini theater in almost all of my residences. I know I spend too much time watching them, but it's my way to unwind."

Claire was surprised by the phrase 'all my residences' but

didn't comment. She knew he was wealthy, traveled frequently, and watching him over the last months had revealed a sharp intelligence and fair leadership. His confidence in business was unshakable, but she had seen it falter here, in this unknown arena.

"I noticed you looked a little ill when you first arrived," Claire blurted out, words following her mind's wanderings.

Surprised at the change of subject, he took a slow sip before responding. "I was in an accident at home. A rather serious one, and my heart stopped for a few seconds. It made me slow down, look a little more closely at my priorities."

"An accident," she said softly, "and it reminded you of your dad."

"Yes," he swirled the wine in his glass and looked thoughtfully at the red liquid. "I realized everything I've started, I've finished. Except the house. I inherited it and left it, avoided it and the memories." He paused, swirling the light golden wine in his glass. "He died December 22."

"Oh Cole," she breathed, "no wonder."

He looked up at her and shrugged. "It's been a long time. It's not as fresh..."

"But it's strong. You may be more affected than you thought. Have you ever wondered why no major manifestations occurred until you got here? You're part of the family; you resemble him so much you could have been his twin, and you're grieving. It's no wonder they were stirred back up. They feel you. And they feel me."

He looked skeptical, but she could see the doubt in his eyes lifting. Slowly he drained his cup and set it aside.

"We're getting bogged down again. I thought we were going to try to think of something more cheerful."

She silently agreed and helped him clean up. "So, what are you doing for Christmas?"

"Going to see Grandma in Chicago. I haven't seen her for almost a month, and I promised I'd go up there."

"She sounds like she's important to you."

"She's all I've got," he said softly, frankly.

He played for her again on the piano that night, the music deliberately light and fluid. She felt herself sliding, falling. She knew she loved him, the fresh heady feeling that made the entire world seem different, lighter. But she also knew there were incredible things going on, things out of their control that made the relationship impossible. Not to mention the fact no words had passed between them that gave a clue to his feelings.

When the music ended, she jerked her head up, feeling her cheeks and neck burn.

"Falling asleep?" he asked softly.

"A little, I guess. I should head up, get some real sleep before trying to dig out of here tomorrow."

He smiled, holding the door open for her. "I'll lock up and come up later. Are you sure you're okay by yourself?"

"I'm fine, thanks," she said, hurrying up the stairs. She could hear the soft strains of a Christmas melody floating up behind her. She closed her door softly against the sound and raised chilled hands to her warm cheeks.

"Stupid, stupid. I wish I could be a little less obvious. Talk about wearing your heart on your sleeve. I'll dig out of here if I have to use my bare hands before I embarrass myself further," she muttered to herself, and then grinned when she saw Leta had woke and was perched on the footboard of her bed. At least she wouldn't be spending the rest of the night alone.

CHAPTER TWENTY

The room was hot, stifling. The window was open, the curtains lying lifeless without a breath of breeze. A trickle of sweat slid down her back, tracing over her ribs to soak into the heavy fabric of her gown. A slamming of the door had her jerking upright. Oh, God, someone was coming! She stumbled to her feet, pushing the heavy covers free so she could move quickly.

A cold sweat had beaded on her upper lip and at her hairline. She paused at the doorway, her cold fingers clinging to the frame, leaving wet prints as she passed.

She turned down the hall, toward the stairs. Door after door, closed and locked as she tried the knobs. *SOMEONE HELP. PLEASE HELP.* Her sweat slicked fingers slid on the knobs, her face frozen with sweat and tears. She panted through her open mouth, her heart pounding so hard it throbbed in her throat.

NO. NO, HE CAN'T BE BACK. I KNOW HE'S NOT HERE, BUT I FEEL IT. THE FINGERS, HARD AND FLESHLESS. OH GOD, THE SMELL!

She could feel it now, the sharp tugging at her gown. She could hear the hiss of breath, his mouth open in a soundless scream, lips pulled back to reveal ravaged teeth.

I'M SORRY, I'M SORRY. OH GOD, I NEVER MEANT...

But the words never came, and she felt her mouth open as the fingers finally touched flesh, and he was there, grabbing and ripping...

Further down the hallway she saw another figure, the beloved face, a mask of terror and despair.

MICHAEL, MICHAEL HELP ME!

But the figure turned away, and she felt the pull of death take her, down and down.

"Claire! Christ, Claire wake up. No, don't fight. It's me, it's me."

She felt herself emerge, draw a ragged breath and realized the ringing in her ears was caused by the sound of her voice.

Hands soothed her, smoothed her back and drew her close until her head sunk against the hard warm chest. Her breath hiccupped in ragged breaths, her face soaked with tears. Her gown was damp, the cool air causing her skin to pucker and shudders to overtake her slender frame.

"Okay, okay. You're going to be fine. You're not alone. It's just me. Easy," his words were murmured, rumbling deep in his chest as his arms tightened. With one fluid movement, he eased an arm beneath her knees and swung her up until he settled in the chair, resting her comfortably in his lap. He pulled the blanket tighter and wrapped it around her back and shoulders, tucking it under her legs.

Warm, finally, she thought vaguely. Her sobs died to shuddering breaths. Her face was pressed against his bare neck, her tears drying slowly against his skin.

"Claire, were they here? Did you see them?"

Slowly she turned her face up, feeling his warm breath feathering over her cheeks. His eyes were shadowed, a gleam reflecting deep.

"No," she said softly, her voice alien to her in its rasping. "I think it was just a dream." Her smile was tremulous, her chin quivering. "A nightmare."

"Easy," he said softly, easing one warm hand over her face from cheekbone to chin.

She nodded, a fresh tear slipping down her cheek. She was slightly embarrassed by her weakness, by the spectacle she had made of herself.

He carefully wiped the tear away with his thumb, reaching in his pocket and handing her a handkerchief, faintly scented and expensive. Unrepentant, she wiped her face and blew her nose, keeping her head lowered.

Feeling more composed, she looked up into his visage, the planes of his face sliced with ribbons of darkness so his expression was unreadable.

"Claire," his voice soothed, his hand again moving up to cup her cheek, to slide beneath the heavy curtain of her hair.

Their lips met, his mouth slanting over hers, firm and smooth. Her breath hitched as her blood heated, the chill of fear erased by the intoxication of passion.

The kiss changed from tender to hungry, hot and aching, wanting and demanding. She felt her hands curl into the silky strands of hair at the back of his head, and he drew her closer in his embrace. His mouth slowly eased down her damp cheeks to the smooth column of her throat. The kiss seemed to last forever, but she realized it was only a moment, just long enough to seal her love.

With a gentle pull, he raised his head, smoothing his hands through her hair.

"Let's go downstairs," he said softly, "or do you want to try to go back to bed."

She looked confused, her tear stained face highlighted by the moonlit glow.

"I'd love to stay, right here, like this. But I don't have the self-control for this." He smiled ruefully. "If it's any consolation, I'll stay with you if you want, hold your hand," he laughed softly, "I'd like to hold more."

He stood slowly with her in his arms, his limp returning as he walked the few short steps to her bed. Easing her down, he pulled the blankets back in place.

"Feel better?"

"Much, thanks," she said softly, her mind foggy, exhausted.

He pulled up the chair, easing next to her and slowly pushing the silky hair from her forehead. "Go to sleep. I'll stay."

She closed her eyes, amazed at how swiftly her mind drifted. He continued to touch her, his hand a steady weight on her arm as she let her mind go free.

The morning dawned with a fierce glare from the frosty world out the French doors. The curtains hung open, a chill drifting in despite the furnace working overtime to maintain warmth. Claire sat up slowly, rubbing a hand warily through her hair.

Her fingers froze as she noted the blankets pooled on the floor. The night before flashed though her mind, her fear, desperation, and passion. Had she really clung to him? Had she betrayed her feelings?

She felt her stomach turn and sicken. What if she had embarrassed him, to put him in such a place? He was her employer for goodness sake; their personal relationship was so fragile, so new. Her face felt hot as she lay back in her bed, groaning aloud. She forced herself to rise, avoiding the mirror so she wouldn't have to see the naked vulnerability in her eyes.

Her second thought chased quickly on the first. What about Leta? What had happened to the little bird? She remembered the dove guarding her bed as she fell asleep. She couldn't recall if she had seen her later in the night. Now, in the harsh light of morning, she could see the makeshift nest, the seeds spread on the desk, the towel protecting the surface, but no bird. And the balcony doors were closed. But the bird did have the habit of coming and going at will. So perhaps she had escaped into the night? For now, she would just have to keep her eyes open, and ears tuned to listen for the coo that would clue her into the bird's location.

After her shower, she quickly dressed but stopped to take a little extra time on her hair. When she had brushed it to a smooth shiny curtain and had added a little color to her cheeks, she stiffened her spine and opened the door.

The spicy scent of cooking sausage mingled with the rich smell of brewing coffee and greeted her at the head of the stairs. She had abandoned the side stairs for the front ones in the last few days since it had been some time since the last spiritual encounter. This particular morning, she was amazed by her recovered equilibrium.

This morning she wasn't even thinking of ghosts or spooks. She was dreading facing Cole, looking into those eyes after she had broken down in front of him, actually on him, and kissed him. Wow and what a kiss it had been!

She sighed and forced herself to walk briskly into the kitchen. He was standing at the stove, a plate of sausages in front of him and eggs frying in the pan at his left. A cup of coffee was on the counter and he took a sip while Claire watched him in silence. Even in her dread of embarrassment, she enjoyed watching him, his soft, lightly curling hair, finely arched brows, and long lashes. The carved beauty of his face, so different from any man she knew. He even seemed different from the man she had first met. Or could it be her feelings had added an attractiveness to him?

She was smiling at herself when he turned, and his returning smile was warm.

"I figured I could lure you down with food," he joked, doling the meal out on plates. "How do you feel?"

"Fine," she responded, trying not to stiffen. "Can I help you with anything?"

"Just drinks. Juice, coffee if you like."

She obediently helped him set the table and get their full glasses before sitting down. She picked up her fork, toying with her food.

He set his food down and walked around behind her, his fingers hovering over the shiny silk of her hair. "You look pale. Are you sure you feel alright?"

She nodded, feeling the familiar flush under his careful scrutiny.

"Claire, can I get you anything else?"

She shook her head mutely, smiling weakly, a forced expression. She felt like such an idiot. She wished he would just sit down, let her be embarrassed in peace.

"Claire," he was beside her now, his voice deep, caressing. She looked up into his eyes, watched them darken as he smiled. "Can I kiss you?"

Again, she nodded until he cupped her cheek and gave her a soft, tender kiss, a mere brush of lips.

"Just because we're in this situation doesn't mean..."

"I thought you didn't, I mean, you weren't interested." Their voices mingled, his words tripping over hers. He paused as he digested what she had said and smiled, openly and warmly.

He laughed softly. "Interested? I'm very interested. But I know the timing is poor. I don't want to rush you or..."

Claire found herself smiling back. "Slow is fine."

"Good," he murmured, kissing her lightly again. "Now eat. I intend to work you hard to get us out of here. I want Grandma's Christmas cookies."

The world was crisp with a biting wind that brushed over the surface of the snow and whipped up into their faces. Claire's nose reddened almost immediately, and she was grateful for her knitted cap and the heavy scarf she had borrowed from Cole.

She held a shovel and watched as Cole began immediately digging a path down the porch steps. Claire descended after him, gingerly holding the rail as she walked. There was no way she would ruin her holiday by falling and breaking a bone.

The sun had already started melting the snow, compacting it until it was twice as heavy as the day before. The surface of the lawn was marred only by the light tracks of birds and squirrels as they foraged for forgotten food. Claire grimaced as she lifted the first shovel full. It was going to be a long day, considering the weight of the snow and the expanse of the driveway.

With Cole leading, they started by clearing a path around his car and taking the bulk of the snow off the hood and roof.

Next, they moved behind the car to clear a path. Claire soon found sweat gathering under her arms and down her back as she heaved her snow-laden shovel. Her fingers and nose grew numb with cold, but she was reassured at the sun's warmth at her back. Just one more day of this, and the snow would almost melt on its own.

She found her mind wandering as she completed her task. Since Cole's kiss, she had been thinking only of him. The way he smiled, the way he felt and tasted. She appreciated the gentle concern he had shown her and the tender way he shielded her. She couldn't deny the tiny bud of hope she felt blooming. The chance of a new love, this love, felt good and right. It was all so frightening, but she felt as though she was at the edge of a precipice. What lay beyond was glorious, breathless, and grand.

She paused, hands at her aching back. Checking her watch, she noticed it was almost noon. A thud on her back caused her to jerk around in surprise.

"What the?"

A second snowball nailed her in the stomach and she squatted, grinning, to gather ammunition. The childish battle lasted only a few minutes when she slipped in the snow, landing heavily on her backside.

"Are you okay?" His expression was concerned and he stretched out a gloved hand to help her up. She caught his hand firmly and yanked, upsetting his balance and pulling him down next to her, his astonished face inches from hers.

"Fine, and you?" she said, grinning.

"You play dirty."

"I play to win," she replied, easing into a kneeling position.

"Okay," he said, pressing a chilled kiss to her lips, "you win." He stood and helped her up. "Let's go in and get lunch."

By the time they had finished lunch and cleaned up, the sun had dimmed, heavy gray clouds obscuring the sky.

Claire looked up, concerned. It looked like rain, or snow. The temperature felt like it had dropped slightly.

"Oh, Lord, not more snow," she sighed, standing in the doorway.

"It said chance of rain. As long as the temperature holds steady, we're fine."

She ducked her head in agreement, but her heart was sinking. She could smell it. The cold wet soil, icy wind, the scent of winter.

Sighing again she started to dig, arms aching. They worked until the darkness hovered, but the path through the heaped snow reached the gates and Cole was able to move his car close to allow easier exit. They had even cleared around the gates so they could pull them open, a welcome sight like an open mouth to the rest of the world.

Dinner was canned soup and coffee. Cole persuaded her to eat a second bowl before retiring to the music room again. She avoided the wine, fearing a repeat of the nightmare. They played two hands of rummy, and when Claire felt her eyes growing heavy while Cole dealt the cards, she decided to go to bed.

"I'll go up too," Cole said quickly, placing the cards in a neat stack on the table.

"You don't have to."

"I know. I'm tired too."

He followed her up the staircase, standing in the doorway as she entered her room.

"My door will be open. If you need me, just call," he said softly, his eyes dark and intense. The kiss on her forehead was more fatherly than passionate.

Sleep was almost immediate and deep. She woke once, hearing the sharp patter of rain on the window.

She was relieved and energized after a dreamless night of sleep. She was also not surprised when she looked out the window. A solid sheet of ice coated the window when she pulled the curtain open.

She first worked at the French doors, and a sudden thought made her fingers clumsy. What of Leta? She hadn't seen her at all the night before. She had combed the room, looking even down the hallway in case the bird had escaped without her knowing. But she hadn't found the bird anywhere, and now she just wished she knew where the dove had stayed the night.

In the crystal morning, the balcony was empty, the expanse of the woods glittering like fairy lights among the trees. But no dove.

She showered and dressed, descending the stairs slowly. She opened the front door, her eyes widening in dismay. The ice was everywhere. The trees were encased, each single branch as fragile as glass. The piles of snow they had carelessly thrown were frozen in place, a crust of ice sheeting the white peaks. Worst of all was Cole's car, the ice so thick it was difficult to discern where the hood ended and the bumper began.

"No cookies today," Cole said softly, standing close behind her.

"No, not unless you know how to make some."

He pulled her gently to face him, his hands cupping her jaw tenderly.

"Are you all right? I feel like I'm always asking you that. I know you're disappointed..."

"I'm fine. I slept like a baby, really."

She covered his hands with her own. He bent to give her a gentle kiss, sending her heart fluttering to her throat.

"Good morning," he said softly.

With shaking hands, she linked her fingers behind his neck. The second kiss was hungry and desperate. She broke away herself, ducking her head in embarrassment.

He pulled her close again in a warm embrace, cradling her head against his shoulder.

"We'll be fine. You know that, don't you?"

"It's not over," she said softly, feeling the shift deep within her bones. Something was waking.

He went out after lunch and returned with a spindly pine tree.

"Is that our Christmas tree?" she asked incredulously.

"Temporary tree. Temporary. You'll be at home with your family for Christmas morning," he replied firmly. "Besides, it was the only one I could find that wasn't iced over. The woods are a mess out there, broken branches everywhere. It's amazing we still have power."

"Quiet," she said scolding. "Don't even think it."

"I have a generator," he replied consoling. "And we need to get busy with this!" He gestured to the tree.

"So, what will we decorate with?" she asked, watching as he propped the tree in the corner.

"There is stuff in the attic."

They went up together, pleased to find the Christmas decorations neatly boxed and labeled. Cole carried down two of the boxes, and Claire began unpacking as he went back up. When he returned she saw he carried a familiar trunk from the attic.

"Is that from the turret room?"

He nodded, setting it down gingerly. "Since we had the letters and portraits here, I thought I'd bring this down too. I just saw the trunk and decided to get it out of there."

She said nothing but was mildly surprised. She had almost forgotten the rest of the contents of the trunk. And since the hauntings had apparently stopped, she had thought no more about Henry and his wife's tragic love affair. To see the tray of bottles, their colored glass catching the light, made her shiver slightly.

"Yes, I guess we should get rid of those. There's something, I don't know, strange about them." She brushed her fingers over the corks, listening to the harsh clink of glass against glass.

"Okay, let's get going," Cole said, pulling her back to the moment. She forced a smile and left the box of bottles, an uncomfortable doubt preying at the back of her mind.

CHAPTER TWENTY-ONE

They spent the remainder of the afternoon decorating the tree. Claire was delighted by the lovely old ornaments, the light catching their polished surfaces like gems. After much deliberation, they decided to set the tree up in the music room since it was their favorite place to relax. They used antique beads for a makeshift garland and unwrapped each ornament reverently, hanging the heavier ones on the lower boughs to assure they would not fall and break. Topping the concoction with a foil star, they sat back to admire their work. The limbs hung heavy beneath the weight of the antique glass balls and the only illumination came from the lights around the tree, but it was still special.

Cole made coffee, hot and strong, and they stayed in the music room until dinnertime, talking and reading.

"You never mentioned where you live. I mean, when you're not here," Claire said casually, her eyes studying the warm mug in her hands.

"A little bit in New York, but I spend the bulk of my time in a house on the California coast. I travel a lot for business and for pleasure." He leaned against the chair back, as relaxed as Claire had ever seen him. "I'm not sure what I'll do after the renovation is done. I enjoy traveling but not as much as when I was younger."

"So, you just do your business where ever you happen to be."

"We have headquarters in five different cities. I can work out of any of them, or at home. Computers have revolutionized our industry along with everything else."

"And what do you do?" Claire asked, studying his face.

"I'm the boss."

Claire resisted the urge to probe deeper into his life and curled her legs up under her. Cole walked casually around the room, pausing briefly to pick out a few notes on the piano. Next, he stopped at the antique box, his long fingers skimming over the rows of bottles.

"What do you suppose these are?" he asked quietly, almost as though speaking to himself.

"Medicines, herbs," Claire said, looking up from a book she had picked up.

"Poisons."

She looked up, curiously. "Some herbs were poisonous given the wrong dosage. Is that what you were thinking of?"

"Isn't it a woman's typical means of murder? Slowly poison the poor man to death in his gruel?"

Claire got up and squatted next to him, pulling out a bottle at random. "Do you suppose they were Beatrice's? Or Etta's? I don't know how much the upper crust dabbled in this stuff, but I know this wouldn't have been hard to find."

He put the bottles back in neatly. "We may never know what happened, but I think it's time to get rid of this stuff."

"What do you mean?"

"Tomorrow we're going to take all of it and burn it. I'm tired of having this shadowing us. We need to get rid of all of Beatrice's things, even the letters."

Claire felt a prickly sensation at the back of her neck but said nothing. Her fingers went to the crucifix around her neck. They had come so far. Perhaps it was time to close the mystery. With the removal of Henry's body, the spirits had quieted. Now if they just got rid of the rest of the items from the Hagen's legacy, they could move on.

Feeling mildly uneasy, Claire said nothing. When she went to bed she left a dim light burning and checked the cross above her bed. On impulse, she also pulled out her suitcase and donned her favorite nightshirt her mom had given her years ago, wrapping it around her like a big good luck charm. She eagerly burrowed under the covers and pulled out the romance novel she was currently reading. She had read only two pages when she heard the sharp rap outside her door in the hallway, and her eyes jerked up to the closed panel. Slowly she climbed out of bed and crossed the room on chilled toes, suddenly anxious. She couldn't decide if she was fearful if the spirits were stirring outside her door, or if it was Cole, wandering the halls in an evening vigil. She paused and laid an ear against the smooth surface of the door, and when she heard nothing outside, she turned the knob. Squinting up and down the corridor, she stepped onto the worn runner and stood frozen.

Nothing. She turned hastily and returned to her bed, her heart pounding uncomfortably in her chest. If she made the supposition it was Cole, was she being foolish, hopeful? She would much prefer a late-night guardian than a menacing one, but she realized it was not hers to choose.

The door to the outside balcony remain a blur of ice with no pale shadows dancing behind the pane. Her dove had not returned either.

Sleep was difficult, and she found her mind racing. Finally, she settled down with her book again and read until her eyes grew heavy. Despite her concerns, she slept deeply and soundly until the sun finally rose.

By morning, the ice showed signs of melting slightly although the day seemed overcast. Claire had more hope for leaving and went down the stairs with a lighter heart. Her good mood was ruined, however, when she saw Cole's activities. He had assembled a large number of items in the parlor and was building a fire in the huge fireplace.

"What in the world," she muttered, watching him gather more kindling.

"I decided to get it over with. The weather seems to be warming up, and I've called into the city. We may be leaving this afternoon."

Claire felt a wave of relief so strong it was almost palpable. "Oh, that's great. Thank God. Not that this hasn't been fun but..."

"Yes, waiting for the other shoe to drop is fun. I just want to get rid of these things quickly."

"Well, I'm going to grab some coffee. I'll be back in a minute."

She left quickly, anxious as he to have done with the gristly tasks. She had the sudden urge to put the letters in the flames herself. No matter what had happened to Beatrice, Claire had a deep abiding fear she hadn't killed her husband and left to live happily ever after. Even if her lover had turned up, happy and healthy, she doubted Beatrice's fate had been as sweet.

The kitchen light was off, the only illumination seeping through the window shade. The light on the coffee maker blinked red, and Claire inhaled the aroma appreciatively.

She grabbed the mug off the counter, left by Cole as he had taken to doing over the last several days, and poured. Adding sugar with quick strokes, she smiled absently, thinking of her mother's strong coffee.

She turned toward the refrigerator to grab some cream when a movement caught her attention. She walked to the dining room door, freezing when she saw her. The figure was as clear as it had been in her room. It was a young woman dressed in an archaic gown of indiscriminate color, the lines straight and plain as it swept to the dusty floor. Her hair was pulled back into a modest bun, and her hands were clasped before her, pale fingers fidgeting in the still air. It was Etta. Claire had little doubt. She looked almost exactly as she had in the photo from the little book. Although she may have been slightly older, the clothes were similar, and her expression was the same intense concentration.

She looked directly at Claire, her mouth moving in a soundless plea. The cup slipped from Claire's fingers, smashing on the floor when it struck. The ghost of Etta stood firm, her hands raised and she shook her head vehemently, her expression becoming anguished. She was there a moment longer, then, like a storm cloud, dispersed into nothingness.

Claire stood, her face pale in the reflection of the windows. She saw movement behind her and spun again, relieved to see Cole standing quietly.

"What? What did you see?" He approached her quickly, step-ping around the splattered coffee and shards of china to catch her shoulders in his hands. "Did you see them? The ghosts?"

"I saw Etta," Claire replied, looking blankly at the mess at her feet. "She was talking, trying to say something. She kept shaking her head. I think she was scared."

"Of what? She's dead, for Christ's sake. What can she be scared of now?"

"She doesn't want you to burn it."

His eyebrows rose with curiosity. "I thought you didn't know exactly what she said."

"I didn't. I don't. I just feel like, I don't know..." Claire looked uncertainly at the dining room, its emptiness haunting her.

"Well, unfortunately I'm not taking any more crap from these spirit friends of yours, pardon my impatience. Come on, we've got some things to burn."

He turned on his heel, heading for the parlor without waiting for her. She followed, uncomfortable and feeling like she was trapped between two very strong and determined forces. She had never seen him like that, so determined and almost angry.

She felt color flood her cheeks as she stepped over the china and coffee and followed him. If he was angry, she wanted him to face her, talk to her. The sheer ambivalence in the atmosphere was over-whelming, almost as though the house was holding its breath in anticipation.

The parlor was flooded with heat, the fire licking the sides and back of the fireplace, the greedy flames leaping over the heavy wooden frame of the painting Cole was thrusting inside. His stack had grown to include the portraits of the Hagens as well as their other pictures, several heavy books, and a trunk full of clothing. The letters and bottles lay by themselves to the side, waiting for the last call.

As Claire watched, he picked up a heavy book and tossed it on the flames.

"Who are you so angry with?" she asked loudly from the doorway.

"Angry? I'm not angry. Tired, frustrated, fed up -- okay, a little angry. I'm not letting them do this. Pop in to mess you up and pop back out, leaving you floundering. It's not right they try to control us. No, control me through you. That's what it's been. They're trying to get to me, the last of the family, and they're doing it by messing with you." His face looked dark and set. "You hear me!" he shouted, looking toward the ceiling. "Deal with me!"

The silence was deafening, the crackle of fire the only sound.

He took up the portraits and shoved them both in at once, watching the flames lick their faces, bubbling the paint and black-ening Beatrice's softly curling hair. The frame crumbled under the abuse of the fire and the poker, the canvases gradually folding in on themselves until the images were totally obscured.

Cole moved more swiftly, pushing the rest of the books in the huge fireplace. When the stack was cleared, he grabbed the box of bottles, snatching them one at a time and hurling them into the flames. The glass shattered, powdery contents scattering within the brick cavern.

Claire herself picked up the letters. She folded them reverently and wrapped them with the time-faded ribbon. Carefully tying the bow, she handed the packet to Cole feeling suddenly soiled by handling them. He didn't pause, but tossed them into the fire. As the flames greedily spread over the fragile paper, a mild tremor shook the floor.

Claire's hands caught the chair behind her, and she backed away from the fireplace. Cole moved to her side, reaching out to grasp her hand as a pungent smell permeated the room. Claire gagged and covered her face with her hand, and then reaching up to grasp the cross hung around her neck. She looked up quickly; staring with horror as a form began to develop.

It grew, dark and huge, becoming more distinct. As before, it seemed to separate into two entities. The temperature in the room dropped as the searing heat from the fire dissipated, and a chill settled.

Claire felt her teeth chattering and a grinding pain in her hand she realized was a result of Cole's tightening grip.

As her eyes widened in silent horror, the figures continued to evolve. The one on the left growing taller, bulkier, but still a mere shadow.

The second began to take on a more human form, the limbs lengthening until arms could be seen. Within seconds it was fully recognizable. Bulbous breasts and exaggerated hips made a cruel farce of the female form. The face was a dark sketch of her once lovely features, and her hair curled like writhing snakes around her head. Her eyes were distinct, yellowish lights sunk in a putrid face.

"You," the sibilant whisper rippled over Claire's scalp. "Destroying my things! How dare you."

Her head whipped around with unworldly speed and she pinned her gaze on Cole. An odd change came over her features. "Michael? Oh Michael, you came back for me." Her words were slurred and breathy, sounds coming from a long dead throat.

Cole stood stone still, his face a mask of disbelief.

"Don't you know me? Can't you see me? I thought I'd never see you again." Her face changed again, the expression unreadable. "Why didn't you help me? You knew he was after me? You knew he had come back, even after all we'd done to him. Why didn't you save me? Michael? Michael did you kill me? Did you?!" The voice rose to a shriek.

Cole was stumbling back, his hand clamped hard over Claire's arm, pulling her back with him. "I'm not Michael."

The spirit seemed not to hear him but turned with furious speed, her horrid eyes, sunk into the twisted face, following Cole's every move.

"You locked me here with him. You left me here with him. I killed for you." The floor was trembling again, the plaster from the ceiling raining down on them in thick white dust.

Claire realized the spirit was caught in her own web of disillusionment and sheer insanity. She felt the eerie awareness of having lived in this creature's mind. She was sure, in that moment, that the nightmare had not been just a figment of her fertile imagination but a replay of this woman's final moments when her mind finally betrayed her. Chased by her guilt, she had raced down the shadowy hallway with the spirit of her own twisted crime breathing down her neck. Had she fallen then? Or had she heaved her body over the rail to land in a broken heap on the cold tile floor?

"Beatrice, you're dead now. You need to leave," Claire said loudly, her voice high and trembling.

"This is my home. I will never leave here!"

"Not anymore. You're dead. You've been dead for a very long time. Let Henry go. You need to leave and let Henry leave too."

The spirit looked back to Cole. "Michael?" Her voice, a hot whisper, was imploring, somehow confused.

"I'm not Michael. He's been dead for a long, long time. Beatrice, leave."

"I can't. I'm here!"

The floor shook with an undulating motion, the fury causing Cole to grab Claire's upper arm to steady her. Claire yanked the chain from around her neck and tossed the cross at the creature, saying a breathless prayer as she stumbled backwards on unsteady legs.

"We've got to get out of here. She's pulling the whole place down."

They staggered into the foyer, tripping on the tiles, broken, uprooted, and scattered. Claire froze, her eyes on the floor. Beneath the stairway, the exact area where John's body had laid after his fall, the tiles were flipped over, yanked free. In the gaping hole was a body. Claire knew who it was before she approached it, pulling away from Cole's firm grip.

"It's Beatrice." The blond hair looked like shredded yarn, the mouth pulled in a parody of a grin full of yellow teeth. "She truly did die here. Michael just left her. Left her to rot while her husband lay one floor above."

A roar of anger, frustration and madness burst out of the parlor, sending the air into a cyclone around them. The fragile bones rattled with the tremor of the earth and the rotted dress stirred around skeletal feet in the makeshift tomb.

Cole grabbed Claire, pushing her out the front door as a wedge of ceiling broke free from above and tumbled down.

The ice was a solid sheet on the porch, and Claire barely felt the wood strike as her feet slipped from beneath her.

"Claire, darling Claire. Please wake up. Please God."

Claire opened her eyes to see Cole's gray face hovering above her. His arms held her tight, his breath coming in steamy puffs in the chilled air.

"Can you hear me?"

"Yes," her voice sounded hoarse to her own ears. "I'm okay, I think."

She slowly became aware of the pain. It shot up her arm and into her shoulder, becoming an ache in the cold.

"I think I broke my arm," she said softly.

"It's okay. I'm here. I won't leave you, and help will be here soon."

She didn't ask how, or what he knew that made him so certain they wouldn't be stranded on the ice slicked porch. She just lay in his arms, feeling his soft kiss linger on her lips.

She heard the soft coo of a voice over their heads and her eyes focus on the carved lip of the doorway. Perched in a small niche was a familiar cream-colored shape, the dark eye gazing at her with strange intelligence.

"Leta," she breathed softly.

"What?" Cole's breath pearled in the air.

When she smiled faintly, he held her tighter.

As she opened her eyes she expected to see the house, the beautiful antique bed with the lovely carvings, the French doors shaded by the heavy curtains, and the huge fireplace, empty but for a few spent ashes.

But the room was painted a bland green, the curtains a straight fall of tan, and the bed had metal rails caging her from head to foot.

When she turned her head, a bloom of pain spread from the back of her head up to her temples, causing tears to spring to her eyes.

Cole sat in a straight-backed chair next to the window. His arm rested on the sill and his head rested on one hand, eyes closed and seemingly asleep. At her gasp of pain, his eyes blinked open and stared at her with glassy eyes. He looked terrible, his hair rumpled for the first time in their acquaintance, his clothes wrinkled. A shadow of whiskers covered his cheeks and chin, and his eyes were reddened.

He got up quickly and bent close, his hand brushing her cheek.

"Does it hurt?"

"I have a headache," she responded, sounding a little cross. "What happened?"

"You got hit by a piece of the ceiling as we went out the door." He ran his hand through his hair, his face drawn. "I guess I wasn't quick enough. Then we hit the ice and slid down the steps."

Claire frowned, taking inventory of her aches and pains. "Are you hurt?"

He shook his head slowly. "Sprained ankle, a few cuts and scrapes," He gestured vaguely to a bandage on his hand. "You bore the brunt of it. A concussion and broken arm. The doctor says you'll be fine." He paused, easing his palm against her tender jaw. "Should I call the nurse? Get some pain medication?"

"No, not yet." She covered his hand with her own, blinking back the pain. "What happened to the house? To Beatrice?"

"I don't know. We had been outside for only a few minutes when I heard the plows. I ran down to flag the driver, and they picked us up. They were able to take us down to a clearing where a police officer was stationed. He drove us out to the interstate where the ambulance met us and took us in town. I never looked back."

Claire closed her eyes, overcome by fatigue. "How long have we been here?"

"Since around 3:00 yesterday. I called Charles and got the

phone number for Noel and your parents. I expect visitors at any time." He smiled wryly, his eyes betraying his concern behind the attempt at humor.

"What time is it now?"

"Almost noon. Your mom was very polite but very short. She said they'd be here as soon as possible and then asked to talk to the doctor. If it hadn't been for the snow, I'm sure she'd be here by now."

"She can be pretty protective when one of us is hurt," Claire responded faintly.

"It's the parent in her. She said she wanted to talk to me. Do you suppose I'm in serious trouble?"

Claire smiled at his second attempt at a joke.

"She'll probably want to know your intentions."

He grinned. "I think I'm more interested in yours." He bent close again, his smile fading. "I was thinking of getting a place nearby, maybe in town. I don't want to stay in that house anymore, but I don't want to leave." She watched as his eyes darkened, betraying his emotion. "I want to stay and be with you. I know you'll need time; we both will."

She raised a weak hand, silencing him with a gesture. "Yes, we may need some time, and I know we said we'd go slow, but don't get carried away. I'm not that fragile."

"You look a little fragile. I feel like I almost lost you, and I don't want to let you go. I want us to have a chance at a relationship."

She took his hand, holding it loosely. "I think that's a wonderful idea. I mean I don't want to tie you down..."

"Maybe I want to be tied down. Besides, I already told Grandma we'd be out there after Christmas to visit. You'll come, won't you?"

"I'll be there," she said softly, yawning. His kiss was infinitely tender as he pulled the blankets up around her shoulders.

"I love you, Claire."

EPILOGUE

The snow lay only an inch deep on the ground. The driveway, now black topped, was shiny slick with melted snow. The loop of the driveway held a new fountain, peaceful deer grazing by a sinuous stream, dry now that the winter freeze had come. In the spring, water would trickle musically over carved stones and delicate flowers etched into the base and pedestal.

The front steps were free of snow and ice, the massive doors already opening as they stepped out of the car.

"Cole," Charles greeted him, taking his hand. "And Claire. Lovely as ever. How are the girls? My daughters can't wait to see them again. They've become quite the babysitters."

Cole held open the door, unbuckling one of the twins while Claire attended to the other. At four, they were becoming very independent, but the drive had made them sleepy.

"Daddy, where's Mr. Pig? I want to take him in."

Cole scooped up the sleepy child, fishing her favorite toy out of the seat and following Charles as he led the way.

Claire took Katrina's slightly damp hand and led her up the stairs into the front door.

The foyer had been restored to all its grandeur, the crystal chandelier casting a glittering illumination over the room. The floor, refinished with gorgeous blue-gray tiles, reflected the light.

The bustle of a busy hotel was all around them, guests and workers alike filling the rooms with chatter and noise. The scent of pine needles and candles was intoxicating, the smell of Christmas in the country.

"Has it been a year since you've visited?" Charles asked, showing them up the stairs. "I guess it was around Christmas time last year."

"Yes, well, we like to keep the kids home when we can," Cole said smoothly, dropping Kathleen to her feet at the head of the stairs.

"You know Noel and Ben are scheduled to be in tomorrow. She said the place would be too dull without her. God, that kid of theirs is a terror." Charles grimaced and led the way up the staircase.

Claire laughed, picturing her five-year-old godson running up and down the frozen aisles of the stately rose gardens out back.

They followed Charles to their rooms; Claire amused by his proprietary air. After becoming manager almost three years ago, Charles had made the place a smashing success. The rooms stayed booked almost a year in advance with men traveling miles for the excellent golf course and ladies enjoying the extensive gardens, numerous shopping choices, and day care for the children. Horses for riding, two swimming pools, and a five-star restaurant were included on the grounds. The proximity to the city, with both Louisville and Lexington in close driving distance, both hosting numerous sporting events as well as cultural affairs, was also a significant draw for the patrons.

Claire sighed with pleasure at the rooms. They always stayed in her old room when they came, the girls through an adjoining door to

Noel's old room. The door had been installed to link the two rooms several years ago, but their rooms had changed very little. The portrait still hung on the wall, the wise eyes of Cole's ancestor watching them as they dropped their things.

"It looks great, Charles, thank you. Maybe after the girls have their nap they can see your daughters. How's your wife?"

After a polite exchange, Charles left, sending a bellboy up with their baggage.

"You feeling well?" Cole asked softly, encircling her with his long arms from behind.

"I'm fine, just a little tired. Stop fretting," she said playfully. "Let's get the girls down and put our feet up." She turned toward the curtained French doors. "Open the doors to let in the birds," she said softly.

He smiled and scooped up the nearest daughter, taking her with him to the door where he threw open the panel. As though they had been waiting for their invitation, a line of four doves, each lovelier than the next, came soaring through the opening. They flew in an arc formation, lighting with barely a flutter on the footboard of the bed. Cole was still smiling as he took his daughter with him into the adjoining room, laying her on the twin bed with all the gentleness of a father's love. Claire could hear them fussing about missing the birds, but she knew they would have plenty of time to visit later. Cole paused to smooth their daughter's blond curls from her cheeks and stooped to kiss her on the forehead. He repeated the procedure with his second daughter before pulling the door partway closed.

"They're out like a light. If Kathleen didn't love the morning so much..."

"And Katrina the night..."

He grinned, "They just have to be different."

Claire laid out her evening clothes, carefully unpacking the outfits for the next few days. She put them in the wardrobe, watching to make sure the birds were nowhere close to the fine fabric.

"I wonder if Etta will approve."

Cole frowned at the dress she had chosen. "I doubt it. She likes brighter colors."

Claire put away the blue dress thoughtfully. Etta and the doves were their only reminder of the horrifying events of that winter. No shadows of Beatrice or Henry remained, and they had discovered later that Michael, the last point of the twisted triangle, had died three states away, a bachelor of 86 years old. It seemed his spirit had apparently rested better than that of his victim or his co-conspirator.

Etta, however, had remained, tending to the one bedroom of the house as she had so many years ago, and visiting the turret room to light the lamp on occasion.

Only certain guests were invited to stay there in the haunted bedroom, and although almost once a year a scandal story was printed in the tabloids about the ghost house, nothing more had come of her continuing presence.

Cole had respectfully had Beatrice's remains buried at the local cemetery, far from her murdered husband or her lover. Claire just hoped she had found some rest, although she was sure now that Beatrice, and not Henry, had caused any evil manifestations.

The painting was the one point of contention between her and Cole. She wanted it left alone, tucked in the little room. The basements were used for storage only, and even then, there were rooms that were not needed.

But Cole had insisted it be removed. Even if it hadn't been her artistic talent, it had been Claire's hand that had painted the picture, and he was strangely proud of it. After much debate, it had been trimmed down and placed in the clubhouse where the men admired the beautiful woman at the window, never realizing what had really lived behind those eyes.

Claire lay on the bed and relaxed, her eyes drooping. She enjoyed these visits now, but they were careful not to allow the girls out of their sight. Both girls had shown an unusual awareness of the history of the house, and Claire was afraid they might have inherited some of her sensitivity.

The year before, while traveling over the newly repaired bridge, Katrina had asked who the man sitting on the rail was. Cole's face had paled but he had calmly asked who she saw. Her response had chilled Claire, but it hadn't frightened the girls at all. "He looked just like you, Daddy."

Claire had seen no more spirits but remained alert to her girls and their pretend play. She knew well one child's imaginary friend may be something much more real.

Claire dozed lightly and woke to find both girls sitting on the bed. Each had a cooing bird on their chubby hand. Cole grinned at her from the chair.

"They wanted to wake you up. They're hungry. Again."

Kathleen studied her critically. "Mommy, when is my baby brother going to come out of your belly?"

Claire stared at her, sitting up.

"Who, sweetheart?"

"My baby brother. He's in your belly, but I want him out so we can play. He's little now. How long until he's big enough to come out?"

Cole got up, walking over to the bed to sit next to Claire and lifting Kathleen onto his lap.

"You're not?" he asked Claire, eyebrows raised.

"I don't know," she replied honestly. "I'm a little late but I never thought..."

Katrina spoke up insistently. "Can we name him Bart?"

"You don't name babies after dogs," Kathleen snapped back.

"But Bart's a good dog!" Katrina insisted.

"Girls, we don't even know if we're going to have another baby," Claire interrupted.

"We know. We've talked about it. He'll be a good baby." Kathleen said, her voice very serious. "But we are not calling him Bart!"

Cole slowly put his arms out, engulfing them in a hug. "I am such a lucky man," he said grinning.

ACKNOWLEDGMENTS

This is an important book for me since it is the first that I completed and has undergone many rewrites. I must thank my readers who are trying out yet another genre with me. I do love a good ghost story!

ABOUT THE AUTHOR

Rachael Rawlings is a full time mother, wife, writer, pet owner, and Speech Language Pathologist. She enjoys writing mystery books with amateur detectives, pets such as her talkative parrots, and a dash of robbery or murder.

She lives with her husband, James, a professional architect; her three children, Faith, Nicholas, and Chase; and two dogs in the small town of Crestwood, Kentucky.

She thrives on great coffee, chocolate, and friends and family.

To learn more about Rachael's work and her upcoming releases, visit her on her website:

http://rachaelrawlings.wix.com/rachael-rawlings

ALSO BY RACHAEL RAWLINGS

Speak to Me

Grave Reminder Series

Dearly Departed

Dearly Remembered

Dearly Beloved

Another Fine-Feathered Mystery Series

The Parrot Told me

The Cockatoo Called

The Macaw Muttered

The Cockatiel Cautioned